The Ghostly Quilts on Main

a novel by
Ann Hazelwood

C&T PUBLISHING

Text © 2014 by Ann Hazelwood
Artwork © 2014 by C&T Publishing, Inc.

Executive Book Editor: Elaine H. Brelsford

Copy Editor: Joann Treece

Proofreader: Chrystal Abhalter

Graphic Design: Sarah Bozone

Cover Design: Michael Buckingham

Photography: Charles R. Lynch

Published by C&T Publishing, Inc., P.O. Box 1456, Lafayette, CA 94549

Library of Congress Cataloging-in-Publication Data
Hazelwood, Ann Watkins.
  The Ghostly Quilts on Main / by Ann Hazelwood.
    pages cm. -- (Colebridge Community series ; 4)
  ISBN 978-1-60460-160-2 (alk. paper)
  1. Quilting--Fiction. 2. Missouri--Fiction. I. Title.
  PS3608.A98846G48 2014
  813'.54--dc23
                                    2014018820

Printed in the USA

10 9 8 7 6 5 4 3 2 1

"I fell in love with Anne's characters! I would love to see the Taylor House, plus I love flowers, gardens, and gazebos! I am wishing I had the next book to read."
—Marianne Rudisel, Terre Haute, Indiana

"Considering the fact that I'm not a "reader," I've become so involved with the Colebridge characters that I have to pace myself, so I don't read each book too fast."
—Terry Doyle, Rantoul, Illinois

"I moved to Colebridge! I have become Anne Brown! If only I could step over to Grandmother Davis's position to advise Anne before the next page turns. Ann Hazelwood has captured me into the beloved Colebridge series."
—Jackie Reeves, Angels Camp, California

"I waited anxiously for *The Jane Austen Quilt Club* and was not disappointed. This book renewed my affection for Jane Austen. Once again, I felt as though I had come home to wonderful characters. The adventures of Anne, Sam, and their families are always exciting, heartfelt, and inspiring. I look forward to the next book!"

—Linda Pannier, Perryville, Missouri

"Ann Hazelwood's writing style is so enticing. It draws you right in to the Colebridge Community. I feel like I am right there on Main Street or quilting in the basement with the characters. I have read all of Ann's books so far and I am always left in anticipation of what is going to happen next with the residents."

—Sharon Metzger, Maryland Heights, Missouri

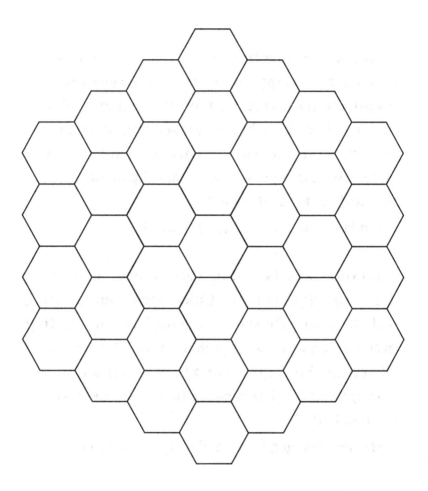

The pattern for this block is available at:

With Appreciation

One does not fulfill one's success without the help of family and friends. I would like to acknowledge and thank the following:

First and utmost, my heartfelt thanks to my husband, Keith Hazelwood, and my sons, Joel and Jason Watkins, who continue to give me love and support. I love you!

My writer's group, The Wee Writers—Jan, Mary, Janet, Hallye, Ann, and Lilah. Their talent and friendship are such an inspiration to me.

My friends and former employees of my former business, Patches etc., who continue to cheer me on and occasionally share my travels.

Last, but certainly not least, is the AQS staff, especially Meredith Schroeder, who believed in this fiction series, and my patient editor, Elaine Brelsford, whose wisdom makes me a better writer. I feel they are on this journey with me and I hope to make them proud.

Dedication

Quilts On Main was a popular outdoor quilt show in St. Charles, Missouri, for many years. I had many dedicated volunteers who planned and displayed over 400 quilts each year. This event could not have happened like clockwork without Valerie Zulewski. My appreciation of her efforts are sprinkled in my latest fiction novel, *The Ghostly Quilts on Main*. Thank you, Valerie!

CHAPTER 1

"ere goes," I said, taking a deep breath. My heart was
pounding loudly like a base drum. "Oh, not pregnant,"
I said aloud to confirm my visual of the home pregnancy
test. "Yes, yes, yes! Thank you, thank you!"

I breathed a big sigh of relief as I watched the latest digital
pregnancy test indicate my outcome. I double-checked
the package instructions to make sure I did it correctly. I
certainly was not ready for any little Dicksons in my life right
now. What kind of person and wife was I that was rejecting
a baby? Was I just not ready or just plain selfish? Did Sam,
my husband, notice my concern about being pregnant and
remain quiet so he wouldn't upset me? Why was I second-
guessing the pill anyway? I had been extremely careful to
swallow my daily pill. Pregnant at just barely married a
year? Not! Pregnant during the restoration of my Brown's
Botanical Flower Shop? Not! Pregnant still trying to restore

our home at 333 Lincoln? Not! Pregnant trying to write a book about the Taylor house? Not! Pregnant and trying to keep up with gardening and my potting shed? Not! Pregnant just to please Sam and our extended family? Not! Okay, I'm done. I am going to forget this little exercise ever happened. I regained my composure in the bathroom off our master bedroom and came downstairs to take care of my daily routine at our home at 333 Lincoln in Colebridge, Missouri.

The devastating heat of the summer in Missouri was not showing any signs of waning in its last months. I could not remember such a hot summer. It was no wonder I was having spells of lightheadedness and a churning stomach. I was actually looking forward to fall for the first time in my life. Watering the grass and grounds of our estate seemed endless. Albert and Marion Taylor, who once owned our place, had a gardener. Knowing that fact eventually convinced Sam to hire Kip Blackstone as our part-time gardener. Kip's background was perfect for us and his results were noticed and appreciated. He was also helping Kevin, my delivery guy at the shop, whenever extra help was needed. I found their close friendship to be a plus.

I had also hired a new cleaning lady by the name of Ella Christian. My former housekeeper, Nora, refused to clean the house after the day I left her there alone. She rapidly left the house when my spirit grandmother created a scene in the little room where I sometimes sat to write about the things that interested me.

Grandmother Davis, now deceased, took it upon herself to remind us of her presence now and then at my former home where she once lived, but she really resided at 333 Lincoln, which remained empty for many years after Albert and Marion Taylor died. The whole town seemed to know about some kind of ghostly presence there. Now that Sam and I had purchased the property, it gave Grandmother some satisfaction, but her unhappiness was still evident. We were now living in the house where her lover and his wife once lived. As a young, single lady, Grandmother had an affair with her boss, Albert Taylor. When she became pregnant, he denied the affair and simply ignored her. His response seemed to be enough to satisfy Mrs. Taylor, as they remained happily married with a child of their own. Grandmother's anger and jealousy had obviously kept her from moving on, even after her death.

Grandmother seemed to accept the idea of us living there because I had uncovered the secret about her child with Albert and the adoption that followed. It was revealed in a quilt Marion Taylor made which I discovered in the estate's potting shed, where cut-up letters in the piecing revealed her story. The result was a happy reunion with our family after we found Mary and her two children, William and Amanda. We were briefly one big happy family until we lost Aunt Mary recently due to a heart attack. I patiently put up with Grandmother's mysterious maneuvers, but others, like my husband, seemed to be running out of patience with her mysterious behaviors.

Each morning, I looked forward to my walk either in my hilly neighborhood, located on the top of the hill, or on the beautiful trail along the Missouri River near to where I work. Walking was my time to count my blessings to the Lord above and to plan my very busy life that had just gotten busier when I married Sam. Leaving the residence of my widowed mother, Sylvia Brown, wasn't easy to do. Prior to my marriage, I had never lived away from home. I was very spoiled domestically, which left me more time to run my successful flower shop on historic Main Street.

Today, as I arrived at the parking lot by the river's edge, I had even more to be thankful for as I started my walk in the morning of the heated day. A reminder of remaining childless did give me a bounce of relief as I stepped along. There was always a breeze along the river, which was why I rarely walked along the brick sidewalks of all the storefronts on Main Street. I loved nature and the wild things that grew along the way. The heat of our summer was causing leaves to drop earlier on some trees and many flowers were giving up their blooms way too soon.

Having a flower shop was the perfect career for me. The success of Brown's Botanical also allowed me to begin to expand to be able to handle large weddings and events, where the better profit was to be made. My able manager, Sally, was able to convince me with her research that our bottom line could at least double in size. Jean, my English transplant employee, was also a gift from God with her charm and more traditional ideas. Abbey, the most recent employee at the shop, because of being single, wild, and out of the box, made our team quite diverse and yet like family.

Checking my watch was routine in my walk and I found it to be annoying, but necessary. I knew a full day was ahead of me at the shop as well as a merchants' meeting to follow this evening. These meetings were tempting to miss because of the constant dissension among the shop owners. A sense of guilt regarding not doing my part on the street usually won out, and so tonight, I had decided to attend. Sam was out of town on business, which happened frequently, so I felt

I should take advantage of the opportunity. As vice-president of sales and marketing, Sam traveled much of the time and was basically promised the title of president of Martingale when the current president retired. Having him gone so much was a mixed blessing, as it freed me up to do my work without feeling I was neglecting him. We both knew of our work obligations when we married, so we had to make the best of our situation. Our time together was precious and very happy.

CHAPTER 2

❧

I welcomed the cool shower when I returned home. From the nightstand in my bedroom, I saw the message light blinking on my phone. It was Jason Cunningham's voice. He was the architect for my shop expansion and would oversee the development of the project. He was also scheduling meetings required by the city to achieve a parking variance and gain permission to make exterior changes to my shop. We would need to obtain the approval of the Historic Landmarks Board. We already had a letter from one of the "no" people on the street complaining that we were taking away green space and that the addition should not be approved. Jason and I did consider the problem, but felt we were making up for the lost space with a better designed landscape. No one would consider that element more than I. I wanted the green and color on Main Street to remain. Making things more beautiful was my business. I made a mental note to return his call later in the day.

When I walked into the shop, Sally was quite pleased to see me. Another phone call was waiting to be answered. It seemed that customers not only preferred phone orders, but many insisted on talking to me personally in order to achieve their mission. I guessed they thought their order would be quicker, supersized, cheaper, and of course more beautiful. It made me wonder if I was emotionally ready for the additional drama of adding large weddings to our services. We certainly were kept busy without it. Sally said she would gladly take on that responsibility, but the buck would still stop with me if there were any problems. My thoughts were then interrupted by the ringing of my cell phone.

"Hey, sweet Annie," Sam's voice called out. "Am I calling at a bad time?"

"Oh, not in the least, honey," I answered, trying to convey a smile over the phone. "I just walked in the shop and it's a little crazy here right now. Sally's a little overwhelmed and Jean isn't due in until noon."

"Well, I won't keep you," he said with a comforting tone in his voice. "I wanted to call you last night, but it got so late. I'll be home tomorrow for dinner I suppose. I'm pleased to say we closed the deal here, so it was worth the trip."

"Great!" I said with as much enthusiasm as I could. I wanted to share my personal joy of not being pregnant, but that definitely could not happen. Sam was eager to have a family, but he didn't have a clue as to how disruptive it would be to our careers. I knew it would fall on me to make it work. He would have been hurt that I didn't share my worry and that it took the drugstore test to confirm it. I opted to change the subject. "I have a merchants' meeting after work today, so if you call tonight, I'm not sure when I'll be home or what kind of mood I'll be in."

He laughed, as he knew my dread of controversy. "You need to be a player on that street, Anne," he said, trying to console me. "Be patient. Remember, you need as much support as you can get with your expansion plans. Don't work too hard and get some rest. How are you feeling today, by the way? Has your stomach settled down?"

Oh boy. I had hoped he would have put any memory of my nervous stomach and fatigue complaints out of his mind. "Yes, indeed it has," I replied, picturing the beautiful color of blue in the test. "I'm feeling great! Need to run now! Talk to you later. Love you!"

"Love you too, Annie," Sam sweetly said, ending the call. I never got tired of hearing that.

I started my e-mails when the bustle of business stopped for a moment. On top of the e-mail list was one from my best friend, Nancy Barrister. It read: *Need to see you as soon as possible, my dear friend. I have news to share. Call me when you can get free for lunch.*

Nancy's goal in life was to have a family. She was married to Richard Barrister whose family started Barrister Funeral Home here in Colebridge. They recently moved from Boston to take over the business from his father who had retired. They had it all, you might say. They had it all, except a child. Nancy was obsessed with the thought, even wanting to start adoption proceedings. Richard did not want to adopt, so the conflict put pressure on them. It would be great if Nancy made a pregnancy announcement, but not be so great if Sam escalated his desire for us to have children after hearing such news. I e-mailed her back that I would meet her tomorrow for lunch at Charley's, a three-story restaurant on the corner of my block here on Main Street. It is a popular spot in Colebridge and handy for my purposes.

The rest of day moved quickly as interruptions ceased. Sally graciously agreed to meet with an unexpected salesman. She loved picking out accessories for our gift area. My personal contribution was finding antique and retro flowerpots for people to purchase for vintage-style arrangements. I purchased them at flea markets and garage sales. It gave my customers a unique choice that no other flower shop offered. Sally was always trying to expand our accessories that could be add-on purchases, especially with walk-in customers.

Jean was providing Sally with her opinion. When I did the ordering, I typically scheduled appointments with salespeople when I was alone in the shop so I wouldn't be influenced to purchase products that I really didn't need or want.

"I would venture that these stunning floral doodads for the light would sell well, don't you, Miss Anne?" Jean asked, showing me a sample that she held in her hand.

"Oh, the stained glass ornaments?" I questioned.

"I suspect a gallery of these in the window would bring about a sale or two, right?" she said eagerly.

I couldn't help but smile inside at her many ways of communicating in her English way. "Why yes, the floral ones only, of course," I noted. "What do you think, Sally?"

"I think for gift buying during the Christmas season, they may sell very well, but Gayle has something similar in her shop next door, so maybe just a few," Sally said, holding one to the light. "These colorful gardening tool ornaments are a hoot. You can get them in sets, which might make a nice gift. I also like these herb identification sticks since we're using more herbs in our arrangements. What do you think, you all?"

"I'd say let's give it a go!" Jean exclaimed. All of our hands went up in a vote of support!

Finally, at five thirty, everyone had gone home so I finally returned Jason's call.

Jason had already left for the day, but his secretary said she was to pass on the message that we were scheduled for the Historic Landmarks Board meeting on Monday night at seven. He would also touch base with me on Monday morning regarding what he intended to present. Okay, that was moving forward. Now, I just had to face inquiring minds and voices at the merchants' meeting.

CHAPTER 3

At the shop next door, I knocked on Gayle's door to see if she was also going to the meeting. She was just getting ready to leave so I waited for us to go together. Her glassworks shop was a colorful and creative place in which she took great pride. I marveled at the art form, but had no interest in attempting it. It was a good addition to the street.

"So, can't we stop to get a drink before we do this dirty deed?" she teased.

"Oh I wish, but then I may not hold my tongue at the meeting," I responded with a laugh.

We walked into the Soup Tureen Café where everyone was gathering around their reserved tables. The charming café was only open for lunch, so it worked out well for the group to occasionally meet there. Maggie, its owner, always prepared wonderful soups and desserts.

Gayle and I grabbed two chairs so we could sit next to

one another. We shared many opinions and I always enjoyed her sense of humor. Phil from Main Street Collectables was quick to join us. George, the owner of the Water Wheel, was president of the group. He was beginning to use his gavel, but to no avail. It was a very good turnout for a change and everyone was chattering away.

"I'm so glad you are here, Anne," Phil said. "We put off calling you today in hopes that you would be here this evening. I want to visit with you before you go."

I nodded and wondered what in the world it could be. Phil was a quiet, well-liked shop owner who at had been on the street long before me. His shop's silk flowers and expensive collectibles were delightful and I always admired his displays. Sharon, his right-hand person, was younger and very creative in her own right. I think someone said she was perhaps a relative of Phil's and hoped to take over the shop one day.

The chatter finally settled into business. After George's welcome, Kathy from The Cat's Meow gave the treasurer's report. She complained of low funds and said that if we did not come up with some fund-raising, we would have to increase our dues. Voices from every table responded negatively to her remarks. That idle threat was the wrong thing to say to this group.

Phil spoke up and said, "We need new ideas instead of doing the same things every year."

Nick Notto from Nick's Bakery jumped in and said, "Well, don't think it'll be the Oktoberfest that's coming up in a couple of months, because it does nothing but take away sales with all the booths they have on the street."

Many agreed as George tried to quiet the others from speaking.

"He's right," chimed in Kathy. "Most of the vendors are from out of town and don't pay the taxes that we do every year."

George didn't want the meeting to turn into a big gripe session, but he agreed that our events were like many other communities and that we needed to think of something unique. He encouraged everyone to bring some innovative ideas to the next meeting. He then went on to hear other committee reports.

"Before we adjourn, I hear there's an expansion about to happen on the street!" George announced, looking straight at me. "Can you fill us in on that, Anne?"

I was unprepared and surprised. What could I tell them? Silence in the room prevailed as they waited for my response. "All I can really tell you is that I do hope to expand, but I am still going through the process and am not able to give you many details," I said, shrugging my shoulders. "My store is very crowded and I have wanted to expand for some time. I think I have a good plan, so we'll see how it goes. You all know about the hoops we have to jump through." Responses and questions were blurted out, but I ignored them. "Stay tuned." I smiled and turned my back to them. Oh dear, why did I come?

Finally, the meeting was adjourned. As the crowd began to clear out, Phil asked if I could join him for dinner at Charley's.

"Sounds great. Sam is out of town and I can always use a debriefing after these meetings," I joked.

Gayle and I said our good-byes and I headed toward

Charley's. When I walked in the door, the large crowd indicated there would likely be a waiting list, so I went to the bar area to look for Phil. Looking straight at me when I got to the bar was Ted Collins, my former boyfriend for two years. I was the one who had finally ended the relationship with Ted when I met Sam. I was not happy with Ted. I was, in fact, rather bored with the relationship and I certainly didn't want to get married, which seemed to be his goal.

"Well, look who's here!" Ted said in a more-than-friendly tone. "Out with the girls again, are you?" His words were slurred and I felt he might even be drunk. He came closer with a big grin on his face. The bar space was crowded and I felt I had no escape. This was not going to be good, I told myself.

"Hi, Ted," I managed to say softly. "I'm here to meet Phil from Main Street, but I don't see him. Do you know him?" I tried to walk to the end of the bar to gain a little distance, but he followed.

"Another guy? Well, that beats all!" he said with a laugh.

I looked at him, feeling quite puzzled.

"Brad, bring this girl a merlot. I guess you still have a taste for it, or did that change, too?" He snickered with a sloppy grin. "I guess Sam is out of town again?"

"No need to do that, Ted. He'll be home just before dinner," I explained as I moved a bit more away from him. "Phil and I just came from our merchants' meeting." Why did I even bother telling him that much? It was none of his business. In seconds, Brad put a glass of merlot in my hands and gave me a wink.

"Well, Brad, don't leave me out," Ted said sloppily. "I'll have another."

"I don't think so, Ted," he said, to my surprise. "I think you've had enough. Do you have a ride when you leave or should I call you a cab?"

Oh boy, this was not a good scene, so I pretended not to hear.

"Okeydokey then, Mr. Brad," he answered smartly. "I'll bet this nice young lady here will give me a ride. She seems to be fancy free tonight."

"No, Ted, I can't. I have plans," I quickly responded. "Please don't try to drive. Have Brad call a cab." If looks could kill, he did just that.

"I should have known," he said, shaking his head. "What's gotten into you, Anne? Looks like you are still just thinking of yourself. What a pity for that Mr. Dickson."

This was just going to get worse. I turned away in disgust, without a response, and walked to the receptionist. Phil was now coming in the door. We greeted one another, and luckily a table was ready for us.

"I am really glad to see you," I said, feeling a bit out of breath. "I ran into an old friend at the bar, and it didn't go well." The bewildered look on his face implored me to explain, but I didn't want to.

"I got detained talking to Nick," Phil said. "Sorry I kept you waiting. Man, this place is crowded! Glad you got our name in for a table."

"No problem, really," I said, taking a deep breath. "Since I already have my merlot in hand, I'd just like to order an appetizer. What about you? I'm not really hungry." He agreed with the idea and so we ordered an assortment of fried and unhealthy delights.

CHAPTER 4

So, what's going on?" I asked, in order to get to the point.
"How can I help you?"

He grinned as he raised his glass to make a toast.

"Cheers!" we said together as we clinked our glasses.
"Well, I suppose I should begin by asking you, and I know
this is quite out of the blue, if you knew I enjoyed making
quilts."

What? Was I hearing him correctly? "You do?" I
responded, a bit jolted by the unexpected confession. "No,
I didn't know that, but I must say how cool that is! How
long have you been quilting? Isabella at the quilt shop said
she is getting more and more men quilters coming in. I'm a
newbie at quilting, but I have family that quilts."

He was now looking embarrassed. "I've been doing this
for the last five years, I guess," he blushed. "Besides flower
arranging, of course, I was more of a painter. I moved from

oil to watercolor, but now I love working with textiles much better. I do some really strange pieces. They are mostly for the wall." His face began to light up as he described his work.

"That is so cool, Phil. I never knew you painted, either."

"Back to the purpose here, Anne," he said as he cleared his throat. "I've been thinking about our fund-raising problem here on the street and wondered what you thought about making a raffle quilt to raise some money. I know groups who profit quite well from them. Sharon and I were talking and wondered if the two of us could whip up something interesting. I already talked to Isabella and she said she would donate the supplies. Sharon is quite good at sewing. She has even made a quilt or two, so I know she would help. I think my aunt would quilt it for us, and possibly do it free of charge. You belong to that Jane Austen Quilt Club that meets at Isabella's, don't you?"

I was trying hard to follow where he was going with this. "First, let me say what an awesome idea I think this is. I do not quilt unless I am helping in Mother's basement. I don't have the time. I like the social excuse we use to get together. I no longer attend the club at Isabella's because it just became too much. I do belong to the Jane Austen Literary Club and enjoy that immensely. Many dropped out of the quilt club once we got the Jane Austen quilt finished. I think Isabella has changed the name to the Colebridge Quilt Club. You may want to look into joining that, by the way. I think I am a writer, Phil. When I get a spare minute, I feel my hands itching to write. Isn't that strange? I started a book about the Taylor house where I live. I'm not very far along because I have no extra time to speak of."

17

His interest perked up considerably. "Wow, Anne," he replied, grinning with admiration. "I didn't know that. You amaze me. Someone told me you are quite the gardener too! Isabella raves about you and your mother. I guess you both were really there for her when the Jane Austen quilt was missing."

"I think she is a very special person as well," I said firmly. "She went through a really tough time when customers and friends were deserting her. They were starting to blame her for losing the quilt. I'm glad it all worked out."

"Yeah, we heard it was the foul play by one of her employees," he interjected, fishing for more information.

I shrugged my shoulders. I didn't want to hear more and decided to change the subject. "I think you should move ahead with your plan for a raffle quilt. Do George and the rest of the board know your intentions? I can't imagine who would be against it, unless they felt the raffle process itself was an issue."

"No, I haven't said anything to the board. I just felt I wanted to explore the idea first. We need something very different, so the quilt shouldn't be anything ordinary. We need an event unlike any other. This raffle quilt could generate income for a few months, especially during Oktoberfest. We might as well take advantage of that crowd."

"I agree, and I'll figure out some ideas for you," I promised, getting excited. "I seem to always be good for ideas, Phil, but I'll admit that I don't always have the time to fulfill them."

He nodded in agreement like he knew exactly what I was talking about.

We ended our pleasant chat and made our way to the door. I went purposely to the bar to see if Ted was still there. Thankfully, he was not. I asked Brad if Ted got a ride home.

"Yup, I have the taxi on speed dial for him," he muttered, shaking his head in disgust.

"What do you mean by that?"

"He's been hitting the bottle pretty hard lately," Brad said softly, looking at the floor. "He's in here almost every night now. He brings up your name a lot, Anne. He's always asking if I've seen you. It's none of my business, but I don't think he ever got over you."

I cringed at the thought. "Oh Brad, enough! This is awful. What happened to his darling Wendy?"

"That's been over for some time," Brad offered, grinning. "The way he tells it, he broke up with her. I think 'possessive' is one of the nicer words he's used to describe her." He laughed.

I shook my head, feeling sad for Ted. I said good-bye to Brad. On the drive home, I tried to digest it all. There was more to Ted's unhappiness then the absence of yours truly. Maybe the recent death of his mother was really due to an overdose, as rumor had it. That would certainly be hard to deal with. Ted was always so sensible and worried about what people thought. It was hard for me to see him not in control. I couldn't believe I was actually feeling sorry for him.

CHAPTER 5

✹

I turned off the alarm as I walked into the empty house. The sadness I felt for Ted made me want to run into Sam's arms. I was so lucky to have chosen Sam for my husband. I really wanted happiness for Ted. His family was always so nice to me. I sensed they hoped I would marry into the family.

I checked my messages, and one was from Ella reminding me she was coming to clean tomorrow. The other was from my dear mother that I was definitely ignoring, although it was completely unintentional.

I was ready for a cup of chamomile tea to sooth the sadness of the evening and to help me sleep. I took it upstairs and sipped on it as I changed into my cotton pajamas for the evening. I took my china teacup into "the waiting room," as I called it. It was a small but charming room off our master bedroom, most likely used years ago for a sitting room. I called it such because everyone seemed to have plans for that little room. It seemed to be waiting for whatever use we decided to give it at any given time. Sam always called it the nursery. The bedroom across the hall would make a much larger nursery, however. Thank goodness this will continue to be my own little room for writing, as well as a convenient packing area for Sam as he prepares for his trips. It had a charming little desk and chair from my family that was perfect. It was waiting for me to come and write. Right now, I couldn't even picture a little baby, in a little crib, in this little room, for a long, long time!

Could I muster writing some words tonight? I really just wanted to relax so I wouldn't think about Ted or how I would get out of a new project on the street. If I were to start writing about the Taylors, I knew there was likely information on them waiting for me in that spooky, dark attic upstairs. I just couldn't make myself go up there, for some reason. Sam said there were some things he saw in the attic when he looked at the property while we were first considering purchasing the house. There were lots of areas and nooks and crannies that I still had not yet explored in this big house. When Nora, my previous cleaning lady, and I both attempted to go up the stairs, the lights went out, leaving us in total darkness. We had to feel our way back to the hallway. One day when she was cleaning our home and was alone, Nora got so scared that she ran out of the house and vowed she'd never be back! She said papers flew everywhere from my desk in this room. She was right. Grandmother did not want her here or up in the attic. When I returned home that day after Nora's frantic call, I found papers scattered everywhere. I knew there must be something in the attic that Grandmother did not want me to know or see. Her dislike for Marion Taylor was quite evident at times.

I walked from my desk to call Mother on my cell phone. "How are you, sweetie?" I heard Mother asking in her caring voice. "Is everything okay? You know, we have just a bit of quilting to do on Jean's quilt. Can you come over Sunday afternoon?"

"I think that should be okay," I replied, sounding rather sad. "We've had the quilt too long and we need to get it done. How are you doing, by the way? I'm sorry you haven't heard from me, but with the shop expansion and all, it seems time gets eaten up quickly."

"I'm fine," Mother said and then paused. "No one knows better than I how busy you are. You sound worried, Anne. Is everything okay?"

Oh dear. She knew me so well. "Yes, I just had a long day and then a merchants' meeting that got attached to it," I explained, hearing the exhaustion in my own voice. "How is Harry Stone, by the way?" Harry was the manager at Pointer's Book Store where Mother had once worked part-time, and Mother had started seeing one another, which was, in a way, kind of cute. I couldn't quite say the word dating, but she was certainly enjoying his company.

"He's just great," she said, sounding perkier. "We are thinking about taking a little trip soon. He has some time off and I haven't been out of Colebridge for some time." She paused, waiting for me to respond.

I was numb. I guess that meant an overnight stay. This was much more serious than I had ever thought. "Oh, how nice. Where are you thinking of going?"

"Well, we haven't decided as yet, but he loves museums and Kansas City is one place on his bucket list."

"Yes, they have some great museums and it is not that far," I found myself saying, trying to be happy for her. I made a decision to change the subject back to our Sunday quilting plans. "I'll be there Sunday, Mother. I hope all the others will show up."

"I've already talked to Julia. I'll call the others. I sure hope Jean can be there for the final stitches. We'll have to get a picture of that." Many Kodak moments had taken place in that basement of my home. Mother always referred to special or happy pictures as "Kodak moments." I had picked up the practice of taking note of those moments myself.

"Oh, she'll be there for sure, Mother. She will be so excited. Don't forget to include Isabella. She seemed to enjoy it so the last time we were quilting together."

"Yes, you're right, I will! I'll see you then, Anne. Get some rest, honey. Did you say Sam will be home tomorrow?"

"Yes, and I can't wait," I affirmed. Within a few minutes, we ended our call.

I usually let Sam make the call to me at night because of his schedule, but now I really wanted to talk to him. I called his cell and got a recording to leave a message. Was he working late again? Maybe it really wasn't that late for him, but I was exhausted. As soon as I brushed my teeth, I turned out the light. The thought of my mother traveling with another man besides my father was certainly something for me to visualize and absorb. Seeing Ted drunk at the bar and slurring his words was a sight I'm not sure I'd ever imagined as something he would do. When did be become an alcoholic? Was I so busy that these changes, and most likely others, were happening without my notice? What else didn't I know? Where was my husband tonight? Maybe I should start there. Hmmm...

CHAPTER 6

After a surprisingly good night's sleep, I awoke to thoughts of Ella coming to clean. She didn't have a key, so I had to be there on her first day. I showered, dressed, and tidied up a few rooms. Sam usually made the coffee when he was home, but on mornings he was not, Starbucks was my best friend.

Ella arrived ten minutes early and her appearance was professional, to say the least. She appeared more to be the lady of the house instead of the cleaning lady. I told her that when she finished, I'd like her to assess the attic and see what needed to be done there. I said if she could bring anything down, I would also be very appreciative. She assured me there would be no problem with that. As we continued with some small talk, she said she had cleaned my mother's house last week.

"Well, that's a first," I commented. "Was she feeling okay? She never liked the idea of someone coming in and cleaning her things."

Ella grinned. "Let's just say that Mr. Stone had a bit to do with that, Anne."

I laughed. "He's having quite an influence on her, isn't he?" I asked, not really wanting an answer.

"They are both wonderful people that are enjoying each other. He's trying to be helpful to her, and thanks to your mother, I am here today to help you!"

I had to admit that she was right.

I was finally able to slip away from 333 Lincoln and make my stop at Starbucks to pick my usual blend and purchase a few muffins for the staff. Waiting in line, my cell phone rang, announcing my call from Sam.

"Sorry, Anne, another late night, I'm afraid," he immediately reported.

"Mr. Dickson, I am not sure I am falling for this late night at work story. You have a lot of making up to do."

"You're certainly right." His voice sounded very sweet on the other end of the line. "I plan to do just that. I'll meet you at home and we'll go to dinner. I'm sorry, I have to run. I'll see you tonight! Love you!"

Hmmm...

It was Friday, which meant Sally, Abbey, and Jean would all be working to make sure we had things covered for the weekend. I typically ordered lunch for everyone on busy days. Kevin always made sure he was there to indulge as well. They were already busy with chatter when I walked in.

"Good morning, Miss Anne," Jean said first. "Your mother gave me a ring first thing this morning about Sunday's quilting. I am exceedingly grateful for everyone's help. It's quite a blessing to have such friends! I have taken a shine to start another quilt real soon."

"Mother loves it, of course, as well as I," I responded. "It's a great way to catch up with everyone. I'm surprised she has time to quilt, as busy as she is with Harry."

"She's still seeing him?" asked Sally from the front room.

"Oh yes, and she announced last night that they were taking a little trip to Kansas City to see some museums," I shared with a sarcastic tone. "Her casual dinners have now advanced to a sleepover!"

Everyone erupted into laughter.

"Now, Miss Anne, as we used to say, 'She's pulling up her widow weeds and getting on with life,'" Jean said smartly with her English accent.

"She's right, Anne," chimed in Abbey. "You should be happy for her. She is still a very bright and attractive lady."

"I know you're right, but she's just so different since I moved out," I shared. "Here I thought she would be pining away with my absence, but instead, she has reinvented herself."

"That's what a man will do for you!" teased Abbey.

They all agreed and made their own comments.

"Is the Historic Landmarks Board meeting still scheduled for Monday night?" asked Sally.

"Yes, and Jason will meet with us that morning to go over the latest information," I said for all to hear. "If anyone else wants to go, it's at seven."

Work orders continued to come in the rest of the day. The soup and salad lunch from Charley's was a big hit. It seemed they all were working harder now, knowing an expansion was in the works. Kevin ended up asking Kip to help toward the end of the day. The phone rang again with no one to answer. I picked it up to hear Ella's voice on the other end.

"Anne," Ella said distinctly, "I think you'd better come home now before I leave. I have some things we need to talk about."

"What's wrong, Ella?" I asked, rather shaken up. There was a pause. I knew it had to be serious for her to call. "Just stay there, Ella. I'll be right home." I hung up. This call was almost as bad as one I had gotten from Nora when she stayed alone to clean at the house. Please let it not be Grandmother again, I prayed.

"Something's wrong at home, Sally. I have to go," I announced as I grabbed my purse from my desk. "Can you stay to close?"

"Go. Go, Anne," she said. "We'll be fine."

As I drove home, I knew quickly in my mind that Grandmother was going to be the topic. When I walked in the front door, all appeared normal as I called out to Ella.

"I'm in the kitchen, Anne," she said calmly, sitting at the kitchen table. "Sit down. We have to talk," she paused as she took a sip of tea, then continued, "about the spirit you have in this house." There was another pause. "Do you know who she is? I feel it's a she. Am I right?"

Here we go, I thought. I sat down to join her.

"Oh, Ella, I am so sorry," I began. "It's my unhappy Grandmother. Someday, I will tell you the whole story, but in short, this house used to belong to her lover, who did not marry her when she became pregnant with his child. What did she do now?"

"I could feel her here all day," she said, her voice more elevated. "She became active when I was cleaning your bedroom and that little office area of yours. Papers started blowing off your desk and your chair was positioned on its side. It was not like that when I went in the room. I went about my business picking up things. After I vacuumed the hall rug upstairs, I decided I would check the attic, as you requested. The stairway bulb had burned out, but I saw some light coming from one of the windows up there. I got to the top and walked about. It's a mighty big room, full of dust and plain clutter. There are a few things in one corner. Are you aware of that?"

"No, Ella, I haven't been all the way up there because there is no light." I knew it was a foolish statement.

"You haven't been up there? Are you afraid?"

"Yes, you could say that, I suppose," I confessed, feeling embarrassed. "When the bulb stopped working as I was going up, it was terribly dark and I couldn't get down fast enough. I don't want to ask Sam because he thinks I make too much about Grandmother the way it is. I will be sure to do it soon. I know it's dumb. It's my house now, for heaven's sake."

She gave me a sympathetic look. "Well, I saw this old suitcase by the window and thought I'd bring it down for you." She continued, "I started to go down the stairs with it and felt someone give me a push. I nearly went down, but fell against the stair wall, which gave me my balance. It really scared me, to say the least, but I made it down."

"Goodness gracious, Ella. You poor thing! I'm so sorry. Are you all right?"

"I am, and if you don't mind me saying so, she is not going to get the best of me, Anne," she stated firmly. "No ghostly spirit is going to chase me away! Is there something in the attic she doesn't want you to know or find?"

"Obviously!" I didn't know how much to keep telling her. "I feel she is not too keen on me writing about the Taylors, either. I'm sure she'd be pleased if I wrote about her unhappy story, but I'm more interested in this house and the beautiful grounds and potting shed. There is so much good history here. It is such a mystery to so many folks in this town because it is so private here on the hill. As I grew up, I wondered about it, like everyone else. No one seemed to come up here, so the rumors of it being haunted prevail and are quite exaggerated."

Ella listened intently.

"She and I will eventually get things settled here, don't you worry, Anne," Ella said with conviction. "I'll be leaving now. I hope you will find my work satisfactory. I'll be back next week. I'm sorry I had to have you come home, but I didn't want to discuss this over the phone."

"Oh, no problem, Ella," I said, consoling her. "I'm so glad you didn't get hurt and I commend you for not being angry or quitting. Thanks for understanding. Not everyone would do that."

She went calmly out the door as I watched her get in her car. I couldn't believe she didn't quit. I shut the front door behind me and looked up the grand staircase that I loved. "Grandmother, this has got to stop now! No one will continue to love you when you behave so badly. You must not harm anyone, do you hear? I am the only one here to defend you. Please, please stop. Don't send me any lilies either. It won't help."

Grandmother had a habit of placing live lily arrangements around when she was sorry about something. It was her favorite flower and she didn't let anyone forget it. I went to the kitchen to pour myself a drink and checked my watch. Sam should be home any time now. I had to gather my thoughts on so many things. Hmmm...

CHAPTER 7

I took my drink to the south porch where the Taylors had enjoyed lemonade and the Dicksons continued the same practice into the current generation. The grand porch displayed white wicker furniture just like the Taylors described in old letters that Albert had written to Marion. I thought of them every time I sat down to visit, enjoy a drink, or simply have a cup of coffee. As I started to review my thoughts from the day, Sam drove up and parked on the circle drive, thinking we'd be going to dinner.

Out of his car he hopped, with a big grin on his face, carrying red and white long-stemmed roses. He loved to surprise me. That was my Sam. It was a Kodak moment I'd want to remember. He pulled me out of my chair and embraced me with all his might. It was wonderful!

"Sam, you are the only man who has ever brought me flowers," I said, pushing him back to observe the beauties.

"They are beautiful! How did you know to bring red and white?" We both laughed, knowing those were my favorite colors.

"You should always have flowers, my sweet Annie," he said as he kissed me on my neck. "I love you, baby, and it is so good to be home. I'll be around here at least a week or two. Can you stand it?"

"I just miss talking to you each day," I started to pout. "My day is not complete unless I do."

We held onto each other until he went in to get himself a drink. He was talking a mile a minute as we went back on the porch. He was on a particular high with his new business account. When he paused to give me a chance to talk, I didn't know where to start. I began by telling him about Mother and Harry going on a little overnight trip. The whole time, Sam was smiling, giving his approval but not saying a word. Finally, I had to tell him about Ella's first day. He listened intently and his smile went away. When I mentioned that she was pushed, the look intensified on his face.

"Annie, we're lucky she still wants to come back to work here." He got up, his frustration evident. "She could have really hurt herself. Then what? That's about all I am going to say on that subject." He paused and looked at my sad expression. "Are you hungry?"

"Not really," I was confused about his silence and anger.

"Well, you will be when I fix you one of my amazing omelets, by golly," he said, pulling me out of my chair to join him inside.

Sam loved to cook, unlike me, who never learned in the first place. He knew we both were not in a festive mood to go out. I loved watching him cook. When we started remodeling

333 Lincoln, Sam made sure the kitchen had the latest and greatest equipment. I'll never forget some of the wonderful things he has cooked for me from the time we started dating and now into our marriage. He puts so much love into it. He could pull whatever from our pantry, throw it in a pot or pan, and it would be delicious. He was right. When I saw the fluffy omelet with freshly sliced tomatoes on the side, I became famished. We touched on many topics as we ate and then decided to turn in early. I followed him upstairs and watched him unpack, listening to his every word. I just wanted Sam near me and I could tell he missed me as well. As we crawled in bed to snuggle once again, I kept thinking about how much I loved this guy. It was the last thing I remembered until the next morning.

The bright sun and the aroma of Sam's freshly brewed coffee were typical morning starts to our married life. He was an early riser, and by the time I would get downstairs, he would be reading the paper or working on the computer. It was a pleasant thought that today was Saturday and Jean and Abbey would be working until noon when the shop closed. I took my time pulling on my shorts and T-shirt. It was still plenty warm this time of morning for my walk. Sam gave me a whistle when I walked into the kitchen.

He was reading the paper next to my vase of roses. How striking they were. I wonder where he purchased them, of course. He offered me a piece of toast and honey, which looked very appealing, so I joined him. He then handed me a section of the paper.

"Here's something you will likely be interested in, Anne!" he offered as he showed me an article on a specific page. "The Colebridge Historical Society is having a fund-raiser by having a cemetery tour. Isn't that where the Taylors are buried?"

I looked at the article to read it for myself. "Yes, it is." I began to read aloud, "Actors will be dressed as the deceased persons listed on the tombstones and tell you about themselves on the tour. Many buried here are famous and have contributed in significant ways to the Colebridge community. A twenty-dollar fee per person will be charged when you enter the grounds. No cell phones or recorders are allowed. Hot cider will be served at the end of the tour. Call for reservations." Hmmm...

"Well, it sounds like you will likely meet the Taylors, don't you think?" I couldn't miss the humor in his voice. "Sounds like it could be helpful as you write your book."

"Oh, it does, Sam. I will not miss this! Will you be up for it?"

"Not in the least, honey," Sam confirmed, shaking his head. "Why don't you take Grandmother Davis with you and leave her there!"

We both had to giggle over that one.

Sam added, "I'm sure she wouldn't mind paying a visit to her old boyfriend, Albert!" It was a rather cruel statement, but I hoped she was listening.

"Sam, don't talk like that. I'll have to take someone, that's for sure. Maybe this would be a good field trip for my staff. They would find this fascinating, I'm sure." I also made a mental note to tell Phil about the event. Why didn't our group think of this kind of fund-raiser? We could not duplicate the idea, but we needed something out of the ordinary, just like they were doing. Hmmm...

CHAPTER 8

W alking the neighborhood hills this morning worked up a good sweat. I wondered if Marion or Albert used to do the walk for exercise. Huffing and puffing, I headed for the shower as soon as I came in the door. Going into my bathroom, I saw something out of the corner of my eye in the waiting room. It was an old brownish and gold suitcase sitting on the floor. Of course, how could I forget that Ella had brought it down from the attic? How could I have waited this long to peek inside? I decided to shower first and think about what the contents might be. After dressing for the day, I would have time to look. Why did I feel kind of strange about it?

Sam was busy in the garage so I finally scooped up the courage to sit on the floor and open it. If things were awful or filthy, it would be best opened on the floor. It felt like heavy things were inside. The locks flipped open quite easily and I was thankful the case was not locked.

The first thing I saw was folded clothing. I picked up a small, cream, knitted baby sweater. It had a little hood and was tied with a ribbon. Despite how yellowed it had become, it was sweet. This was no doubt something Miranda Sue Taylor had worn as a baby. Next were two folded white dresses that perhaps a one-year-old little girl would wear. The delicate scalloped edges on the thin cotton fabric had also become yellowed with age and were quite wrinkled. A third long dress followed that was quite fancy. It had christening dress written all over it. The lace was so intricate and the buttons were the smallest I had ever seen. A tiny cap was tied to its neckline. I placed them carefully side by side to better view them together. What a keepsake for Miranda Sue's mother, who perhaps hoped it would go to her grown daughter someday. Why hadn't someone from the family taken these? The Taylors lost Miranda Sue at the age of six, I had remembered reading. I wonder what could have caused her death. I checked the cloth pockets on the side of the case and discovered a tiny pair of white satin baby shoes. They would have been worn with the christening gown, I surmised. In another pocket was something hard. It was wrapped very securely. When I opened the yellowed tissue, out came a tarnished little fork and spoon. How precious they were! The last pocket held tied-up fancy ribbons that were folded quite nicely. This was a puzzle. They were gathered together and tied with another ribbon into a bow. They were saved from some special occasion, no doubt. They weren't ordinary ribbons. They were more like what I remembered as funeral ribbons. I'll bet Nancy could verify if these were funeral ribbons. Would Marion have saved ribbons from

Miranda Sue's funeral?

"Miranda Sue Taylor, this must be all about you." I took a deep breath, in case she was listening. At that moment, a cold rush of air came around me. It made me shiver. Somehow, I knew it was from something related to this house.

I carefully held each item. I wanted to cry for her and Albert and Marion. I'm sure I was not supposed to be the one to end up with these heirlooms. I got up to get my camera out of the closet so I could take some good pictures to refer to as I wrote each item on a piece of paper. These things will have to carefully be put back in the suitcase. They didn't belong to me. I told myself I would be the caretaker until I found whom to give them to. After I took a few pictures, I started putting everything back as I had found it and closed the lid. Why were these things kept in a suitcase? How did they get left behind?

"Anne, are you up here?" Sam was calling from the hallway. The suddenness of his voice scared me and I became more chilled.

"Yes, honey, I'm here in the waiting room looking at the contents of the suitcase that Ella brought down from the attic."

When he walked in and saw me on the floor with my camera, he looked quite puzzled.

I reopened the case and didn't say a word.

"Baby things, I take it?"

I nodded sadly. "Yes, I think they belonged to the Taylor's little girl. I got them all out and took some pictures."

"Why do you have it so darn cold in here?"

I was glad I wasn't the only one to notice. "I didn't have anything to do with it. It just suddenly got very cold."

Sam did not respond. He just had that look that I was seeing on him way too often. I knew Sam was never going to connect emotionally to the Taylors as much as I. For Sam, it was the uniqueness of the house's architecture that he loved and not the former residents of 333 Lincoln. He was also not going to succumb to believing any spiritual activity, if he could help it.

I pointed out to Sam each and every item without taking them out of the suitcase. He could see how emotional it was for me and he did not respond. I told him I would keep this in the waiting room closet. I felt all my Taylor research items needed to be where I would be writing about them. It was also where I stored Marion's Potting Shed Quilt that Grandmother so despised.

Sam kissed me as if to comfort me and then said he had to run some errands. I got up, putting the suitcase near my desk. I decided to get outdoors to my gardens and potting shed, which was always good therapy for me. It would clear my head about what all may have taken place inside this house. I couldn't get the picture of a little Taylor baby wearing that christening outfit out of my mind. Perhaps my waiting room had been her nursery.

I entered my potting shed and glanced at my cacti, which were perfectly lined up in little clay pots. The hot dryness of the shed was perfect for them. They thrived in the summer heat. I went to the herb garden to gather some chocolate mint and couldn't help but notice the handiwork of Kip, our part-time gardener. He had a way of keeping things tidy and groomed, which was what I needed. For some reason, I liked pulling weeds, and there were always plenty of them to attract my eye. I was always amazed at how, in the dead of summer, a weed could appear overnight. The rosebushes were still blooming profusely, despite the ending of summer. I loved their strength and hardiness. This was all my therapy. September would be here shortly, which meant fall would begin its colorful splendor. September 12 was our wedding anniversary. Time was going by too quickly. Fall unfortunately would lead to bitter winter which I hated, but it did, however, treat me to my favorite holiday, Christmas. After Christmas it was like a dark hole for me until spring. How could I ever find enough joy in each season to welcome it? Buds of green and lilies were hopes of spring, summer was memories of roses and my wedding, fall was a break for all to snuggle and watch colors change, and winter was all about Christmas. I had to remember that change was good in all things, even the seasons.

CHAPTER 9

O n Sunday mornings, I usually walked on Main Street so I could make a quick stop at my shop to check on things. I loved looking at the shop windows to see their display ideas. Some were great about changing them frequently and some were not. There were so many memories as I looked at each shop. It was easy for me to remember who previously rented or owned each one. Even before I had my flower shop, I fell in love with Main Street and had my favorite shops. One was a tiny needlepoint shop called the Miner's Daughter. The attractive and spry owner had talent beyond belief and I was envious of her little haven and how she marketed her products. Another shop was the Corner Country Store, where Buttons and Bows is now located. She had unique things that had such appeal to me. It was where I bought my first red-and-white quilt that had redwork embroidery on it. It was considered a summer quilt and had no batting.

It had been expensive for me to purchase, but I have never been sorry about the monetary cost. Isabella had shared historic information with me about redwork that made me appreciate it even more. When Turkey red thread became dye fast in 1880, it encouraged stitchers to stitch in that one color because they no longer had to worry about it bleeding. The same was true for solid red fabric. The timeline for red-and-white quilts was from 1880 to 1930. She thought mine was made around 1920, judging by the embroidery designs in the quilt blocks. Soon, I must display that in one in my red and white guest room, I reminded myself.

As I walked along, I could also point out buildings where someone claimed that ghosts inhabited the interiors. Many of these ghosts were already documented in published books on ghosts. Most building owners embraced their ghost with humor and some kept knowledge of their spirit under wraps, if they felt it would hurt their business. Donna at Donna's Tea Room repeated her love for her mother-in-law ghost to anyone who would listen

Brown's Botanical didn't have a ghost, or at least not yet. My fear was that Grandmother would choose to hang out at my workplace as well. She first became active at my home on Melrose Street and then at 333 Lincoln where she was most famous around town. Her presence never frightened me, but her recent activity with Ella was much more of a concern now.

I reached the shop, grabbed some cold water, inhaled the cool air, and admired all the living things that grew before my very eyes. I sat to rest and look at my e-mails. The first was from Jean, reminding members of the Jane Austen Literary Club meeting this week. There was always a pleasant e-mail or two, thanking me for something wonderful we had sent to customers. I felt really lucky when we were able to produce what someone had imagined and wished for in their mind. I had created a short file of good customers who liked certain colors or flowers. It came in handy many times. They also liked it when I told them to come in on their birthday to receive a free flower. These thoughts reminded me that a group e-mail needed to be sent soon. They loved it when I added hints on gardening or included Main Street news.

One e-mail jumped out at me from my list. It was from Ted. I quickly clicked on it to find only two words: *I'm sorry.* I guess he was referring to when I saw him drunk at Charley's. That was all he said. No way was I going to respond to this one. Hmmm...

The cloudy and humid Sunday afternoon was perfect for an air-conditioned quilting at Mother's house. Sam was playing golf with his best friend who happened to also be my Uncle Jim. Uncle Jim used to be married to my Aunt Julia. We all were grateful that Uncle Jim and Aunt Julia had a congenial relationship for the sake of their teenage daughter, Sarah, and our extended family. They truly enjoyed each other, or at least it seemed that way to us.

When I reached Mother's home, I walked in with my cousin Sue and her three-year-old adopted daughter, Mia. Her dark complexion revealed her heritage from Honduras, where Sue went to adopt her. Sue's parents, Uncle Ken and Aunt Joyce, lived in Ohio. Sue chose to remain here after college, where she was employed as a secretary and also sometimes worked at my flower shop. Now that she had Mia, she seldom was able to help me, however. I also had chosen Sue as my maid of honor in my small wedding. I was still determined to find Sue a man someday. She loved our small family and enjoyed quilting with us. Frequently, she brought her little dog, Muffin. Mia and Muffin always knew Mother would have a treat for them. We were especially important to them since they didn't have any other family nearby. Sue had become the sister I never had.

"Hey everyone!" I greeted as I came in the door. Aunt Julia and Sarah were arranging some cookies on a platter and Mother was putting on a pot of coffee. "Did you remember to call Isabella, Mother?" I asked as I kissed her cheek.

"Yes I did," she quickly responded. "She said she will bring Jean because Al has the car today. They have one car in the shop. Oh, here they are now. As soon as they come in, we can take all this downstairs."

"Tallyho!" Jean said in her English greeting.

"What's this?" I asked, peeking under the foil platter cover.

"My heavenly scones, of course," she teased. "You all fuss over them so!"

"Oh, yummy," said Aunt Julia. "Isabella, how nice it is to see you again. It's nice to have a *real* quilter in the bunch." Others responded in confirmation.

"I'm thrilled to be here to actually practice my rusty quilting," she explained. "It seems like I just get to talk about quilts and never make them. Watching you all quilt together reminded me how much fun one could have quilting. I may put one together myself one day and have you all help me quilt it. Oh! Here are some sugared pecans that I love so much. My recipe makes way too many."

"Thank you so much!" Mother said, taking them from

her. "You just let us know when you have that quilt ready, by golly."

Everyone took seats where they had sat before. Sarah didn't always quilt when Mia was present. She much preferred to play with Mia and Muffin, unless she was talking on her cell phone. Sarah was very interested in the arts, so she did have a level of interest in what we were doing at the quilt frame and quilted with us once in a while.

Everyone settled in with their refreshments and coffee. Being together created a sense of comfortableness for each one of us. The memory of Aunt Marie continued to be with us when we gathered here. She taught us all to quilt so we could help Aunt Julia finish her quilt top. The day we finished that quilt, Aunt Marie had a heart attack as she was leaving our house. We still felt her spirit here with us. She had to feel warm and fuzzy knowing we were still all here quilting together, unlike Grandmother Davis who was unsettled and had to keep reminding us that she was around.

CHAPTER 10

*

"You must allow me to tell you how much I fancy having all of your stitches in my quilt," Jean said before she sat down. "I venture to say we might be able to pop this out today. You'll carry on then with another quilt, right Sylvia?"

"I hope it might be one for Isabella if she can 'pop one out' soon enough," Mother joked, looking at Isabella. "If not, I have some unfinished tops from Marie. I'm sure she'd be thrilled for us to quilt them up so we could pass them on to family like Sarah, Mia, and even Amanda and William, Mary's children."

"Splendid thought, Miss Sylvia," Jean said. "I would venture I shall have another, one day. I fancy we'll want to stich a friendship quilt one day like Miss Nancy suggested. I cherished her idea, did you not?"

"I do fancy that idea, Jean," Aunt Julia agreed. "Believe it or not, I do have another quilt started. It's for Sarah and she's the one that picked out the pattern at Isabella's. It has more of a modern look to it with its big squares. It's called something like Bold and Beautiful, I think."

"Yes, it's a quick sew and a look that a lot of young people like these days," bragged Isabella. "I remember I recommended all solid colors, which is so popular now. It really shows the quilting so much more."

"Indeed," agreed Jean. "What colors might they be?"

"Purples and teals. They are very striking together," Aunt Julia described. "I've only pieced a few vertical rows. It goes quickly."

"It sounds great!" said Sue when she stopped stitching. "I would like something simple like that for my wall in the living room. My taste is more contemporary, as you know, even though my house is from 1929. I could probably do it myself, but I keep pretty busy making those coffin baby quilts for Nancy. I never get tired if it when I think how precious it becomes to the parents of these babies. I know Nancy really appreciates it, too."

"Yes, she does, Sue," I said, looking up from my quilting, "She comments now and then how she is using those little quilts more and more frequently."

"I agree, Sue. You are doing something that is so appreciated," Isabella added. "It's good to see quilters doing more and more charity-related projects."

"By the way, I am having lunch with Nancy this week and she said she had something exciting to share with me," I boasted. "I'll bet anything she is going to tell me she's pregnant. I sure hope so."

Everyone stopped quilting to take in this comment.

"Wouldn't that be jolly?" Jean said happily.

"Indeed, it would," joined in Isabella. "It's all she talks about. Let's keep our fingers crossed."

"What's the latest with the expansion, Anne?" Mother asked, filling her coffee cup.

"Tomorrow night, we go before the Historic Landmarks Board to get approval for the drawings and site plan," I shared, not expecting the question to come from Mother. "I'm hopeful they will like what Jason has come up with. I'm also hopeful that there will be no objections. They do not let people put expansions onto a historic building very easily, which I understand. Jason said each building should reflect something from each owner, as long it doesn't take away from the integrity of the original structure. Sally will be going with us, for sure."

"I cannot devise going along as yet," said Jean with some disappointment in her voice. "I've been ever so worried we may have to go car shopping."

"Not to worry, Jean. You and Al have other things to worry about," I said as I sipped some more of my coffee.

"Well, I'm no help," confessed Sue. "I would love to participate, but don't like leaving Mia any more than I have to."

"Is that mother of mine behaving herself, Anne?" Aunt Julia asked with sarcasm in her voice.

I paused, not knowing quite how to answer. Leave it to Aunt Julia to bring up the subject. Mother gave me one of those keep-your-mouth-shut looks.

"Actually, she's not!" I stated.

Everyone stopped to hear what I had to say.

"She chased away my cleaning lady, Nora, and now she's trying to get rid of my new one, Ella."

They wanted to hear more.

"Ella? Don't tell me!" Mother quickly responded. "She did a beautiful job cleaning here last week. What happened? Did she quit?"

"No, she didn't, thank goodness," I assured them. "She's a pretty tough cookie and she said no spirit is going to intimidate her."

"She certainly rattles those chains now then to get a rise, does she not?" asked Jean.

"What did Mother do now?" asked Aunt Julia.

"Never mind," I said, wanting to change the subject.

"She needs to move on," said Sue as she revisited the subject of Grandmother. "Does she really think hanging around her old lover's house is going to bring them back together again? I guess if Albert was in heaven, she'd want to move on, but maybe he isn't there!"

More laughter followed. Mother remained quiet.

"That is all so strange," said Isabella, who did not know the whole story of Grandmother Davis. "You all talk about her as if she really is here. Do you realize that?"

I ignored her question, as did the others.

"Our Main Street is full of those spirits or ghosts, Isabella," I revealed. "I was just thinking of them as I approached each building this morning when I took my walk."

"I just know about the mother-in-law ghost at Donna's Tea Room," Isabella said. "Donna loves to tell the story and it's all quite quaint, rather than scary. I think it adds charm and history to the area. I suppose in my strip mall, I'm likely to never have one!"

We all chucked.

"Many spirits twirl in their graves in England and it doesn't matter none," Jean shared.

The thought of such a sight was humorous. We all agreed that it was just what each person made of such activity. The longer we talked about the ghosts, the more animated everyone became. I did notice it was true for everyone except Mother.

"Charlotte from The Cookie Shop said they sometimes see a lady in a black coat hanging out on their outside bench. Isn't that creepy?" asked Sue. "I always think of that when I go there. That building is creepy too, I think."

"She really existed at one time, Sue," I shared. "I'm told she was homeless and she would sit there all day until someone brought out a cookie for her. From what they said, she was an attractive gray-haired lady that wore a black coat, no matter what the weather. She had excellent posture and sat there on the bench like a distinguished lady. That place may have been one of her fondest life's memories. No wonder she still hangs out there!"

Everyone laughed and agreed.

"Jean, would you pass the scones again?" requested Mother, wanting to move on from the subject matter. "They are so light. Can Mia have one, Sue?"

"Sure, but she'll just feed it to Muffin like she always does," she said with humor in her voice.

"Anne, did you see where there is going to be a cemetery tour sponsored by the Colebridge Historical Society?" asked Mother. "Since you seem to like all that ghostly stuff, I thought you'd be interested in visiting the Taylors' graves once again."

"I sure would," I confirmed. "Sam already pointed out the notice in the paper, so I'm going. I may ask around and see who wants to go with me. Speaking of the Taylors, Ella brought down a suitcase from the attic and it was filled with baby things. There is a darling christening gown and cap. I guess it was worn by their daughter. I don't know anyone to pass it on to. How sad. If I end up keeping it, I'd like to have it preserved and framed. It belongs in the house. It's the least I can do."

They were all ears as I described each item in the suitcase. They all agreed that it was a sad representation of what might have been left from someone they cared so deeply about.

Mia broke our intense conversation by her unexpected screaming. Muffin had done something she wasn't happy with so Mia was crying. Sue decided to end the afternoon. Others followed. Just as at so many quiltings, the conversation was diverse. It was another way for friends and family to connect. It was no wonder the quilting bees from the past were so popular. I needed that for myself, I discovered. It was a good thing!

CHAPTER 11

The dreaded, yet exciting, Monday was now here as my eyes opened halfway. Sam reached over to give me a kiss.

"Today is the day of reckoning, Mrs. Dickson," Sam teased. "Will Brown's Botanical Flower Shop be allowed to grow like their flowers or will they be put out to pasture to wither and die?"

"Stop! Go away," I said, burrowing my head into the pillow. "You're cruel!"

Sam laughed as he nudged against me.

"I brought you some coffee and a muffin to save you some time this morning," he murmured, kissing me on the neck. "You said you wouldn't be walking this morning, right? What time are you meeting Jason?"

I turned toward my husband and pushed myself into a sitting position. His dark, gorgeous eyes were looking right at my face, which was completely void of makeup. How can he love me, I continued to wonder. I reached for the coffee.

"Thanks, honey, that was sweet of you. I'm going to need this! He'll be at the shop at eight to meet with Sally and me. I need to shower and get going."

He reassured me once again that I would do fine and that I had a habit of convincing folks to do what I wanted. Sam looked at me and smiled. I wasn't sure if I agreed with that remark.

I got to the shop at seven thirty. That left time for me to put on some coffee and check out the work timeline for the day ahead. Sally arrived in a chipper mood and commented on what a beautiful day it was.

"Wow, this Rose Patterson funeral seems to be a big one," Sally noted as she looked at the order sheet. "Did you know her?"

"No, not really, but Mother did. She'll likely go to the funeral. Ms. Patterson was quite the advocate for women all her life, in Colebridge as well as regionally. She never married and kept herself busy with civic matters and always donated a lot of money to nonprofit organizations, which is why so many are acknowledging her now. How old was she?"

"I'm not sure. I haven't read the obituary," Sally said as she let Jason in the front door.

"Good morning, ladies," said Jason in a positive voice. "This won't take long. I just wanted you to see their agenda and my outline. I've talked to most of the members and I think they look at it all quite positively. Thank goodness most are pro growth and want to see businesses expand here." He laid out the agenda of the committee and then went item by item through his presentation. "I will present, but they may ask you some questions, Anne. Keep in mind that even though they may be quite supportive of your project, they have to put forth a good effort to appear as though they are looking out for the street's best interests. Don't let any of them throw off your confidence."

By the time he left, I was feeling much better, and even a bit excited.

Watching Sally's interest and hearing her comments reminded me again how much she had invested in Brown's Botanical Flower Shop. As soon as Jean, Abbey, and Kevin arrived, she had them instantly informed of their responsibilities. That used to be me, I remembered. Was this new manager now their boss? Hmmm...

I went to the computer to read e-mails and fill any Internet orders. There was an e-mail from Phil. He wanted me to join him, Sharon, and George, the president of the group, for lunch on Tuesday. Somehow, responding to this e-mail told me I was getting myself involved in something I likely did not have time for. Of course, I agreed to a quick lunch and would meet them at Charley's around noon.

Finally, the shop closed and I was starting to feel the pressure, anticipating what I might experience in the next few hours. Sam rang on my cell phone.

"How was your day, sweetie?" he asked, like always. "I just wanted to wish you luck and see if you had changed your mind about wanting me to be there."

"No, honey, but thanks," I replied, sounding confident. "We have a good team and will hopefully get a good result." It was an answer Sam was used to hearing.

Sally and I arrived early. We met up with Jason in the small conference room. As I viewed the committee members sitting in their chairs waiting for us, I was sure they were all customers at one time or another. One male was part owner of a business on Main Street, I recalled. There was only one woman on the council, which seemed strange to me. Our mayor was very pro growth, so I hoped that would carry some influence. I sat quietly with an internal mix of nervousness and confidence as they started the meeting. The first item on the agenda was a sign approval for an existing business. They were then ready to hear our proposal.

Jason began his presentation with much professionalism as I watched the faces of each committee member. When he got to the part about taking up more green space, I could see concern on a couple of faces. Jason immediately picked up on it, giving a detailed description of actually beautifying more of the area than what previously had been done. He also told them we had approval from nearby neighbors who were not objecting to our expansion. When they asked if we had our parking variance, Jason explained we would be approaching the Planning Department after this step, since the meeting times were not coordinated. I took a deep breath, hoping they would not postpone our approval until that was in place. The male business member from Main Street questioned if we had the cart before the horse. He carried on a bit about the area not having enough parking as it was. Now we could be in trouble, I thought, until the one councilwoman spoke up quickly in our defense.

"Things don't always flow the way we want them to, but I know one thing for certain. We need to get this approved and going," she said quite firmly. "Brown's Botanical Flower Shop has needed to expand for some time. They provide a service and are a wonderful presence on our street. It will be done just as they say, and perhaps even better. I doubt a parking variance will be denied when half of the other businesses on that street don't have the adequate parking they should. We need to be working with these folks in every way possible. Therefore, I move that we approve the drawings and the site plan as presented."

I gasped as Sally squeezed my hand. I had to stay calm.

"I second it," said a somber elderly council member that had walked in with the aid of a cane.

When the vote was taken, it was unanimous! I could not believe it. Now it was certain the expansion would happen. I wanted to do my happy dance, but Sally and I remained calm as Jason turned to shake our hands. I stood, wanting to show my gratitude. I walked toward the podium.

"I would like to thank all of you, if I may," I stated, out of turn. "This is why I love doing business in Colebridge. I promise not to disappoint you." They nodded and I turned back to my winning team. Jason then gave me a hug and I hugged Sally.

"Good luck," another member said as we walked toward the door. "We look forward to seeing it happen." They quickly announced the next item on the agenda.

All three of us left the room in relief as they continued their meeting. I was so very happy. If there weren't so many people around, I would have done my happy dance right in front of them. We followed Jason to his car, and he offered to buy us a celebratory drink at Charley's. We accepted, of course. I called Sam on the way to Charley's and asked him to meet us there. He was thrilled to accept, as he had been waiting at his office to hear from us.

"You can't wait until morning to tell Jean, Abbey, and Kevin," Sally said excitedly. "They are at their homes, waiting on pins and needles."

She was right. It was not just my dream to celebrate.

By the time we entered Charley's, I had contacted everyone, which included Mother. She seemed to be especially thrilled that I would think of her in such a moment. To her credit, she did not remind me about what a major undertaking I had ahead of me. I felt she was truly happy for me.

Sam was getting out of his car at just the same time as we were, and he greeted me with a big hug. He congratulated Jason on his achievement. Kevin was the only other one that said he was dropping everything to join us.

Brad greeted us all as we grabbed one of the small stand-up tables left near the bar. I told him I would be accepting the tab but Jason argued that it was his treat.

"I think you'd better know, Anne, that Ted is at the end of the bar, in case you haven't seen him," said Brad in nearly a whisper.

Oh great, I thought. I'll just pretend I don't see him. Would that work, I wondered.

Sam wanted to know all the details, so just when Jason started to tell him, Ted approached us.

"Sounds like we're celebrating something here," Ted said. His words were slurred.

We all stopped our conversation. I wasn't sure if Jason knew him.

"Hi there, Ted," Sam said, quickly knowing I would be thrown for something to say. "Anne's had some good luck with the city tonight on getting approval for her expansion, so we thought we'd have a drink to celebrate. Would you like

55

to join us?"

Oh, no. Did Sam just ask that?

"No, no, I'd better not," he said with a snicker. "Besides, your bride may not approve and Brad cut me off awhile ago, so I'd better head on home. Congratulations, Anne. I always knew you were unstoppable. You all have some fun."

Jason looked at me strangely.

Out the door he went. I didn't say thank you or good-bye. I would need to explain Ted's drinking problem to Sam later. Everyone else ignored the interruption as they received their drinks. Sam was quite the man to offer that Ted join us. That was the kind of guy he was, and I loved him for it. I joined in the celebration because nothing was going to spoil this odd, yet significant, Kodak moment. Anne Dickson and Brown's Botanical had taken a big leap tonight!

CHAPTER 12

O ur conversation on the way home was kept to a minimum until we arrived home and went upstairs to our bedroom. I sat on the side of the bed and began explaining how I found out about Ted's drinking problem. Sam listened intently without interrupting.

"I'd be drinking, too, if I didn't have my sweet Annie," Sam said, half grinning. He then gave me a light hug.

I was so lucky Sam never showed any jealously when it came to Ted. It would have been very easy for me to have played it safe with Ted during that early part of the relationship between Sam and me. Instead, I chose to take a gamble with Sam, who provided me with real feelings of true love. However, in this case, I came to Ted's defense and reminded Sam that Ted had just lost his mother. Her death had come as a shock, I am sure.

The next morning when I arrived at the shop, big

congratulations and *good luck* balloons were tied to my desk. Jean made a homemade sign that read, *You go, girl,* in all capital letters. I loved my little shop family and appreciated their excitement. "Remember, guys, we now have to get busy and pay for this addition!" I reminded them. I remember Donna Howard telling me that it gets harder to keep success than to get there. Perhaps it was also like the saying about being careful what you wish for because you may get it.

Nick and Gayle came in the door together to find out what happened at the meeting. They were delighted to hear our good news. However, I reminded Nick that there might be some inconveniences that may make him unhappy along the way. They were about to go out the door when Mother entered the shop.

"I just had to tell you in person how happy I am for all of you," she cheered. "What can I do to help?" She gave me a little squeeze that meant the world to me at that moment.

"Keep me focused and grounded, Mother," I said, shaking my head and feeling a bit worried. "You know I am not a patient person, and this will be quite challenging. I sure hope we don't have much loss of income in the process."

"Don't you worry about that, Anne," said Sally, who was easily able to overhear our conversation. "I've been thinking about that and have some ideas." Sally knew she was partly responsible for me making this move. I was so glad she was stepping up to the plate with this new undertaking.

Reviewing my schedule for the day, I realized that shortly I had to meet Phil, Sharon, and George for lunch. Why had I agreed to do this? I had to plan an expansion, for heaven's sake!

It was great having Charley's at the end of the block. It was so convenient for quick lunches. When I entered the door, Phil, Sharon, and George were all waiting for me at the reception desk.

"We heard about your good news, Anne. That's terrific!" said George as he patted me on the shoulder. "I knew you'd have no problem."

"Thanks," I said modestly. "We still have some work to do, but I feel really good about it all now."

After we placed our food orders, Phil began explaining his purpose for getting us together.

"Sharon and I decided that we will do the raffle quilt for the group, if they approve. In talking to George and some other folks on Main Street, we decided that to get the most bang for our buck with this quilt, we need to do a quilt show." Phil lit up with excitement as he spoke.

This was the last thing I expected to hear from them. "Where would you do this?" I had so many questions running through my mind.

"Right on Main Street," said Phil. "Where else? Since fall and winter are coming, we have to play it safe and have the quilts indoors. However, it would have been nice to hang them off our balconies and porches like I've heard some places do. I figure each shop can at least come up with one quilt to display with their merchandise. If they have more, that's even better."

"If a shop prefers not to participate, that's okay, too. We just won't put them on the map which we will provide," explained Sharon. "I don't think anyone will want to be left off the map."

I tried to visualize the idea. "So far, so good. It would

certainly be a way to get customers in each shop," I concurred. "You have really given this some thought, haven't you? We really do need something for when the colder weather starts. Last winter was horrible! One could always borrow a quilt from someone else if they don't have one. Isabella knows lots of quilters and you said she's offered to help, right? This is going to be a lot of work, you guys!" But my mind was already racing. Oh, please don't let them think I will be involved in this! I've tried to be a good listener and I always try to provide support for anyone taking an idea and running with it.

"We're working on naming a chairman," shared George. "Frankly, I think the biggest job will be coordinating the publicity, even though Phil and Sharon are really doing the hard work of making the quilt. The raffle quilt will have to be the big draw and will have to be something really unique."

"Yes, Phil and I are still figuring that out," revealed Sharon. "We have to get started soon! Isabella will be helpful, to a point. She is giving us some supplies and we will list her as a sponsor. Some of the restaurants have offered some sponsorship help, so that's all good."

We thought of some other businesses off Main Street to help promote it as well," added George. "The organization has no money to speak of. I think it's worth a try."

"I'm scared to find out where I come in on this, but I will share a crazy idea I had the other morning when I was walking," I said as I tried to think how to explain what I had in mind. "We have Halloween coming up, which seems to get bigger and bigger every year. It's second to Christmas in the retail world, as you all know from your own shops. The Colebridge Historical Society has jumped on this theme with a cemetery tour this year, which is a marvelous idea."

They all agreed.

"What if you did a quilt about the ghosts on Main Street? We have plenty of them, you know."

They looked at me like I was crazy.

"Say you do ten quilt blocks or so, picking out ten of our most famous ghosts on Main Street. You can find one in nearly every building. An example would be the mother-in-law ghost from Donna's Tea Room. Donna has that great silhouette of her ghost that she uses on her menu. I can see that appliquéd in a block."

They each had mysterious looks on their faces. I couldn't tell if they were following me or not.

"The quilt could really set up the excitement for the show. Folks will definitely want to visit those shops haunted by ghosts. You could have a guide telling about each shop and a bit about the shop's ghost. At the cemetery tour, they are even dressing like the person whose grave they are visiting."

Their looks still had not changed.

"You could call it The Ghostly Quilts on Main or The Ghostly Quilts Inside Main. They will be curious, for sure!"

"George, this is a fantastic idea!" Phil said loudly. "Anne, you are a genius!"

"Is this doable?" asked Sharon. "How cool that would be!"

"It is quite unique and that's what we want," added Phil. "No one has ever done a quilt like this that I've heard of! The next question is whether someone will want to take a chance on a ghostly raffle quilt."

We all laughed.

"This won't be a quilt you'd want on your bed, that's for sure," Sharon joked. Everyone laughed and contributed some crazy comments. After hearing their remarks, I wondered if

61

the idea was a bit too crazy.

"I'd look at it as quite a unique collectable if I won it," I said, still thinking. "I suppose if I won it, I'd donate it to an organization or something like that because I have enough ghost activity at my house."

They all looked shocked and somewhat confused.

"Really, Anne?" George asked. "So it's true about that house you have on the hill?"

"It's no big deal. We think it's my grandmother, but it's not a bad thing," I said, not thinking about what I had just said. It gave them all something to think about. Hmmm...

"I say we try to do this, George. What do you think?" Phil said boldly. We all looked at George.

"What the heck," he said, as if he could hardly believe his own words. "We can do the norm, but I think the public would expect something out of the box from Main Street, don't you? Who else could pull this off? I don't know another street with ghosts, do you?"

Sharon was now laughing hysterically.

"Now that I've got you in this mess, I have to confess that I have my hands full with my expansion, remember?" I said as they all stared at me.

"Anne, you just gave us the biggest help of all with this idea," George acknowledged. "Now I know why you have such a successful business. You have to be on this committee, even if you just share your ghost stories with us. Most of us don't know them like you do. You can be our consultant. What do you think?"

I felt trapped. This is how I always get myself into trouble. "Sure, in name only," I told them.

They all left, but not before plenty of time was spent brainstorming, working out some details, and feeling very excited. I did think it could work, and I knew Sharon and Phil were just artistic enough to pull off this ghostly quilt. How would Grandmother Davis feel about a ghostly quilt, I wondered. Hmmm...

CHAPTER 13

I arrived home that evening to an empty house. Sam was working late and had also been working way too hard lately. He hadn't complained about having pains while breathing for some time, so I suppose that is a good thing. I hadn't asked him any questions about it.

The evening's weather was perfect, with just the right temperature. I got comfortable in my wicker chair and was happily sipping my drink on the south porch. I needed these moments to myself so I could reflect on the events of the last couple of days. I loved looking at the gazebo that we enjoyed so much. I noticed Kip had pulled the heat-wrenched geraniums from the flower boxes around the gazebo and put in early red and yellow mums. This move was aggressive on his part, but right then in my life, I appreciated his effort to keep 333 Lincoln looking well kept and beautiful.

Sam's call was ringing on my cell phone. He said he'd

pick up Chinese food on the way home, which sounded great. I thought of lunch tomorrow with Nancy. If she announced she was pregnant, it would be great—except then the pressure and attention would turn toward me to be the next victim. Did I just think the word *victim*?

I hoped there was no assignment for our Jane Austen Literary Club tomorrow night. I always tried to keep the club on my calendar because I promised Mother it would be something we could do together each month. Plus, I loved Jean, her English tea, and Jane Austen, of course. Jane Austen would approve of Anne Dickson moving forward in her business. That thought brought a smile to my face.

By the time Sam arrived, I had his drink waiting and had situated placemats on our wicker coffee table to suffice for our Chinese meal. We stayed on the porch as we shared the details about our activities of the day. He had a good laugh when I told him about The Ghostly Quilts on Main promotion.

"Have you given any thought about what you'd like to do on our upcoming anniversary?"

His question caught me off guard, but I had a ready answer. "Yes, I have. I want to go back to the Quarry House where we honeymooned. I think it was perfect and it would be a nice tradition to go there each year."

"Yes, it is pretty special all right, but it was where we also had our first fight regarding when to have children and where I had my first chest pains coming down that blasted cliff!" he shared with gusto in his voice.

I had to grin, hoping he was being sarcastic.

"We mustn't forget about London, Anne. I know how much you want to go there." London was a Christmas gift that was postponed by Sam's heart attack and hospitalization. "I'd like to do something extra special and get you far away from the flower shop."

"I dream of going to London! This year, however, going to the Quarry House is perfect for us. I don't want to be so far away from home with the expansion at the shop going on. I suspect things will be torn up by then. It will not be a good time to leave for that amount of time."

"Sally can handle that." He paused. "Well, if you insist, the Quarry House it will be, sweet Annie. I hope I can get it reserved at this late date. The colors are starting to turn early this year and I imagine it is a hot spot during the fall season."

I was relieved I had convinced him regarding the Quarry House. We were both exhausted, so we turned in to our beautiful bedroom upstairs to read before we fell asleep in each other's arms.

The busy morning at the shop nearly had me late for my lunch with Nancy. We had an incorrect shipment to straighten out and some rush orders at the counter. The best feature of a small business was customer service, but it was also the most difficult part to accomplish with limited resources.

Donna's Tea Room was perfect for visiting, unless you ran into half the town having lunch there. If I didn't know them, Nancy did. You couldn't ignore anyone. I was determined not to ask about her excitement, but halfway through our soup and salad, Nancy said, "I'm sure you probably guessed what news I have."

We grinned at each other.

"You're pregnant, right?" I boldly guessed.

"At this very moment, yes," she said in a soft voice.

"Nancy, this is awesome!" I wanted to stand and give her a hug. "Do you want me to do my happy dance right here in the middle of the restaurant?"

She giggled and then got a serious look on her face. "I almost didn't tell you at all because the doctor is very worried I may not carry the baby to full term. He knows all about my past history."

"Why would he say that? How far along are you?"

She looked so bewildered. "About three months." Her face had a look of sadness. "I wanted to tell you sooner, but Richard said I should wait three months to say anything. I can't really explain everything, but the doctor practically wants me on bed rest. He has frightened me so much, I'm afraid to do anything! Richard and I have waited so long for this. I feel that if I get too excited, it may raise my blood pressure and everything." She looked like she could faint just talking about it.

"Good heavens, Nancy. What doctor would scare a patient like that? Perhaps you're making too much of it and he's just trying to caution you. A positive attitude like yours would go a long way, I would think. Many people have miscarriages before they deliver a full-term baby. At least that's what I understand from my little knowledge." I shouldn't have said that.

"I just don't want to get my hopes up too high. That's Richard's worry, of course, that I will be disappointed, not that we might lose the baby. I just had to tell you, Anne. We're going to wait awhile before we say anything to anyone else."

"Oh, Nancy, I am so happy for the two of you. You have always been able to put your mind to anything you have ever wanted, and this will be the same. You have got to think positively. I won't say a word to anyone if that is what you really want, but I would like to share this with Sam, if you don't mind."

"Sure, just tell him not to say anything to anyone. I will be spending more time at home, so will you come see me?"

"Of course," I replied, giving her a big smile. "Is there anything else I can do?"

"No, Anne. Just be there. I don't even want to know the sex of the baby for a while. It helps to make it less real."

How sad for my sweet friend. It sounded like she was half pregnant.

We turned down Donna's complimentary coconut cream pie. It contained calories we both didn't need right now. We went our separate ways with our minds racing. I was truly happy for my best friend and knew she would have the smartest and prettiest baby in the world. I must try to help her stay focused on the months ahead. How could I not feel guilty about my negative thoughts of a baby for myself when Nancy would give anything to see her pregnancy through to a healthy delivery? Hmmm...

CHAPTER 14

I felt I was going through the motions the rest of the afternoon. I couldn't stop thinking about poor, yet happy, Nancy. Mother called and broke my thoughts, reminding me to pick her up later. When I returned to my floral arrangement in process, I realized that my distraction had created a floral piece I wasn't proud of, so I took out half of the flowers and began to work on the project again.

Sally was watching me as she began the floor sweep for the day. "You know you and Jean can leave early, since tonight is club night," she offered. "This is the last piece of the day, and Kevin should be back soon to take it to the funeral home."

"I should be delighted to get on then," Jean said, putting away her broom. "I get a bit of nerves on this night, if you get my meaning."

"You do a wonderful job, Jean. By the way, what's tonight's topic?" I asked before she headed to the door.

"Julia will employ herself to discuss the fashion styles of the Austen era," she revealed. "It should be quite grand. I'll be off then, Miss Anne. Cheerio!"

So it was about fashion. That was certainly something I had not allowed myself to think much about lately. I hadn't gone clothes shopping in ages and it probably showed. If I wasn't in my sloppy walking attire, I was dressed in conservative garb for the shop. I had no idea of the latest trends. Sam was such a great dresser and paid close attention to detail. I knew he took advantage of buying clothes when he was out of town and had free time on his hands. Sam mentioned there would be an anniversary dinner and dance coming up for Martingale's anniversary. Perhaps I should buy something smashingly sexy for the occasion. Poor Sam deserved to see that side of me once in a while, and, frankly, so did I.

Mother saw me pull up in front of her home, and like always, she was eager and ready. She slipped gracefully into my car.

"Is that a new outfit, Mother?" I asked as she closed the car door.

"As a matter of fact, it is. Do you like it?" She had a big grin on her face.

"That magenta color is wonderful on you! Tonight's program is on fashion. You'll fit right in! Clothes shopping has been something I have been neglecting, I'm afraid."

"To be honest, I had to buy some new things since I gained a few pounds. Harry loves to eat out and loves my cooking, so you know what happens then!"

Really? That much eating? "Well, that's one problem we don't have, since I'm not in the kitchen. You look fine to me.

So, things are still good with Harry?"

"Sure," she blushed. "What an easy man to be around—so intelligent and even well traveled, which I'm discovering."

I let the subject drop before my inquisitive side erupted.

Mother and I sat down next to Sue after we got our cups of tea. I noticed immediately that Nancy was not there. She loved coming to this club, so she must not be feeling well. Jean introduced Aunt Julia and the topic. She said we should jump in with our comments and questions. Everyone settled down to hear what Aunt Julia had to say.

Aunt Julia began, "Like it or not, the Georgian fashions of the early 1800s were very fancy, but not necessarily uncomfortable, as you can see from the copies of the fashions I have passed out to you. They had a layered look, as we would say today. I suspect it was also a way for them to look a little different with some of the same basic garments. This was also why their accessories were so important. It was a less expensive way to change the outfit. Just look at the high waistlines. You could be pregnant for some time before you had to tell anyone."

Everyone laughed. I thought of Nancy.

"Back to the accessories. The hats must have always been the talk of the town," she continued. "They couldn't embellish them enough. They had feathers, ribbons, flowers, and even tassels. I would bet most of them were homemade. Fans, of course, were commonly used to accessorize their gowns. Fan etiquette prevailed and had its purpose, ranging from flirting to hot flashes."

Another touch of laughter came from around the room.

"It looks like in some of these photos, they inserted ruffles and collars to hide their cleavage, or maybe it was for warmth," observed Sue. "I guess we would call them dickeys today!"

Jean had a look like the word "dickey" was foreign to her.

"Yes, indeed, from what I could devise," Aunt Julia said, "they were not blouses as we might think. Lace collars and lots and lots of ruffles prevailed. I don't think we would have seen our Anne wearing one of those, however."

Chatter and more side comments erupted as they looked at me. They knew they would not find me wearing a ruffle.

"Right on!" I agreed.

"In the course of the day, I fancy that their apron was the main accessory," added Jean.

"I do like the necklace effect they used, whether it was a ribbon from their garment or the choker style," commented Paige.

"Yes, cameos, pearls, and single stones were attached to velvet ribbons, giving them a variety of looks," Aunt Julia continued. "Remember in *Pride and Prejudice*, the Bennet girls go into town and want to buy ribbons. Elizabeth denies her younger siblings the money to purchase any ribbons, but Mr. Wickham gives the girls a coin, and off they happily go to purchase them. They were displayed by hanging them from the ceiling in the shop. A pretty clever way to create a display, I might add."

"Oh yes," said Sue. "They also grabbed ribbons to put around their waist when they had unexpected visitors, like Mr. Bingley and Mr. Dorsey, remember?" It was also my favorite scene from that book.

"What I remember more was how they tweaked their cheeks to bring instant color to their faces," remarked Sally in fun.

Everyone did remember that moment and laughed among themselves.

Aunt Julia made a few more comments about the handouts given to us and then encouraged everyone to have more refreshments. She thanked Paige for bringing Nick's famous mini cannolis and for Jean's tea and hospitality. We all clapped in appreciation of a very fun evening. Aunt Julia did a nice job and I could tell that she was pleased.

"I loved this, did you not?" asked Jean to those of us standing near her.

"Oh yes," said Mother. "Jean, did you get your binding on your quilt?"

"I did directly, Sylvia," she responded. "I do love it so. My Al says it's made for our bed, so perhaps it must be so. Many thanks for all of your stitches. Please let me know when you stitch again."

Mother and I left the evening feeling good about our visit. It was also a good time for us to catch up with each other. Since Mother started seeing Harry, she was no longer complaining about her knees or legs. Her appearance was sharper and the new wardrobe was thought provoking for me. Hmmm...

CHAPTER 15

The next morning before my walk, I took a few minutes to visit with Sam while he was having his coffee. It was not the best time to interrupt him, as I had learned. We both were not talkative people in the morning, thank goodness. This was his time to gather his thoughts for the day, like I did on my walks each day.

"Jason goes to the city to get approval for our parking variance tonight," I casually shared. "He said I needn't go, so I guess I won't. Do you agree?" I looked at him for a response.

Sam finally looked up from his paper. "That is what he gets paid the big bucks for."

"If we do get the variance as planned, he said he would be in the next day to schedule the construction. He said they would start from the back and work toward the front so we could continue to do business." I wasn't sure he was listening.

Sam was not responding, which I should have expected.

This was my baby, as he had pointed out to me. I checked my laptop before I went out the door. There was an e-mail from Phil asking me for my preferred ghosts on the street. I had to snicker to myself. He suggested going with nine blocks for the quilt, so it created a nice square quilt for hanging purposes. The merchants' group had already announced The Ghostly Quilts on Main Street as the raffle quilt, and that the proceeds would go to their organization. Now they just needed to pull a committee together to plan a quilt show. The reminder of the quilt show reminded me that Brown's Botanical needed to participate. I was in luck with the botanical quilt that Mother had made for my wall in the shop. It was already quite the conversation piece in my shop and would serve as my show and tell for the show.

Did I dare bring my crazy quilt from home that I had to hide from Grandmother Davis? It would be a true ghostly quilt for sure. We all referred to it as the Potting Shed Quilt, because the Taylors had left it in the potting shed at 333 Lincoln. The quilt had revealed many things in its paper lining. We learned of my mother having another sister named Mary and she had two children named William and Amanda. They lived not far from us in Illinois, but our visits were sparse since our emotional reunion. Recently, their mother passed away, and we hadn't seen William and Amanda since Sam's birthday party in July. I must make it a priority soon to contact them.

Sally and I worked through the day, barely acknowledging the important city meeting scheduled for the evening. Like always, if I kept myself busy, I wouldn't worry as much.

"What's plan B if this doesn't go through this evening?" Sally finally asked in a nervous voice.

"There is no plan B." I nodded my head in the affirmative. "It will go through. I trust Jason's analysis of this meeting. He said he would call as soon as he knew anything."

"I'm meeting some friends at the Water Wheel if you'd like to join us. It might do you good. I hate to wait for things."

"Perhaps another time." I took a deep sigh. "If we can get this done, we will have plenty of time to celebrate, but thanks anyway. So, are any of these so-called friends male, by chance?"

Sally shook her head with a grin. "Oh, knowing Paige, there might be." She giggled. "She never gives up trying to set me up, but I, for one, am just happy with the way things are. Men just complicate things. She has a really nice guy that is crazy about her, but she treats him so poorly, I don't know why he hangs around."

"Oh, what's his name?" I queried, wondering if I knew him.

"I just know him as Tim. Not sure what his last name is. I think he's a high school coach of some kind. He's cute, polite, and quite muscular. I tease her about playing hard to get, but she blows it off saying he's not her type."

"Sounds like he's more your type. Would I be wrong?" I asked teasingly.

"He doesn't even see me when Paige is around."

"I hear what you're saying, Sally. I think it's human nature to want more of what you can't have than what might be available. I know with Ted, everyone wanted him but me. He wasn't a challenge mentally for me. He was transparent to me. I wasted too much of his time and mine to see if anything exciting could develop, and it never did. I'm sure Paige is looking for someone that will get her attention, and then she'll fall hook, line, and sinker for him."

"Right on, as Jean would say," Sally returned, using an English brogue. "I just feel bad for Tim. When there's nothing much going on, she'll go to a movie or something with him. I'm sure he thinks he'll eventually win her over. He tries to talk to me about her, fishing for some encouragement. I am so tempted to tell him to wake up and move on, but I don't."

"Well, do you think Paige would care if he asked you out?"

"Me? Heavens no," she responded with a laugh. "I think Tim might care, but not Paige!"

Sally had never opened up to me like this before about her personal life. She never mentioned friends until she hooked up with Paige, who seemed to be good for her. The writing was on the wall for me that Sally would give her eyeteeth to have a date with Tim. Perhaps in time he would take a look at Sally.

"Not that you're asking for any advice from me, but I would continue to be a friend to Tim. He sounds like a nice guy that in time will want to meet a nice girl—a girl like you, for instance."

She didn't respond.

"The way you both love sports, it should be a no-brainer."

"In my dreams!" She headed toward the door. "Please give me a call when you hear from Jason. I'm afraid the shop is much more pleasant to dream about."

How sad, I thought as she left. She was dreaming part of my dream. She needed to have her own. Paige was throwing rocks in her own path and was keeping herself from getting to know Tim. I wondered what I could do to help. Sally had done so much for me. Maybe I just helped by pointing out

the obvious to her. She certainly didn't deny my observation!
Hmmm...

CHAPTER 16

I paced the floor of the den while Sam worked on his computer. It was past nine and I was beginning to think this meant bad news about the parking issue. Finally, at nine thirty, my cell phone rang.

"I have my tools in the car if you want me to start on the expansion tonight!" Jason teased.

"What? Can we really do this?" I asked loudly with disbelief obvious in my voice.

"The vote was unanimous, but they made me jump through a few hoops first."

"Oh, Jason, I am so relieved! Thank you so very much. I can't wait to hear more about it. We'll see you first thing in the morning." I was feeling lightheaded with another wave of disbelief.

"Congratulations, Annie," Sam said, getting out of his chair. "I told you that your magic always gets you what you want. I'm happy for you and the whole gang." He embraced my happy and grateful body.

"Sally! I must call Sally!" I practically squealed, breaking away from Sam.

I grabbed my phone again and she answered immediately. She shouted a few choice words over the phone in her excitement. I asked her if she was doing a happy dance. I told her we'd discuss the new expansion first thing in the morning. She was probably the only person who was truly as happy as I.

"I've got to call Mother, too, Sam, despite the late hour." Sam just watched me jump around while he held a smile on his face.

She answered right away, as if she were sitting wide awake by the phone. I quickly told her the great news.

"Way to go, Anne," she said. "It's sure times like this that I think of your father and how proud he would be of his little entrepreneur."

"I know, Mother," I said, thinking of him also. "I hope I didn't wake you but I just had to call."

"No, honey, not at all. Harry and I were just playing a game of canasta and I am not doing so well, so this may be a good time to stop."

"Oh, I won't keep you. Tell him I said hello." I will keep you posted, Mother." We hung up and I sat down to picture the scene in my childhood home. My mother was thinking of my father as she played cards with another man at this late hour. Hmmm...

"She and Harry were playing canasta," I reported to Sam. "He must be there all the time now. Surely he goes home!"

Sam smiled, getting a kick out of my comment.

"Sounds great, Anne." Sam was trying to make light of what he knew was disturbing to me. "She could be alone tonight, you know. I'm happy she has someone to share her time with."

"Oh my word, what if she ends up marrying the guy?" I spewed, letting my imagination run away.

Sam came near me and put his hands on my shoulders.

"Be happy for her, Anne. She was happy for you, remember?"

I didn't respond. My own happy dance of the expansion's next step had just been deflated for the time being. I left the room to head upstairs to really be alone with my thoughts.

I sat down at my writing desk in the waiting room. I looked down at my notebook on the Taylors. All of a sudden, a very cold chill surrounded me, just like the day I was unpacking the Taylor's suitcase. I knew it was Grandmother. I wondered what she was making of Mother's new beau. Was she acting up at Mother's house as well? I got up to get warm. I changed into pajamas and crawled into bed. The light was still on when Sam came in to join me.

"Man, it's too cold in here, woman!" he complained, trying to sound macho. "I need to have the air-conditioning checked up here."

He still didn't get the cold thing, I decided.

He soon joined me under the covers and held me closely. He knew me so well that he didn't have to ask or say much more.

My mind began to wonder down the "what if" road. I knew that once that started, I would never get to sleep. When Sam fell into his light snoring pattern, I slid out of bed and went over to sit in the bay window. The temperature was back to normal, but I still draped my chenille robe around my shoulders. As I looked out down the hill, the lights still twinkled in the town of Colebridge. It was still early enough that folks were enjoying their night life. Was my mother still playing cards with Harry? I could see the stars, which reminded me I was living a wonderful dream and that I had a lot to be thankful for. Mother should have her own dream as well. Tomorrow would be the start of the new Brown's Botanical renovation. Kevin was going to revamp the delivery system and we would have to clear outdoor clutter for them to start. It was too much to think about. Where would we start? The thought it was hard to imagine, but I knew Jason had a plan for us.

As I did many nights, I made a list of tasks for the next day. Since I had agreed to be helpful on the quilt show, I had to begin deciding which ghosts of Main Street to pick for Phil and Sharon. First things first, I reminded myself, despite my expansion. They needed every spare minute to get this quilt made, so my decision would have to be made in the next couple of days. The street was lucky to have the talents of Phil and Sharon and their willingness to share their time. If I dared to schedule an early morning walk tomorrow, I could take notes as I quickly walked down Main Street. If I didn't hurry and get some sleep, that walk would never happen.

CHAPTER 17

Luckily, I heard Sam crawl out of bed at his usual hour. My body was dreadfully tired from getting little sleep, but I knew if I could manage to get up now, a walk was possible before going to the shop.

"Anne, you should try to get a little more sleep," Sam called from the bathroom. "I heard you stirring in the night. Are you okay?"

"I'll be fine. There's a lot on my plate today." Yes, it was very full and Sam knew it, too!

As I dressed in my walking clothes, Sam went down to make coffee. The thought of that first cup sounded really good right now and it would help me come alive. When I came down, it was waiting for me in a to-go cup. Sam knew me so well. He knew exactly what was on my mind today. He was also a type A personality, and when he was focused on something, he behaved the same way I was behaving this morning.

"I have a light day today, Anne, so I'll cook something on the grill tonight for us when you get home. How's that?" Sam asked, picking up his paper to read.

"Awesome, honey," I agreed, nodding my approval. "I will try hard to leave when the shop closes." In my mind, I knew that rarely happened and so did he.

As I went out the door, Kip was driving up to the house. He quickly told me he was there to do some trimming and plant some bulbs. I gave him the good news from city hall and then went on my way. The thought of doing Kip's task today made me envious. I didn't want to give up control of my gardens and the potting shed. I wanted to do it all.

I parked on the south end of Main Street where there was hardly a car in sight. I loved the quiet early mornings that reminded me of being on a historic movie set. The cup of hot coffee helped me tolerate the morning chill. I hated that some of the trees were dropping their leaves. The ghosts were probably still asleep. I got out of my car, still carrying my coffee, plus holding paper and a pen. In some of these places, I would have to do interviews with the current owners. Sometimes "hearsay" could be totally inaccurate. When tales are told over and over, who knows what or who the ghost is and what it really is doing?

Of course, the Soup Tureen Café had to be one of the chosen locations for the quilt. The historic stucco building had become known as the "Witches House." For many years, well-known witches occupied the house and had a school of witchcraft. I remembered hearing stories of the married couple who appeared quite normal. They were quite intelligent and they had a young child. There were always stories about them in the newspaper and they openly talked about their witchcraft. Later owners of the building complained of hearing cackling laughter that sounded like witches. Maggie, the café owner, didn't mind the witch story and even had a sign in the restaurant that read, "The witch is in." Perhaps a witch silhouette would be appropriate for the quilt block. I wrote down my suggestion and thought it was quite clever.

I jotted some notes as I walked along drinking my coffee. The Water Wheel along the creek was certainly worth including. The first renovators of the building told of a brother and sister growing up there alone along the creek. The creepy part was that they would hoard any kind of trash they could find during the day and drag it home to this building and along the creek. It took the renovators a long time to haul and clear the debris. A chicken coop was found on the premises as well, with a few live chickens running around. The current renters of the building had done a wonderful job of landscaping amid their outdoor seating. It was relaxing to hear the water trickle along the creek. The large water wheel left behind from a mill next door was a welcomed landmark for them. There were various emblems that could be used on the quilt. Their biggest complaint from the current owners was that things always seemed to turn up missing. Their first thought was to blame the brother and sister. Perhaps they were still hoarding the missing items. Hmmm...

I passed by buildings that had little to say of such ghosts, but some customers would notice unusual things. Not everyone was keen on letting the world know about such activity, in case it would make folks feel uncomfortable. Sometimes people just plain refused to believe in ghosts.

The Cat's Meow building changed renters every year, it seemed. Was it because of their ghost, high rent, or was it just hexed? Their story claimed to have a lady cook that died there. The weirdness was that she kept cooking. Frequently, there would be strong smells of soup and other food odors that always got a comment from whomever visited the shop. Whenever they talked of the smells of soup, I pictured an old-fashioned black kettle. That visual would be great for the quilt block. I must write that down, I thought. Kathy kept a cat in her shop, and I'll bet the cook kept her cat quite happy. Maybe a black cat would be better to show on the quilt. Animals and children were always more keen at seeing the ghosts, I was told. Kathy was good for our street and worked very hard to have a clever shop. I hoped she could survive longer than the others. I looked at my watch and decided I had time for maybe one more building.

When I came upon the L & L Tobacco Shop, I knew they had to be represented because they claimed more than one type of ghost in their sizable building, which was once a bawdy house of ill repute. Their experiences included a baby crying now and then, floating objects, and a Frenchman. Laura and Larry took it in stride and were free to visit with anyone who was interested in their ghosts. Laura told me once that there must have been a person named Peggy working or living in the building, because now and then someone could be heard calling her name over and over. I'm sure this building that served many travelers and renters had a variety of folks that could have lived or died there. Laura and Larry lived above the beautiful restored building and seemed quite happy in their successful shop. Which ghostly character they would put on the quilt was beyond me. The presence of a baby crying must have created quite the story. We could possibly represent the baby or the Frenchman. If only these buildings could talk! Perhaps they were, in their own way!

I went back to the car and took more notes. I decided time did not allow for me to go home and shower, so I decided to head toward the shop. Once I arrived, I started watering the plants in front of the shop. It seemed that more and more folks began their walks each day accompanied by their dogs. If Sam and I had a dog, the poor thing wouldn't get fed or be walked with our schedules. When would we have time? And, how could we possibly fence in the estate of 333 Lincoln?

After checking the day's orders, I began skimming my e-mails. One from Nancy caught my eye. She said morning sickness was getting the best of her and she was having trouble convincing herself that it was a good sign and that everything was okay. She also said she was bored staying in and that I should stop by. I e-mailed her back, telling her I would visit very soon, and then shared the good news of our expansion.

Sally arrived before Jason and she was flying high with excitement. "Have you told the others?" She was putting her lunch in the refrigerator.

"No I haven't, unless they found out another way! Everyone is scheduled, because Jason may have instructions for us. I know we are going to have to get busy and clear some things out of the back room. Where we'll go with it, I'm not yet sure."

"I've been reading up on bridal consulting. I think I will like most of it, except dealing with the mothers, who, of course, are paying the bill." We laughed.

"Glad you are checking all that out, Sally. I couldn't do

all this without you. We will take it slowly and not commit ourselves to too much."

She nodded as she smiled, indicating her approval.

Jean walked in the back door and said, "Well, it had better be ample good news here today, by golly!"

We all grinned, so she knew it was good news.

Abbey arrived as if she had a hangover and had forgotten about our meeting altogether. She wasn't looking her best lately and seemed to be losing weight. She apologized and then shrieked in joy when she heard the news.

Just then, Kevin walked in. "I take it that the commotion means good news?" he asked, holding his arms up. "Did I miss the happy dance?"

We laughed, wanting to show off. We all clapped and did what we often practiced as a happy dance once a customer left. Sometimes we danced about a good sale and sometimes we danced because of any personal good news. Dancing was always a good thing, whether one could dance or not.

Jason walked in the front door in the midst of our excitement. We clapped, bowed, and sang his praises for getting us to this point. He got a kick out of it and bowed, communicating his acceptance. "I stopped by and picked up a dozen donuts. I happen to know food goes a long way around here!"

We all agreed and didn't waste any time helping ourselves.

CHAPTER 18

Jason got down to business right away and laid out a timeline for us to follow in order to keep the flow of business going. Certain areas like the refrigeration room needed to stay intact, despite working to increase its size. It made my stomach knot, but I knew with my staff's interest, I was not alone in this project. Kevin volunteered to do extra things to be helpful to Jason's work crew. Jason said I would be meeting the foreman when they showed up for construction in a few days. He reminded me that I just had to take one day at a time with this project or I would become overwhelmed. He was getting to know me quite quickly. I also had to remind myself that this was my dream, therefore I would not get much sympathy complaining about anything.

We were able to open on time as Jason went out the door. Abbey and Jean worked diligently on twenty centerpieces for the Shining Star banquet. They all had to go out on Kevin's four o'clock delivery. Sally was our quickest designer, so she was doing all of the smaller miscellaneous orders. I was minding the front counter as folks picked up their orders and selected retail items. They were always happy to see me there instead of behind the computer in the back room. I loved to see what items people were buying. Sales always came easy for me and it was my favorite part of the job besides watering my flowers. The sale of floral and gardening books was picking up, plus my vintage flowerpots were always a hit and needed to be restocked. It had been a while since I had purchased any. Our shop was becoming a place for shop owners to shop as well as locals, when they wanted to quickly pick up a small plant or gift. We gave all the shop owners a ten percent discount, as other shops gladly did as well. They could also pick out a card and were good to go, even though our selection was limited.

We helped Kevin load the van, and I noted that I could indeed be home in time for my husband's dinner.

"Hey, Anne, did you by chance notice that one of those floral pieces was for your mother?" Sally called out.

"You're kidding, "I responded. "Who sent her flowers and why? It's not her birthday and she's not sick."

"It was a phone order, so you can check the message instructions."

I immediately went to the file and found her name. The message read: *In hopes of a good result, Har.* "What kind of result is this Har talking about?" I asked aloud. "I assume Har is Harry, but I wonder if she had some tests done or something. She didn't tell me about it if she did."

"Anne, Anne," Sally said firmly, "this is personal, and I don't think there's anything here to get upset about. He didn't say, 'Love, Har.' Har is probably a nickname she gave him. You've got to chill on this and keep it to yourself or you will upset your mother and lose a customer. I know you well enough to know that you don't want *that* to happen! I shouldn't have said anything. I'm sorry." Sally was trying to make light of it, despite her strong message.

"Okay, I get it," I said as she went out the door.

I locked the shop and headed home, trying not to think any more about the floral order. Sam was grilling out by the gazebo when I pulled up. It smelled wonderful.

"Perfect timing, Annie," Sam said, wearing his familiar man apron with "And He Cooks" on the front of it. "I thought we'd eat on the patio. It's drop-dead gorgeous out. We won't have many of these days left, I'm afraid. I think an early fall is at our doorstep. Is that okay with you?"

"Oh sure. It is perfect out, isn't it?" I said, realizing my ignorance of the outside world today. "Should I make a salad?"

"Done, my dear," Sam bragged with a smile. "I've got some ears of corn on the side of the grill, so it should be a darn good meal."

I went over to give him a kiss and hug. How could I be so very lucky? Even as a married woman, I had someone who kept me out of that kitchen, for which I was grateful!

"I'm going in to change. Would you like a drink, or do you have something?" I guessed I could at least contribute that.

"Sure, bring me another beer and something for you," Sam said as the smoke flared around him. "This is about ready out here."

When I brought the salad, I noticed there was lemonade in the refrigerator again. I'd hoped Grandmother decided to stay in the kitchen and not ruin what looked like a romantic Kodak dinner party.

"Good news," Sam announced when I joined him. "The Quarry House confirmed our reservations today. We'll have three glorious nights to celebrate our anniversary."

"Oh, wonderful," I replied, already calculating in my mind what it would mean at the shop.

I just briefly mentioned the morning meeting with Jason to Sam, so that it would not become a major discussion. I also decided not to talk out of school or tell him about my mother's flower delivery. It was so calming to sit and watch the sun set from where our house sat on the hill. There were silent moments that one could only share with someone they were completely comfortable with. Having a loving soul mate that knew your thoughts and words without ever saying them was more than anyone could ask for.

Later, in the middle of the quiet night, I heard Sam moving about in the room and saw a light on in the bathroom.

"Are you okay, Sam?" I asked, sitting up in bed.

"Just a bit of indigestion, most likely," Sam said. He was wearing his robe like he had been up awhile. "I took one of my pills a while ago, and I think it's getting better."

He wouldn't be taking any of his heart pills if he thought he was really having indigestion. This had to be more, so I got up and turned on the bedside light to size up the situation. By this time, Sam had gone downstairs to the kitchen. I found him opening the refrigerator intending to get a glass of milk.

"Join me?" he asked. He looked at me as if he were embarrassed. "Anne, go back to bed. I'm fine."

"I'll have some of that lemonade, if you don't mind," I told him. "How about we sit for a while on the south porch?"

"Grand idea, sweet Annie," he said, handing me the pitcher of lemonade.

I grabbed a blanket from the couch in the study. We took our drinks to the wicker swing and snuggled as the cool air settled around us. Sam seemed more relaxed as the medicine did its job. I hoped Grandmother's lemonade would calm the waters for both of us as we sat quietly in the darkness on top of the hill at 333 Lincoln.

CHAPTER 19

I hardly slept the rest of the night from worry, but the morning light brought signs of normalcy and hope to the Dickson household. I tried to remember a Biblical saying that truly described the night drama I so often experienced: weeping may endure for a night, but joy cometh in the morning! Sam didn't like to be babied about his health condition, so nothing was mentioned about it. I grabbed a cup of coffee to go and kissed Sam good-bye.

I headed for Main Street, hoping to continue my hunt for ghosts to include in our raffle quilt. The mornings were now a little darker than the glorious summer mornings. Perhaps I should be having this walk after dark if I was truly on a ghost hunt, I kidded myself. Having this little mission for the street merchants would keep me from worrying about Sam, Mother, and the expansion.

I pulled in front of Main Street Collectables. Even though

Phil would be displaying the raffle quilt during the quilt show, I wanted to be sure to recognize their upstairs ghost that rocked in a rocking chair and moved things around on the second floor. Phil, of course, thought it all quite charming, but others were not always intrigued by it. Sharon said it drove her nuts, but Phil said it was like a ticking clock that you got used to. The upstairs was used for storage so no one was permitted up there. Years ago, there was supposedly a lady living above the shop and she spent most of her day in a rocking chair. No rocking chair had been upstairs as long as anyone could remember, but the rocking still occurred. When anyone would go up to check on the noise and rocking, it would usually stop. Phil did recall things being rearranged upstairs when he would go up for store supplies. He often joked with his customers when the noises were occurring, so most folks never took the story too seriously. What was so interesting was that these shop owners couldn't do anything about the happenings if they tried. They just all seemed to take it in stride. I was sure Phil and Sharon would pick a design for the quilt that would reflect the rocking chair.

In the next block, I approached Buttons and Bows. The gray painted brick shop was a cute, small building on the corner that had fashion and sewing accessories that included walls of boxed buttons. It was my favorite antique shop for years, before Barbara, its owner, purchased the building. She bragged about her little girl ghost that was written up in several ghost books. Most of the mischief occurred on a nightly basis when the shop was closed. Barbara was told when she purchased the shop that the ghost was a six-year-old little girl who died in a fire at that building. She was particularly fond of a toy sewing machine that was used for display in a glass showcase. Every day when Barbara would come in, the display case was always a mess. She also talked of things flying or moving once in a while that she couldn't explain. Barbara had a sense of humor and talked to the little girl all the time. Barbara said she had two girls clean the shop one time at night and the little girl scared them out of their wits and they refused to come back. I couldn't recall the name she gave her, but there was no doubt about her presence. Other shop owners would tell her that they spotted seeing the little girl in other locations on the street, but Barbara would discount those rumors.

I took a moment to sit on a bench and drink some of my coffee as I wrote down my notes. It gave me time to reflect on the spirits. They seemed to have some things in common. Many were believed to have died in the buildings where they were still active. None of them were mean spirited, but rather just unsettled. I wondered if they could see each other. It was hard to understand. Grandmother Davis and her spirit friends each had their way of communicating. Could they really feel the love or fear we felt from them? Hmmm...

I remained sitting as I gazed at Donna's Tea Room down the street. She had the most famous ghost of all. Her mother-in-law ghost was written about in many books and tourism advertisements. I read about her ghost long before I opened my shop. The unusually divided historic house was duplicated on each side to house a family and the mother-in-law. The mother-in-law spent her days looking out the side window toward the street. Today, this was one big tea room with the divider now removed. Donna had a table and four chairs placed in front of the window for customers, but she was careful not to seat anyone there because mysterious happenings were known to occur like spilled coffee or flashes of cold air. Donna said she had to come to terms with this mother-in-law early on because Donna made it known she was not happy with her ghostly presence being there, and her business reflected it. So with the suggestion of a psychic, every night when Donna would go home, she started telling the mother-in law that she loved her. It worked instantly. Others say, however, that when Donna is away, the mother-in-law will play. Donna loves to tell her story to tourists and bus tours that have lunch there. The mother-in-law's silhouette is the restaurant's signature on all of Donna's advertising materials. The mother-in-law's face as it is shown on the menu would be perfect for the raffle quilt. I liked her and I'll bet she liked all the attention!

I couldn't help but compare my grandmother ghost with some of the Main Street ghosts. There were times these ghosts had to be reckoned with like children. I checked my watch after jotting down a few more notes and decided it was time to get home and shower. Thinking of this unique quilt, I would have to come up with at least two more block designs. It would be even nicer if Sharon and Phil had extras to choose from. Some of the designs might be too difficult. However, as long as I didn't have to make them, I didn't care.

When I walked in the door at home, I noticed Sam was gone for the day. Right behind me came Ella, who was using her own key for the first time.

"Good morning, Ella," I greeted.

"Good morning to you, Anne." Her voice held a cheerful ring. "It looks a little like rain may be starting with those clouds and all! Sure hate to see fall come in, but it's always beautiful in its own way."

"Yes, but then comes Old Man Winter! I got back from

my walk just in time, it seems!"

"I sure hope it doesn't rain tomorrow because I scheduled the window cleaners to come. I hope that will be okay."

"Oh, sure." No doubt she was going to take charge of this place.

"They come quite early," she warned me. "They were not sure they could be done in one day. I think it depends on how many washers they have. They sure do a fine job. I just had them at Harry's last week."

I stopped midway and turned around. "Speaking of Harry, Ella," I said hesitantly, "did he say anything recently about my mother's health?"

"No, I can't say that he has. Is she all right?" she responded, surprised. "I just saw her last week and she seemed fine."

Why did I open my big mouth? Ella shouldn't be talking about it even if she knew.

She looked at me with a serious expression. "You're concerned about them as a couple, aren't you, Anne?"

Oh dear, it was showing. "I guess Mother and I will always be protective of each other," I offered, feeling embarrassed.

"I don't think they want their relationship to be any different than it is, so don't you worry," she said to comfort me as she walked toward the kitchen. "They're quite lucky, if I have anything to say about it."

Changing the subject, I told her not to leave the window cleaners in the house without her being around. She assured me that I didn't have to worry about anything. She gave me a wink. I didn't know if she was referring to my mother, the window cleaners, or the ghost she would be sharing the day with. Hmmm...

CHAPTER 20

I started packing my overnight bag for our Quarry House visit the next morning. It only seemed like yesterday that we honeymooned there. When I came downstairs to Sam, he reported we were likely to have a stormy day tomorrow.

"Should we postpone?" I asked innocently as I poured my coffee in a to-go cup.

"No ma'am," he murmured, pulling me close to him. "A tornado couldn't keep me away from having a weekend with you. I have to go out of town next week, so this worked out perfectly. We had a storm there before and it was pretty awesome, if I recall."

He was right! "I have so much to do before then," I said, pulling away. "Sally has reassured me she would keep a watchful eye on any construction movement and be at the shop if needed. Thank goodness Sue is willing to help out on Saturday. Aunt Julia is happily taking care of Mia." I sighed.

"It sounds like everything is under control!" Sam grinned. "I've had some luck myself with a deal getting put off until I get back, so that's a load off my mind."

"I had hoped to get by to see Nancy. And then there's Mother," I lamented, feeling frustrated.

"It's nothing that a couple of phone calls can't take care of. You can phone them on the way there. We're not going to be gone that long."

"I suppose," I agreed, thinking it through. "I'll send Nancy some yellow roses since they're her favorite. That should cheer her up a bit."

He nodded with approval.

Sam had a dinner meeting that evening, so the extra time for me today was going to be helpful. I pulled my car in front of the shop just as Phil was parking his car.

"Glad you're here, Phil. I was going to call you today with the information I have so far," I reported as we both went into my shop. "Come on in and sit down. I'll put some coffee on if you want."

"No thanks, Anne," he muttered as he looked out the window. "There's starting to be some activity around here, isn't there? I guess it's all pretty exciting for all of you."

"Yes, but I saw the outline marked for the addition, and it looks so small. Jason said that's typical."

"I'm glad you have something for me," he said, getting back to his mission. "Sharon and I were going to devote the weekend to getting this thing going. Isabella said she just needed a couple of days for the quilter, but she, too, is anxious to get the top. She has really been a big help."

"I thought your aunt was going to quilt it."

"We don't have time for hand quilting, or she would have

been happy to do it. We are really going to have to give Isabella some publicity on this quilt. She is giving us all the supplies and charging us only half price on the quilting and binding. It won't be a bed-size quilt, so that helps. We liked your suggestion of appliquéd silhouettes. The mother-in-law symbol is perfect, so we'll follow suit with the other ghosts. I'm excited. Everyone's going to want their ghost on the quilt I'm afraid."

"I have seven suggestions right now," I said, giving him the list. "These are all wonderful and I won't have a problem getting some more. I'll give you extras so you can pick and choose. Sam and I are leaving for a few days to celebrate our wedding anniversary, so I'll get them to you when I get back."

"Well, happy anniversary." He gave me a big grin. "I still haven't had the pleasure of meeting Mr. Dickson, but he must be a special guy to be married to a great street person. He must have a lot of patience."

"You've got that right Phil," I agreed as he headed toward the door.

"Thanks for getting right on this," he said while clutching my notes. "I'm anxious to read what you wrote. I will make copies for the brochure information." He waved and off he went.

Sally and Abbey arrived shortly and Abbey was blushing and had a big smile on her face.

"There are a couple of hunks walking around out back. Have you seen them?" Abbey teased.

"Leave it to you to check them out," I joked in response. "I hope they belong there. You'd better keep an eye on her today, Sally."

They mumbled a response I couldn't hear.

Sally gave Abbey an assignment and I started to check my e-mails. I had barely gotten through a few of them when Aunt

Julia walked in the door.

"Happy anniversary, Anne," she said, holding out a bottle of champagne for me. "I hope you guys have a great time. Enjoy!" She handed me an elaborately packaged bottle that somehow reminded me of New Year's Eve.

"How sweet of you," I said, giving her a hug. "Sam will love this, too."

"Great news about your mother, huh?" she said, clearly expecting me to know what she was talking about.

"What news?" I asked, hearing the frustration in my own voice.

"The lump on her breast," she said, turning white. "She didn't tell you?"

"I guess that's what Harry's flowers were all about," I said, feeling hurt. "No, she didn't share that with me, but I'm glad it turned out to be nothing." I had to stop a moment to absorb what I had just heard.

"You're always so busy, Anne. I'm sure she just didn't want to worry you," she tried to explain. "Anyway, all is well and I need to get to the dentist. Let's try to get everyone together when you get back. Have a great time." She cheerfully waved while going out the door.

I felt numb. I sat down by my computer, not knowing my true feelings. Was Mother ever going to share that with me? Did she really think I would be too busy to hear about such a serious worry? Should I call her now or pretend I don't know? Who else did she share this with besides Aunt Julia and Harry?

Jean's arrival stopped my self-pity. "How are you getting on with your trip, Miss Anne?" she asked. "I looked about the parking lot and there's plenty of goings on, it seems. I think Abbey has taken a shine to one of the chaps. She's out there having a nibble at her lunch."

"She's not making sales or constructing a bouquet, that's for sure," I said jokingly. "I need to get a start on my errands, Jean. If I don't see you before I go away, help keep it all together, will you?"

"Right on, Miss Anne. Not to worry so," she consoled. "You and Sam have a delightful adventure and think of us not."

When I pulled in the bank parking lot, I punched in Nancy's number on my cell phone. "Hey, mama! How are you doing?" I said as cheerfully as I could.

"I'm bored and tired of being tired," she said in a voice that sounded tired indeed. "Happy anniversary before I forget!"

"Thanks. It came quickly! We missed you at literary club last week. Aunt Julia did a great job on discussing the fashions of the Austen era."

"I heard it was quite interesting," Nancy said between breaths. "Isabella has been here to see me and told me all about it. She is so happy for me. I had to tell her about my pregnancy since I nearly threw up in her shop last week."

"Oh dear," I shuddered, visualizing the mere thought. "I'm so sorry I haven't been by to see you. This expansion has thrown me for a loop. This getaway is really needed, I'm afraid, even though I'd rather pass on it right now."

"You'd better go, Anne," she warned. "That husband of yours has been very patient."

"I hear you!" I agreed, feeling guilty about what I had said. "How is Richard?"

"He's out of town and calling every half hour, I think," she said, jesting. "He'll be back tomorrow and a neighbor is bringing dinner over tonight."

"Good. Take care and we'll get together when I get back," I promised, knowing it may not happen.

CHAPTER 21

&

It was pouring down raining when we pulled up at Starbucks to get coffee for our trip. The day's forecast was stormy, but our mood was pretty chipper at the thought of a getaway. I knew with this weather, no outdoor activity regarding the expansion would be going on at the shop. The drive to the Quarry House was challenging on the winding roads, leaving us less able to enjoy their scenic beauty. The Quarry House was an amazing contemporary guesthouse that was a best-kept secret for most people. It was large enough to accommodate a small conference with guests, but Sam reserved the whole place, just as he did for our quick honeymoon. It came with a cook and a handyman. By the time we arrived in the late afternoon, we were exhausted from the slow stressful drive. After our bags were brought in, we asked for some refreshments before we took a nap before dinner. We felt we deserved it after arriving safe and sound.

Our first dinner was elegant and well planned. Sam had made menu and wine suggestions as before, so it was nearly perfect. I often wondered if Sam had not missed his calling by not owning his own restaurant. The lightning, thunder, and rain continued through the night, creating quite a show for us as we looked out into the top of the massive quarry. Since we were located high on a hill with many trees nearby, it was easy to feel concerned about lightning. It was also great weather for snuggling and feeling close to the one I loved.

The next morning, the sun was up. I was so relieved the storm was over and we could make plans for enjoying the beautiful outdoors. We slept in late, which was a big change for Sam's early rising habit. I was feeling this visit could be even better than the original. After a healthy breakfast, we first settled our stomachs by touring the modern structure with all its colorful glasswork that showed through the sunlight. We enjoyed seeing paintings from local artists. Some of them were for sale. This time, I was going to bring home a piece of red glass that I had admired from our honeymoon. It was the Turkey red like our carpet in the hallway and stairs. I was sure one of the tables would be glad to hold the delicate structure. Sam was all for it, of course. Even though we were not far away from Colebridge, it may as well have been across the country the way it felt so much different than our daily life.

Before we arrived, I had determined within myself to avoid any controversial subjects like pregnancy and shop expansions. This was going to be about our feelings for one another that were so often pushed aside because of our busy schedules.

We walked around outdoors for a while on some of the

shorter walking trails. Touches of color were starting to peek out on some of the fire bushes and trees. I preferred this time of fall with its splashes of green as compared to massive ranges of orange and gold. I loved the color green and wanted to enjoy it all year long.

After a light lunch of a delicious crab salad, we settled indoors the rest of the afternoon with a glass of iced tea and some of their many interesting books. It was good to read without feeling guilty. I wasn't choosy about the subject matter. Some of the classics were there, but I wanted a short read. I had forgotten to bring one of my chosen books that were stacked on my coffee table in the study. Just as in our last trip, there were trendy magazines displayed in nearly every room. This was a treat for me! It was good to see what colors and designs were in and out!

The cook prepared a candlelight dinner on the porch, affording us one of the greatest views known to mankind. We took our time, enjoying the cook's recommendation of wine choices with each course. Sam's interest in food and cooking were evident throughout as he asked many questions. Ultimately, it was so good to talk about us and the moment we were in, instead of where we were going and what we were doing. This place had that kind of effect. It was a good place to be still, meditate, or just be. Hmmm...

The next morning, we dressed for our hike up the quarry hill. It had a wonderful trail of rocks, wildflowers, and early fall colors. I wasn't going to mention that it was coming down on this trail that Sam had his first chest pains, which scared me terribly. Our cook had packed us a light lunch with bottles of water and a tablecloth. When we arrived at the top, we found a shady spot to rest that looked out onto the most amazing view. We could see valleys of farms and a patchwork of colors. The conversation was easy between us. We did discuss Mother and Harry; and, to my surprise, Sam understood completely how my feelings were hurt when Mother kept her secret from me. We talked about his family and his concerns for his mother in the future. His sister had taken on most of the responsibility with her since Sam's father had died. Helen was still independent, but Sam was her only son and she was extra close to him. We talked about how easy it was to go about our lives and not think of them. Sam wisely pointed out how good Harry was for Mother. We didn't stay long on each subject, which was wise.

"How did Ella do this week with Grandmother?" Sam asked with a touch of humor in his tone. I laughed at the thought of Sam bringing up her name. He usually did not want to discuss anything affiliated with her.

"Well, the cookie jar fell off the refrigerator and broke," I announced, matching his good humor. Ella said she was sure it was supposed to hit her on the head, which it almost did. She seemed to take it in good stride, but she felt bad that the cookie jar broke. I didn't make too much of it when she told me, but I loved the cookie jar. I brought it from home, remember? It was always filled with cookies of some kind— until it started living at 333 Lincoln anyway!"

He nodded with a smile. "Well, so not much loss, right?" Sam teased.

I nudged his arm playfully.

"Why doesn't your grandmother do something productive like *make* cookies instead of being such a nuisance?"

"Now wait. What about the lemonade that keeps showing up in the refrigerator?" I teased back.

He shook his head in disgust.

I dropped the subject and suggested we head back. The sunsets were so amazing here and there was nothing better than to witness one with some good company on the deck.

We slowly took our time heading down the trail. Tonight was our last night and our official anniversary dinner. We showered and dressed as if we were heading to the Ritz. Leave it to Sam to suggest dressing well for the occasion. I brought a simple black three-quarter-length dress and all my pearl accessories. It was a classic look that I loved. Sam chose a classic look too as he sported his black suit and red tie. We watched the sunset that happened to be at its best as we enjoyed relaxing before dinner. We took photos as we soaked in this Kodak moment on our anniversary.

When we walked into the dining room that still gave us a view, I noticed the table was once again candlelit and adorned with red and white flowers. It looked so very inviting. It was no coincidence since I am sure Sam had arranged it all in advance.

Also, Sam and I had earlier agreed that we would not give each other gifts, but I requested that we write each other a love letter. He reluctantly agreed, saying it was not a fair request since I was the writer between the two of us. It was something I would want to keep and reread. He understood and said he'd give it a try. After our first course wine was poured, Sam made a lovely toast to many more happy years, which we followed by exchanging our letters before we tasted our first course.

Mine to Sam was intended to be sarcastic, but kind and loving. I read aloud how I loved all the little things about him that he was not aware of, like the way he lined up paper clips on his desk in the study. I described how he ate his pasta so carefully and neatly, the soft rhythm when he snored, and how one foot of his peeked out of the covers at night. He listened, amused, as I went on and on. I really did give it all some thought. He was touched!

Sam's letter to me was awkward for him, but he managed to say it in a lively tone that won my heart. His message was short, but the best part was how proud he was of me and that our first year together was the happiest he had ever been in his life. Having the words in his handwriting was precious to me. The piped in music gave the romantic dinner the perfect feel, as if we were in a movie. The delicious four-course pork tenderloin dinner with its delicious sides and wine was fit for a king and queen. A chocolate soufflé with raspberries and whipped cream had a sprinkled message that read *Happy Anniversary* placed in the whipped cream. My love for chocolate and merlot was not amiss. Someone who loved me certainly played a role in the planning.

After dinner, we went out onto the deck that showed a completely dark view of the world we left behind. Tomorrow, the light would reveal the world we really lived in. Everything would be waiting for us. Nothing would have changed, but perhaps how we react to the same old world would be better and different. We both had mentioned how much had happened in just one year together. We both congratulated ourselves about turning off our phones for the weekend and enjoying the few days of just being together in this perfect place.

"Where did the time go?" Sam asked, snuggling close to me as we sat on the loveseat by the fire that had been lit for us. The chill in the evenings was deepening as expected in

September. "It was so great having you here all to myself. This getaway doesn't take you off the hook for doing a little more traveling with me, you know."

I nodded and smiled like a good wife appeasing her husband. "It's been wonderful Sam. Aren't you glad I suggested coming back here again?" I said, kissing him on the cheek. "What can I do to make this Kodak moment last a little longer?"

"I think I just thought of something," he murmured as he led me toward our room upstairs.

CHAPTER 22

The drive back was quiet. We were reflecting as well as anticipating what was waiting for us when we arrived home. I knew we were both making mental lists in our heads until we reached 333 Lincoln. When Sam unlocked the front door, he put down his bag and suddenly reached around to pick me up in his arms.

"If I remember, it's a bridegroom's duty to get his bride across the threshold properly," Sam said with a grunt in his voice.

"Oh, yes indeed," I gushed, surprised. I was barely hanging on to make it into the entry hall. I had to admit to myself, I loved a guy with a few spontaneous moves! We laughed about being a few pounds heavier than last year when he carried me in the door. I suddenly thought about how Sam's heart condition may not approve of our silliness.

We both didn't waste any time changing clothes and unpacking our bags. Sam was already on his cell talking to people at his office. I went downstairs into the den to touch base with Sally on my cell.

"We're fine here, Anne," Sally said convincingly. "It's a really slow day here, and there's nothing to report on the expansion, so you may as well do what you have to do at home. Don't get me wrong, there's been traffic with different workers like the electricians and carpenters, but nothing to look at, I'm afraid."

I first felt a bit of disappointment. Why did I think because of a decision being made to move forward that miracles would happen? Even though we were just gone for a bit of time, I was hoping for a flurry of business sounding in the background and that I would be hearing about how much I was missed. I took a deep breath and told myself to get over myself.

I went outdoors to check on the potting shed and noticed Kip had added a few pots in the shed for the winter. He really was looking out for me and everything on the grounds. It did look quite tidy from his work. The green grass was holding its color despite us not having a sprinkler system like most folks. I hated for summer to leave. I guessed it was why I liked working in a flower shop where things were green and colorful all year long. I pulled a few weeds while going back to the house, but all and all my little park survived without me.

Since I could access business e-mails at home, I decided to do just that. When I scanned the list on my laptop, the e-mails were sparse; in fact, they were very sparse. There were a couple of e-mails from shop owners on the street reminding me of their ghosts and saying they would like to be included in the quilt. I guess my job must now be that of ghost whisperer of Main Street. I closed the computer and decided I would take advantage of the free time, finish my job for Phil, and get in a walk at the same time. Once the list of ghosts was given to Phil, the merchants would likely leave me alone. I could just refer others to him.

I got in my car and drove to the next shop on my list, which was The Cookie Shop. The shop had been a favorite on the street for over twenty years. There was nothing like a good cookie to help someone remember their visit to Main Street. Charlotte, the original owner, had children and now grandchildren helping her in the business as she approached retirement. This was the shop in which a stately groomed, gray-haired lady in a black coat would come from nowhere and sit on the bench in front of the shop every day to get her cookie from Charlotte. No one knew where she lived and she did not respond to any conversation. No matter what the weather, hot or cold, she wore the same black coat. One day, she never returned and was never heard from again. Rumor had it that she had died. After some time, however, her spirit did return, according to Charlotte's family. Some see a glimpse of her in her black coat sitting at the table in the shop or on the bench in front of the shop. She never reacted in any way that they could recall. She just came and went, I suppose as a reminder of her former life there. She knew it was a place where she was treated kindly, but perhaps there was a story we were never aware of. Perhaps Phil could just design her black coat for the quilt.

As I approached the Spice Shop, located across from my shop, I recalled the e-mail sent asking me to consider them for the quilt. They felt they had a ghost, but offered no documentation or experiences as to why they felt they had a ghost. The building certainly was historic. It was where castor oil was developed. The merchant group often joked about having a castor oil festival someday. I didn't feel right about including the Spice Shop in the quilt, especially when so many other ghosts on the street had such living reputations for their activity.

I grabbed my parka and got out of the car to walk and window shop. Phil said the shop owners were responding positively to the planned indoor quilt show and were especially thrilled about the raffle quilt. Phil said he had already printed tickets, even though the quilt wasn't even finished. I told Phil he should say the quilt is ghostly, therefore it can't really be seen. I really felt it would be a good moneymaker and it was time for the street to have fun with something.

Charley's restaurant would probably be the ninth block for the quilt. For years, folks from the famous restaurant would talk about the loud noise coming from the kitchen. The sounds were like dishes being broken and thrown around. No one would ever see or hear anything once they got to the kitchen. Charley's had not always been a restaurant. Mother said she remembered it as a paint store many years ago, with the owners living above the shop. Living above the shops was common many years ago. Someone, likely a cook, bottle washer, or family member, was not happy on the third floor, where the current kitchen was. This symbol may be a challenge for the quilt. Perhaps a broken plate would send a message.

I went back to the car to make some notes and thought about how cool it would be to have one of these ghosts appear on a photograph. No one, not one single shop owner, had proof of their ghost. Everything was hearsay; however, each owner did verify the unusual activities that had no logical explanations. On the brochure, I think it would be helpful to have a photograph of each building that was being described. Perhaps I should make more of an effort to take more photos at 333 Lincoln. I'd love to catch Grandmother in the act sometime. Wouldn't it be something if it turned out to be someone else? Hmmm...

Going to my car, I glanced in the windows of Rose's Relics. It was hard to think that it was once a monument company where tombstones were made years ago. The plaque read *1870*. Its hand-carved stone columns and steps were a signature of the era and history. Rose said it used to be called the May Monument Company. She said there are still some unmarked stones in their basement. The slated floor was a novelty that made it easier to roll the tombstones out onto the wagon. Rose was fairly new to the street, but I could tell she loved the history and was eager to share it with visitors. Main Street had it all, it seemed. It was a thriving place to do business for many years, even after the day you died! Rose claimed she had no sign of a ghost and frankly didn't believe in them. I wondered if Rose's Relics still couldn't be on the quilt because of its direct connection to those who have passed on. A black tombstone on the quilt would be quite appropriate, in my estimation. Rose would have to approve of the idea. She may not like the idea of being included with the other ghostly buildings. First, Phil would have to decide if it was a good idea, and then we'd approach her.

CHAPTER 23

A fter an early morning good-bye to Sam who was leaving on his next trip, I remained awake with plenty on my mind. With Sam away, it took a layer of guilt off of my plate. This meant I could have a totally productive day if I were well organized. My first two priorities were to go see Mother and then stop by Phil's to give him a completed ghost list.

I took my time getting ready for my walk, taking advantage of the early hour. It was quiet and peaceful as I gazed out of our bay window. Another sign that fall was approaching was that we were now using an extra blanket on our bed. I made the bed and got dressed, deciding to take a light jacket. As I headed toward the stairs, I glanced into the waiting room where the Taylor's suitcase sat waiting. I remember reading that William Wordsworth, the poet laureate for Queen Victoria, gave this advice to writers: "Fill your paper with the breathings of your heart." When would I ever have time to breathe all the words I wanted to write about the Taylor house? Was it the actual house I was intrigued with or was it really the people in it that amused me? I didn't even know a lot of basics about the house like when it was built. Old houses like this one were full of life and death. What would I continue to learn? I wanted to record snapshots from its past, but I couldn't seem to get by the present. Was I living the Taylor house story? Was Grandmother going to allow a story to be written about Marion and Albert Taylor? Perhaps tonight before dark I could try peeking into the attic.

On my way to walk on the trail, I stopped by Mother's house, hoping I would find her at the kitchen table. I was right!

"I'm so glad to see you, Anne. What a nice surprise," she exclaimed. "How was your trip?"

"It was great and very relaxing for both of us, I must admit," I replied. I had a big grin on my face.

"That is so good to hear," she said, glowing with approval. "You both need time to yourselves once in a while."

"Now we're both back to the grind," I reflected, pouring my own cup of coffee. "Sam left early this morning and I have a very full day ahead with several funerals."

Mother looked at me curiously. "Sit for a minute, Anne," she said as she poured herself another cup. "Would you like a slice of this coffee cake?"

I wondered what she had on her mind. Was she now going to tell me about her test results, or was I going to have to ask? "Oh, no. It sounds good, but after what I ate the last few days, I may starve for a while," I teased, sitting down to join her. "We had wonderful food and got to really relax. It was a great few days!"

Mother grinned with approval.

"How are you doing, Mother?" I asked, giving her a chance to tell me.

"Good. Staying very busy," she happily responded as she fussed with putting her newspaper aside.

"Aunt Julia told me you had good news concerning a lump in your breast," I finally blurted out.

"Oh, yes, I was very grateful. Why did she tell you?"

"Why didn't you tell me, Mother?" I could hear my voice escalating.

"Anne, Anne, you have so much going on," she said, sounding sad. "You didn't need to concern yourself. Of course, I would have told you if they thought it was malignant. I have a scare like this every now and then. Many of us women do. No point in worrying for nothing. Julia just happened to be here right after I discovered it, so it was a natural reaction to say something to her. There's never been breast cancer in this family, but that doesn't always mean something. We're supposed to die from heart failure, remember?"

I couldn't believe how lighthearted she was about it. "You told Harry, right?" I knew I should have kept my mouth shut on this topic.

"As a matter of fact, I did," she said quietly, sharing like it was supposed to be kept confidential. "At our age, honey, we share things like that. It's part of getting older, I guess you'd say. Every day, there is a new ache and pain for both of us. Some we tell and some we don't tell. Most young folks wouldn't understand." She laughed. "I do feel so much younger and useful in life having Harry as a friend, I can tell you that!"

Now I was feeling like I had pried too much, but there

was no going back.

"You're not going to marry him, are you?" I asked without thinking.

She looked surprised. "No, of course not, Anne." She answered like she hadn't even considered it. "We like things just the way they are. I enjoy having some time alone. I think you can sense that yourself after all these years. We look forward to getting together and that's the way it should be. He is a wonderful friend that I am very grateful for at my age."

What a relief those words were. No wonder she never acted like she missed me so much after I left. For the first time, she could live alone and do exactly what she wanted. I could relate to that. I had never lived alone, either. I went from my home with Mother to a married life with Sam. Perhaps that's why when Sam is gone, I feel more of a sense of independent living.

After clearing the air between us, I practically skipped to work. She knew she had given me relief from an unnecessary worry.

Heading back to Main Street, my mind went back to ghosts. I slowed down to see if Sharon or Phil were at the shop early. Sometimes I would see Phil there when I was taking my walk. Phil was like me in that we knew there were never enough hours in the day to run our businesses. I saw Phil's car and decided to knock on their door.

"Anyone else but you, Anne, and I would have pretended not to hear the knock," Phil teased. "Come on in. I hope you have the rest of the ghosts with you." We both laughed at the thought. "We are really making some good progress. Sharon is a whiz at this."

"Yes, I have them," I said as I handed him a folder. "There's more than you'll need, so you'll have to choose. Like the others, I gave block design suggestions. Don't stress yourself out on any of them. We have more ghosts than we need."

He laughed again. "George said they'll publish a brochure of all the ghosts on the street, whether they are on the quilt or not," he shared. "That way, everyone will be included and folks can come in and visit with them if they choose."

"That's a great idea." I sat down by his counter. "I included the old May Monument Company on my suggestions, Phil. It has no ghost, but the history fits the theme of the departed, you might say."

He nodded and grinned. "Does Rose know you're thinking about this?"

I chuckled and shook my head. "No, but if you choose to include it, I will ask her. She loves the history of the building and may feel honored to be included—or not! Check your thoughts with Sharon. I've got to run. By the way, did they get someone to chair the quilt show?"

"Yes, you're looking at him," he shyly grinned. "I took the title because no one else would, but I have a really good committee. Isabella is included even though she's not located on the street. She'll supply any extra quilts that we might need, and Kathy has offered to do publicity, which is huge. You're my research person, so please, please hang in there. I'll be calling a meeting once I get a handle on this raffle quilt."

"That's really nice of you, Phil. I'll do what I can."

"I couldn't do this without Sharon. Having a quilt show indoors in the cold weather is perfect to get people in our shops. The chamber and tourism office already told Kathy they would help her, plus she knows a truckload of people in this town. You know, if we can pull this off, we could do a spring outdoor show and hang the quilts on the porches, balconies, and windows. Isabella said a lot of towns are doing that. I think you mentioned it as well. Can you imagine how visual and colorful that could be?"

Yes, I could see it. Hmmm... "There are plenty of shops that would like to be included that I don't have down here, so you may get some calls," I suggested as I moved toward the door. "Yikes, the time is getting away from me here."

"Thanks so much, Anne," he said, giving me a hug. "Do you want some raffle tickets to sell? I always heard you could sell the shirt off your back, if you wanted to." I laughed at the well-known phrase the girls told about me. They also told me I could put a push pin in concrete!

"Sure, but if I don't get going, I may have to do just that!" I exclaimed, closing the door.

CHAPTER 24

꙳

When I arrived home, it was becoming more and more evident that summer was going out the door. The thought of getting the addition under roof before the holiday rush was a concern of mine, but Jason assured me they could make it happen. I took a little walk around to see the fall trimming Kip had done on our bushes and trees. He was so good at his work, as well as cleaning up afterwards. The early leaves from our black walnut tree were such a pain and a way-too-early sign of fall. It made me think of our neighbor Mrs. Brody who once mentioned how much she loved to get those walnuts years ago. I imagine as this property sat vacant for years, there were many things she felt entitled to.

As I walked toward the house, I saw Sam pull up and head toward the garage. His return was always a welcome sight. I waited for him on the south porch.

"Hey, sweet Annie," he called like always. He dropped

his bag and came to give me a big hug. He was still wearing his suit, minus the coat and tie. Why was he always in such a good mood? I told him I was inspecting Kip's work and he teased me about the generous amount we were paying Kip.

"How about I get my husband a cold drink?"

"Sounds great, but let me get out of these clothes first," Sam said, with exhaustion in his voice.

I went to get us both a cold drink when the landline phone rang in the kitchen.

"Hello, is this the Dickson residence?" a man's voice asked.

"Yes, how can I help you?"

"My name is Edward Taylor, Jr., and I'm in town on a business matter, but wanted to try to pay a visit to you all before I go home tomorrow."

I gasped, hoping I had heard him correctly.

"I had a realtor represent me when I sold you and your husband the property there at 333 Lincoln. It used to belong to my Uncle Albert and Aunt Marion."

"I knew Mr. Taylor had a brother named Edward," I responded eagerly.

"Yes, I'm his only son, and my father inherited your home when Aunt Marion passed away," he went on to explain. "You may not know they had a young daughter who died when she was only six. I haven't been there for some years, so if it's okay with you, I'd like to stop by before dark today just to take a look at the place and see what you've done. I wanted to call first instead of just showing up at your door, with it being so private up there."

"Oh sure," I masked my surprise and caught Sam trying to listen. "I have been trying to figure out the history of this house and family. My husband, Sam, just got home from being out of town, but we'd love to see you."

I hung up in disbelief of my good fortune. I excitedly explained to Sam who was going to visit very shortly. I couldn't believe we would actually be talking to a Taylor family member.

"Well, it isn't exactly what I had in mind for the rest of the evening," Sam said with some hesitation. "This should be very interesting, however. Did he say where he is from or why he's here?"

"I guess we'll find out!" I realized I didn't look so fresh and the house needed some attention.

A half hour later, a distinguished bearded man pulled up in a beautiful black car. He was wearing khaki pants, a white shirt, and a navy blue blazer. We walked out on the porch to greet him.

"Hello, Edward," Sam said, shaking his hand. "This is Anne. Welcome to our home. Won't you sit and have a drink with us?"

"That sounds mighty good," he replied. Sam immediately went inside while I examined everything about the gentleman.

"I have so many questions for you, Edward," I confessed. "I don't know where to begin."

"Well, I may not be much help, Anne. I never spent much time here."

Sam now joined us with cold drinks. "I went to grade school for a while here in Colebridge, but after my parents divorced, I moved to Oakland, California, with my mother. I did not visit my dad here in Colebridge very often. After my dad's health failed him, I took him back to Oakland and put him in a nursing home. I may have some distant relatives still here, but I did not keep up with any of them."

"Oakland, California. That's where the realtor was from that I worked with," Sam recalled. "So, you were the owner we bought this place from?"

Edward grinned and nodded.

"So you didn't visit here at this house very much?" I asked, feeling disappointment settle over me. "I was hoping you could tell us some things."

"Well, my dad always indicated that Uncle Albert and Aunt Marion didn't get along very well, so I think it's why we never felt comfortable visiting," he explained. "That was his excuse, anyway. I do remember there were always a lot of other kids to play with when we did visit." He started to move about, looking at everything. "I'd like to walk the grounds a bit, if you don't mind. I can't believe how big the trees and bushes have gotten. I don't remember seeing this gazebo, that's for sure. Very nice!"

We got up to join him on the front lawn.

"We have changed a lot of things here, but we've mostly worked on cleaning the place up," I admitted. "With it sitting vacant, it took a beating, I'm afraid."

"I apologize for that," he said quickly. "I had no reason to come back here. I guess it was too easy for me to ignore. I had someone cut the grass, but not much else. You have done an amazing job here."

"Well, Anne has really taken to the yard and enjoyed all the flowers," Sam bragged. "She has a flower shop here in Colebridge."

"Yes, so the realtor said," he recalled. "Oh my, I do remember this little shed," He walked closer to the potting shed. "We used to play hide and seek in there. Uncle Albert had a gardener that used to yell at us for getting in there." He chuckled at the memory.

"See, Sam, I told you they had a gardener," I chimed in. "Do you remember his name? I love this little potting shed. We may not have bought this place if I hadn't seen it. "

He looked at me strangely. "No, I'm afraid I don't remember names much," he admitted. "I do know that when their little girl died, it was a shock to most of us. I'm not sure what she died from. It had to put an extra strain on their marriage, I'm sure."

Oh, I guess he didn't know about the Miss Martha Abbott that entered Albert's life. Hmmm...

"Do you remember anything about her?" I asked, really wanting to know. "I found some of her baby things in the upstairs attic. Did you know there were a few things left upstairs in a suitcase?"

"No, I didn't, he said sadly. " I hope there wasn't too much trash left behind. Just pitch whatever you don't want."

I couldn't believe the coldness regarding his relatives. He walked toward the back yard. "Oh, Aunt Marion loved roses. I remember a lot of roses around here." He looked at the now healthy row of rosebushes.

As we slowly walked back toward the house, Sam asked, "Edward, we're a little confused as to when this house could have been built. Do you know?"

He paused to think as he put his head down. "From what I recall, Uncle Albert had this built about the same time he married Aunt Marion," he said with some uncertainty. "My dad got a kick out of the fact that Uncle Albert wanted to make it look like the Missouri State Capitol they were building at that time. He went to Jefferson City a lot on business and he loved the pillars and peaked roofline in front. One time, my dad referred to it as being his brother's little capitol. He liked to make fun of Uncle Albert."

"Really?" Sam said, trying to figure it out. "If I recall, that construction took place around 1917 to 1918. I'll have to take a look and compare. How could he afford to build a house like this at such a young age?"

Edward grinned in response. "Grandfather Taylor and his two sons did quite well with real estate development," he said casually. Most of their land was in Illinois. I think, if I'm not mistaken, that Uncle Albert even may have had a place in London. He sure went there frequently, my father said. I wish I knew more, but I just wasn't around. I'm sorry."

"London?" I asked, shocked. Then I recalled Albert's many business trips over there when he wrote to his wife, Marion. He might have had a girlfriend over there as well, I maliciously thought. "So, are you suggesting that Albert and your father were not close?"

"I guess you might say that," he nodded in agreement. "There were letters exchanged now and then, but you really didn't know how things were back then. There were many things they didn't talk about. I know my parents were that way."

I could relate.

We walked into the house and Edward was truly amazed.

"I remember having a Christmas dinner in this dining room, but we always had snacks and lunches on the back porch," he said, trying to absorb the surroundings. "Is that still there?"

We walked into the kitchen and he saw how the back

porch had been renovated into an enclosed sun porch. "This kitchen is amazing, Anne."

"Oh, it's not for me," I laughed. "Sam designed it all, as he is quite the cook."

"I am, as well," Edward said as he examined the countertop. "I like this layout and you incorporated the built-ins quite well. The cabinets do look somewhat familiar. Everything seemed so large then."

We walked back toward the entry hall. "Would you like to see the upstairs?" I asked, still milking his memory.

"No, I must be going soon," he said reluctantly. He looked up the grand stairway and said, "I do remember a large Christmas tree that stood right here. We never had a tree that big at our house. I must admit, I think of that tree almost every Christmas."

"There really was?" I asked with chills going down my spine. "We put a large tree there also! I knew that was where to put it, but I had no idea one had been there before." I was delighted to know I had followed a tradition.

"There's no doubt that you are the perfect owners for this house," Edward complimented us. "This makes me feel really good. Sounds like the right owners were worth waiting for."

Sam and I looked at each other in pride.

"Do you have any pictures that would be helpful to us?" I asked as we walked him to the car.

"I don't think so, but I'll check that out," he promised.

"Well, it sure is nice to put a face with who we bought our house from," Sam announced.

I didn't want him to go. Goodness knows when we would ever have another chance to visit personally with a member of the Taylor family. He certainly was anxious to get on his way. We both exchanged contact information and off he went. What a cool happening this was!

"I hope I can remember all of this to put in the Taylor notes," I said to Sam who was still in disbelief. "Now, we know Albert built this house and we now hear again that Albert and Marion were not a happy couple, as I suspected."

"Well, that wasn't hard to figure out. However, I'm surprised it was that obvious to everyone else in the family. With his information, I'll have the building date in no time from the courthouse records. A baby capitol built at 333 Lincoln. How about that, Anne?"

We laughed.

It may have been Albert's capitol, but 333 Lincoln was still my Pemberley!

CHAPTER 25

*

The restless night that came from thinking of Edward Taylor's visit was not helpful for my day ahead. I put off my walk so I could get to the shop early. I knew today would be when construction would begin.

As I parked on the street, I could already hear the commotion in the back of the shop. From the pounding sounds, someone was breaking up our concrete slab. I saw a small Caterpillar moving about as if someone was digging up something. It had begun! When I entered the shop, Sally was already there taking it all in as she peered out the back window.

"Can you believe this, Anne?" she asked in amazement. "They may have this all done in one day the way they are going!" She looked like a kid watching a new toy.

"I don't think I can watch," I said as I went to my desk. "It has too much sentimental meaning to me. Did Kevin come in yet?"

"Yes, he loaded up and went on his way. He has the two deliveries to take to Illinois, remember? There were a few calls on the answering machine for you. Ella is changing her cleaning day to Thursday and Phil has a quilt show meeting planned tomorrow after work. Your mother called just fifteen minutes ago and said for you to turn on your cell phone. I guess she's been trying to reach you."

Keeping my cell off was a bad habit I had to be careful about. What if something happened to Sam and they couldn't reach me? "If I gave you a raise, would you take care of all of them and then answer my e-mails?" I teased as I gave her a sheepish grin.

"Anne, I hate to be so blunt, but you already have me managing this flower shop. You also have a cleaning lady, a gardener, and a husband that cooks. You are a lucky one, I'd say, so don't complain, my dear."

I was so surprised at her response, but she was right, so right.

"Top of the morning to you, ladies," Jean called out as she reported for work. "There's quite a match going off out there I see. I venture you are delighted, Miss Anne, are you not?"

"Yes, I am indeed," I said, handing her an order to fill. "Notice that Mrs. Weber is allergic to lilies. I have it noted on there." That reminded me of Helen, my mother-in-law. She, too, did not want them around.

"Right on," she responded as she hung up her jacket.

"Did you notice that I changed up the flower cart out front, Anne?" asked Sally.

"I barely did, I'm afraid," I answered, embarrassed. "I will look again. I was so distracted by the commotion out back. Put as many mums as you can out there. We have that special still going, right?"

"Yes ma'am," she politely answered. "I also managed to get

the sale listed on the merchants' e-mail list, hoping to pawn off as many as we can to the shop owners on the street."

Good idea.

"The 'mean mister' from next door is out there gazing about the workmen, Miss Anne," Jean reported. "I think I'll go out and distract him by trying to sell him a mum or two."

I snickered at the thought and wished her luck.

"Do it," encouraged Sally. "I was wondering how long it would take him to complain about all this."

Mother walked into the shop as Jean went out. "Morning girls," she greeted cheerfully. "I could hardly find a place to park. There must be at least six men working out back. I was out running errands and just had to drop in and take a peek."

"Too bad Abbey is not working," joked Sally. "She would know all their names before she'd go home tonight."

We laughed.

"She can probably hear the noise all the way down the street to her apartment; it's so loud," I said.

"She's living above that cute little Toodle Do shop, isn't she?" Mother asked, making fun.

"Yes, and she really loves it," I added, talking while I kept working. "What's on your mind today, Mommy dearest?"

"I just went by Isabella's and she said she was going to take us up on helping her quilt a quilt for her," Mother remarked. "She said she had this wonderful antique quilt top that she said needed to be hand quilted. I told her to come by anytime and we could get it set up to quilt. We need another quilt to do and I would love to do something to help her. I know I miss it when I can't go down and do a few stitches every now and then."

Jean came in the door with money in hand to put into the cash register. "I gave him a deal, by golly," she said, holding up her hand of cash. "The meanie went for it. I told him the yellow ones were my favorite, as I gave him a wink. 'Yellow it is,' he said."

We laughed and congratulated her.

"Jean, I am going to have you work the street from now on. How about that?" I suggested with humor. "Mother told me that Isabella is going to have a top in the frame soon for us to quilt, Jean. Will you help?"

"For sure, Miss Sylvia," Jean immediately responded. "She put a stitch to my quilt and I shall be happy to do likewise."

"I'm thinking about next Sunday afternoon," Mother suggested.

"I just can't say right now, but it's a good idea," I said, encouraging her. "She is helping with our raffle quilt for the street so it would be really nice to do something for her. She has a heart of gold."

"I can't say I quite understand anyone wanting a ghost quilt, but it's clever and different, I suppose," Mother said, shaking her head. "Now, the indoor quilt show is a *wonderful* idea. I will make sure we promote it in the bookstore's newsletter."

"Thanks, Mother. By the way, Ella has switched days on me. Does she do that with you and Harry very often? She sure is an independent sort."

"She can afford to be," Mother quipped. "I'm just glad to have her. So, will you try to come on Sunday? I know Julia is coming. You can't be that busy."

"Anne may be pounding a nail or two here on this very spot, if she had her way about it, Miss Sylvia," Jean teased.

Little did they know that I really was going to offer to help the fellows out there. I could clean up after them, if nothing else. I would love every minute of it, and besides, I could do it all, right? Hmmm...

CHAPTER 26

A couple of busy days passed before I remembered my pregnant best friend. I got my cell phone from my purse while I was still in the car and called Nancy. When she answered, I could tell she was in a good mood.

"The doctor is letting me do more now and I'm feeling so much better," she happily reported. "Richard and I are going for the ultrasound today. He's hoping for that boy, of course, so he can take over the business one day. I'm so glad I made it this far."

"This is so exciting, Nancy," I exclaimed, joining her in joy.

"Why don't you come with us, Anne?"

"Oh, I couldn't, Nancy," I said without any hesitation. I knew I would most likely freak out. "This is such a special and private time for you and Richard. I'm so thrilled you are doing much better. Thanks for asking, though."

"Your mother called yesterday and asked if I would help quilt on Isabella's quilt this Sunday. I will absolutely try to do that. It is such fun telling people that I'm pregnant. She's hoping some of the excitement will rub off on you, you know!"

I didn't respond. "Will you be sure to call me later and let me know whether it is a boy or a girl?" I questioned her, sounding eager.

"Immediately!" she promised.

I had to digest it all for a moment. I pictured the nursery that Nancy had decorated since they moved here. She was going to be the best mother ever! Better her than me, for sure!

As expected from me, I pulled up in front of Main Street Collectables for the quilt show meeting and walked in with George and Maggie. Phil had a nice large space he used for both his office and storage where we could all sit at a table. Sharon had made ham-and-cheese rollups and a tray of veggies to nibble on. Sam had a dinner meeting, so this was all very well received, making it my dinner.

George began the meeting by thanking Phil for his offer to be the chairman of the quilt show. Phil then welcomed us and told us he wouldn't have consented to accept the title and responsibilities if it were not for having such a good committee. He had already assigned everyone their duties and also had convinced Gayle to be the shop visitor that makes sure the shops will all have a quilt for display. Isabella will also help make sure they have one if they don't. He was encouraged by having so much help with the project.

"The biggest job is publicity," Phil emphasized. "Kathy will need lots of help. Each shop will need to use their public relations contacts with social media. With this show happening in January, we need to convince everyone that this show will happen, no matter what the weather. That's the whole idea. The excitement of having something for folks to do after Christmas will be a welcome message. George is making fliers for us to put in all the bags during the Christmas season."

"How is that ghostly raffle quilt coming along, Phil?" asked Gayle in a kidding sort of way.

"Great! I couldn't do it without Sharon," he bragged.

Sharon blushed.

"You don't think we need to give this away in the ghostly season?" Gayle was joking once again.

"In case you haven't noticed, Miss Gayle, these ghosts are here all year long!" Maggie said.

Everyone laughed.

"The longer we can sell tickets before we give it away, the better."

My mother was concerned about folks not really wanting a quilt like that," I said, hating to bring up something negative.

"That's true," agreed Kathy. "That's why we're going to sell the cause, not the quilt. You can always tell them to donate it back to the tourism office or sell it. I'm sure even Isabella would love to purchase it."

"This is unique and collectable," added Phil.

Everyone thought the material I had collected on the ghosts was excellent and perfect for the brochure. Kathy assured everyone that their ghost story would be in the brochure, even if it was not represented on the quilt. Most seemed satisfied with that.

Surprisingly, Sam was home when I arrived. He was in

the study on the computer and reported on a good meeting before he looked up at me. Anne, I have to fly to Green Bay, Wisconsin, next month to meet up with a client," he said. "I would really like for you to go with me because Door County is nearby. I'd love for you to see it. It's referred to as the New England of the Midwest. You would love all the shops. When I was there, I could only think of how much you would love it. How about it? We need to get away!"

"Wow, it does sound great," I said in agreement. "I guess you know I have quite a bit happening at the shop right now." I could see him shaking his head as if he knew my answer was coming and knew I would be reluctant to leave at this particular time. "I think I've read about this place. Is it like a thumb-shaped peninsula?"

"It is," he added. "Those guys are going to keep working with or without you, Anne. I have a feeling Sally has a pretty keen eye on what's going on there as much as you. Life went on when we got away for our anniversary! We wouldn't even be gone a week and you need to have a break once in a while. It's a very creative environment that you'll appreciate and the foliage this time of year is spectacular."

It did sound tempting. Just then, my cell phone rang and I could see it was Nancy.

"Anne, Anne, you're not going to believe the news," she nearly shouted. She didn't give me a chance to ask before she yelled, "We're going to have twins! We are getting *two* babies, not one!"

I could hardly grasp what she was saying. "What?" I yelled back. "That is totally awesome, Nancy. No wonder you weren't feeling so well. Hold on." Sam waited patiently for me to explain. "Nancy is having twins!"

Sam grinned from ear to ear.

"He also said from what he can tell right now, one appears to be a girl and one a boy!" she said in her excitement. "I can't believe it!"

"When did he say the due date will be?" I asked impatiently.

"He warned that they could come earlier than the normal time, but right now, it's around February or March," she said like she couldn't believe it herself. "I will have two babies in the springtime. How about that? A little family all at once!" She was really on a high.

"Sam is here and wants me to send his good wishes," I told her. "Please give Richard a hug for me and tell him he did well!" We laughed. "Please take good care, and maybe we'll see you Sunday at Mother's house." I hung up feeling the urge to hug someone. I was so happy.

"This is a miracle for them, no doubt," Sam said as he pulled me close. "What a happy time for them. Babies will do that, you know!"

I looked into his eyes and agreed with him for once!

CHAPTER 27

The next morning, Ella showed up before I left the house. She was dressed as neat as a pin and was in a very chipper mood. "The colors and leaves are early this year it seems," she commented. "That maple tree by the garage is a beautiful sight, have you noticed?"

"Yes, there are so many beautiful sights here on the grounds. I wish that black walnut tree wouldn't shed so early, though. Thanksgiving will be here before we know it and then my very favorite holiday, Christmas, pops right up!"

"Ella, I just have to tell someone that my friend Nancy told us last night that she is expecting twins!" I said, elated. "Nancy and Richard Barrister—do you know them?"

"What a blessing! Is that the Mrs. Barrister from the funeral home?"

"Yes," I indicated, nodding. "They have been trying to get pregnant forever, it seems."

"Well, this house could use a couple pair of twins, if you don't mind me saying so," she grinned.

"Don't you start, Ella," I warned, putting on my jacket. "Since your visit is a little off schedule, would you mind changing the linens today?"

"Sure, and thanks for understanding the adjustment. Harry has some things for me to do when I leave here, so I'd better get a move on it. Have a good day, Anne!"

When I arrived at the shop, I could see much progress had been made as they were framing up the structure. I could see where my little bay window was going to be in my office. Jason talked me into it for more lighting and also for making the room feel larger. I wanted to cut the expense, but then I thought it would be charming, despite it looking toward my "meanie" neighbor next door. There was always something to clean up after the workers left every night. I was so worried that debris would blow into the street and onto the property of other shop owners. All of us tried to keep an eye out throughout the day so we wouldn't receive any complaints.

Jean, Sally, and I worked all day on pieces for the Hofstadter funeral. Foot traffic was light, so we progressed nicely. Around four, as we were taking a bit of a coffee break, I got a phone call on the shop phone from Harry Stone. My first thought was about Mother.

"What a nice surprise, Harry. How are you?" I greeted.

"How are you and that big empire you're building there coming along?" he kindly asked.

"We're doing fine," I replied, sounding confident. "Is everything okay?" I felt concern over his tone.

"Well, Anne, the reason I'm calling is that I wondered if Ella has left your house yet," he nicely asked. "She should have been here by now, but I thought maybe things were taking longer or something."

"Have you called my house?" I questioned. I was beginning to feel a bit worried.

"Yes, I did, and no one answers," he reported. "She usually calls if there's a problem or change of plans." Harry paused and then added, "Well, sorry to trouble you, but if you should hear from her, let her know I called."

"Sure, Harry. Take care," I said, ending the call.

Where was Ella? This didn't sound good. Why wouldn't she answer our phone? Did she leave early to do something else?

"Sally, I think I need to go home and make sure everything is okay," I stated as I grabbed my jacket.

"No problem here, Anne." Sally said, still working. "We're about done, anyway. Kevin should be back for these anytime."

When I arrived at the top of our hill, Ella's car was still parked in the driveway. Why would she still be here? I opened the front door while also calling her name. She was at the bottom of the stairway among her cleaning supplies. My first thought was that she might have had a heart attack. She looked out of it and was not moving at all.

"Ella, Ella, it's Anne," I said in a voice laced with panic. "Are you okay? What happened?"

Her eyes fluttered at the sound of my voice, as if coming out of darkness.

"Don't move and just relax," I instructed. "I'm going to call for help so we can fix what happened here."

She was becoming more alert as she showed pain in her face.

I left her quickly to call 911 on the phone in the study before rushing back to her.

"Oh, Ella, how did you fall?" I first asked. "Where does it

hurt?" I was thinking of her heart like when Sam had fallen.

"I was almost down the stairs when something pushed me," her voice described slowly. "I hit my head I think on the banister. It was like I didn't know what hit me. I feel a bit dizzy, Anne."

"Yes, I'm sure you do," I said sympathetically. "Just relax. I think I hear the ambulance coming."

"Oh, for heaven's sake, not the ambulance," she said with disgust. "I'll be fine. I just need to steady myself." She started to sit up, but then decided otherwise.

I was pushed out the way, just like they did when they arrived for Sam's heart attack Christmas morning of last year. I wanted to go along with her in the ambulance, but they wouldn't let me. Her loud moaning and groaning made me feel so sorry for her. I could tell her pain was in more than one place. I was shaking all over when they finally took her away.

I didn't know what to do first. I picked up the scattered cleaning supplies and took them to the kitchen closet where they belonged. I got myself a drink of water and sat at the kitchen table to gather my thoughts before calling Sam.

I picked up my cell phone to call Sam and told him exactly what happed. He calmly said we needed to go to the hospital and check on her. We agreed to meet there and I knew what he was thinking. It was what I was thinking. I'm sure he first thought of the liability factor but then quickly wondered if my grandmother had something to do with this. The word "pushed" kept going back and forth in my mind. I prayed once again to God. Knowing He protects and loves me, I asked Him to look after her during her scary ride in the ambulance. I prayed, "Please help Ella, and give Sam and me the wisdom to know how to handle this."

CHAPTER 28

Sam and I got to the emergency room around the same time. No one we asked seemed to know anything about Ella's condition. When we sat down, I could tell Sam wanted to interrogate me, as if it were my fault. When I repeated that she said she felt pushed, he got up and walked away with obvious frustration and anger. I had called Harry while in my car on the way to the hospital and he arrived in just a short amount of time. I just told him that she fell near the bottom of the stairs and had hit her head. I was sure wishing that was all there was to it.

"She has a daughter in town. I'd better call her," he said, leaving me alone.

I wanted to cry.

"Have some of this," Sam said as he held out a cup of coffee to me. "I'm sorry, Anne. I didn't mean to take it all out on you. We'll need to address this issue and soon. I feel this is going to result in quite a lawsuit."

I nodded. I had no words, just sadness and a building resentment for what I knew was my grandmother's fault.

It was a good half hour later when an intern approached us with some news. He said she was going to be fine, but very sore. She twisted an ankle, had a bump on her forehead, and likely pulled a muscle in her back, all of which were causing her a lot of pain. He said they were keeping her overnight and that she made it clear she didn't want to see anyone. That I could totally understand, especially if she was going to blame us for her fall. We told the intern to tell her we were all concerned and to let us know if she needed anything.

When Sam and I arrived home, there was a recorded message from Mother asking about Ella. More than likely, Harry had called her right away. I did not want to talk to her or anyone, much like Ella. I went straight up to our bedroom without even telling Sam.

When I got out of the shower, Sam came into the room and encouraged me to eat something. That was not going to happen. Sam sat next to me and put his arm around me.

"Try not to worry, Anne. It appears she is going to be fine in time," he reassured me. "We are lucky this didn't turn out to be worse. I have a feeling she's a pretty tough lady. We may have lost another cleaning lady, but the good news is that right now, she is going to be fine and we have a very clean house."

That wasn't a very comforting thought to me right now. I looked at him, wondering if he thought I should laugh at his remark. I crawled into bed wanting everything to be better. If Grandmother was indeed behind this fall, she was certainly the mean mother Aunt Julia always said she was. I was the last relative that seemed to feel sorry for her. I was the last to keep making excuses for her. I only wanted to believe the good about her. She no longer was going to use me as her source of revenge on her unhappy life. My admiration was now going to be directed toward Marion Taylor who deserved my sympathy and admiration. She fell in love with Albert Taylor who was unfaithful to her and then she lost a lovely little six-year-old child. She lived alone in this big house after Albert died. She may have even died in this house and perhaps in this very room. I never thought to ask anyone that question before. Oh dear, maybe Grandmother scared her to death! Hopefully Edward would know the answer to that. It was because of this turn of events that I decided my story of the Taylor house was going to have a new focus.

Saturday morning as I leisurely got ready for my walk, I opened a very nice thank you note from Edward telling us how much he enjoyed his visit to 333 Lincoln. That was a rare act of etiquette from a man, I thought. Since he appeared so sincere and generous, I decided to make an additional effort to find out more about Albert and Marion and this house. I thought that perhaps compiling a list of questions that I wanted to ask him could be started in my journal that I kept in my desk.

I went downstairs and realized that today was a golf outing for Sam and that he would be gone for most of the day. I sat down at the kitchen table and saw some materials related to Door County, Wisconsin. The photos were enticing, to say the least. Sam must be pretty serious about this trip or he wouldn't have gone to the trouble to leave these for me to see. The scenery did depict New England, just as they said. Sam had circled one of the villages along the peninsula named Fish Creek. It seemed to be in the heart of the county with Peninsula State Park located there. It looked like it could have all the qualities of a real vacation and not just a getaway.

When my cell rang, it was Sally. "Are you coming in today for any reason?"

"I hadn't planned on it. Are you busy?" I asked, becoming more awake.

"Not really, but we did just have a nice walk-in sale of pre-arrangements, so while it's slow, I thought we'd make a few to replace them," she reported. "I guess I just needed to know if there was anything in particular you wanted us to do and wondered if you were going to drop in."

"Well, Miss Sally dearest, since when did I become an authority on giving anyone advice or orders lately?" I joked. "What's going on? Are you alone?" She certainly didn't need to be talking about this with customers in the place. Was something else on her mind?

"Yeah, I'm fine here," she began. "No one's in the shop now, so I was going to tell you that I went to a party last night with Paige. It was at Tim's apartment so, of course, I was dying to see it." She paused.

"Well, that's good. What happened?" I found myself waiting impatiently, as I do so often.

"His place was pretty cool and there were quite a few people there. I think most of them were other teachers he knew. I got to have a nice conversation with him for a change. Paige, as usual, was anywhere but with him. He's thinking that she's kind of his date for the evening, but she's not around half the time. Long story short is that I walked into the kitchen to get another drink and found her kissing this other guy." She took a deep breath. "Can you believe it? Right under Tim's roof!"

"Okay, so Tim had no clue, right?" I jumped in to say.

"No! Of course not! I quickly went out the door and wanted to go over to Tim to tell him what a fool she was playing him for, but instead I left, telling Tim I didn't feel well. I think he thought it odd that I didn't leave with her, but he wasn't thinking about *me*! Was I stupid not to take advantage of my time with him and tell him the truth?"

"You did exactly the right thing," I said, reassuring her. "You would only have been the bad guy if you had told him something like that. Plus, remember you are Paige's friend. You don't want to tattle on her! It will all come to light for both of them. Trust me."

"Yup, thought about that," she said agreeing with me now. "Thanks Anne. I needed a different perspective on this and that's why I was hoping you were coming in. I'm not in high school anymore, or believe me, I would have ratted on her."

We both laughed.

"Just don't call me a 'wise old soul,' " I warned her.

CHAPTER 29

✺

It felt good walking into my old house on Sunday, knowing I was going to see friends and family that I care about. Aunt Julia, Nancy, Sue, and Isabella were already in the kitchen nibbling on some of Mother's treats that were about to be carried downstairs to the basement. Mother had a big hug for me and told me Jean would be a little late in arriving.

"I can't wait to see your quilt top, Isabella," I said with anticipation.

"It's nothing unusual, but I love it and it's from family," she said as she was about to carry a tray of fruit downstairs. We all assisted in taking something down the steps and saw the beautiful quilt top in the frame, waiting to be quilted.

"Oh Isabella, I love this pattern," admired Sue. "I think my mother has a quilt similar to this."

"Now that you have all found a place to sit, I think Isabella needs to tell us about the quilt," suggested Mother.

All eyes and ears were now focused on Isabella.

"Oh dear, I guess I first want to say how honored I am that you are all willing to help me quilt this," she began. "This top has been in my family since the 1930s. My mother gave it to me, but it was made by Aunt Harriet. It's called Grandmother's Flower Garden. I'm told that it took her a long time, and I think you can see why. It's all hand pieced."

Everyone moaned at the mere thought.

"She started it in the 1930s, but I'm not sure when she finished it."

"The pieces are so small, and accurately cut to perfection, right Isabella?" Mother asked as she ran her fingers across the top.

"Yes, they were hand pieced and hand cut," Isabella confirmed. "She fussy cut these hexagons to identify the exact pattern she wanted to show. This takes an incredible amount of time, as you can imagine."

Everyone repeated the term "fussy cut" as if they found it amusing.

"The smaller these pieces are in a quilt, the more likely the value of it will be higher."

"So quilting an old top is okay and it doesn't hurt the value?" I asked out of curiosity.

"It doesn't unless you finish it out of character to the original quilt," she explained. "I chose a plain cotton backing fabric and cotton batting like they would have done back then. When you try to keep to the original look of the quilt, the buyer has less concern. Even if you finish the quilt for your purpose, you want the quilt to look like a 1930s' quilt, not one made last week."

Interesting, I thought. It made sense.

"The flowers made out of hexagons are referred to as rosettes in some quilt books," Isabella shared. "The best way to quilt this pattern is to quilt around each hexagon about one-quarter inch. If you do that, you will miss the seam, making it easier to quilt. It is not marked and you probably noticed that. Once you get started, it will become easier as you quilt."

"You've got to be kidding," said Aunt Julia. "That's a lot of quilting. I don't know if I can quilt it without a line for it."

"I know, but you'll get the hang of it and the results are worth it. Just trust me," she insisted.

"Well, let's get started," Mother said, putting two spools of thread on the quilt. "If that's the way Isabella wants it quilted, that's what we'll do. The practice is good for us! Does everyone have a thimble?"

"I just don't know if I can get in the groove again," I sadly stated.

All of us became very quiet as we made our first attempts.

"Aren't we glad to have the new mama to be with us today?" Mother said, starting the conversation.

"Thanks! It feels good to be here and out of the house!" Nancy said with a big smile.

"With two babies coming in the spring, ladies, we need to get this quilt out of the frame as soon as possible," Mother encouraged. "Those babies are going to need quilts!"

"Oh, Sylvia, how sweet," Nancy said, blushing with joy. "I think Grandma Barrister has already bought out every baby store she can find."

Everyone chuckled.

"Look at each of these hexagons. The roses are so perfect that she cut," noted Sue. "I don't think I have ever seen this done in a quilt."

"My aunt was a fussy person, always doing everything better than my mother," explained Isabella. "I can just see her attempting this. My mother made very simple quilts like the Nine Patch and Dresden Plate. I wish she had lived long enough to know I now have a quilt shop. Thank goodness Aunt Harriet didn't see it happen or I would be under surveillance for sure!" Everyone laughed and agreed that her mother would have been proud of her.

Just then, the wall phone rang in the basement. Mother answered. It was Jean who was calling to tell us she would not be attending. She had friends who dropped by unexpectedly and were not planning to leave anytime soon. Mother told her to be sure to come again and that we would see her at the literary club. We always looked forward to seeing Jean. She was typically so funny and the life of the party.

"Where is Sarah today?" I asked Aunt Julia.

"She's with Jim," she said with some reluctance. "She loves spending time with him now that he has his new loft at the Foundry. I guess you know he lives there now."

"No, I didn't know. Did you, Mother?" I asked. "Wow, he told me some time back that he would have loved to live there, but he couldn't afford it."

"Well, he must have robbed a bank, because Sarah said he's also been looking at new cars," she reported in a sarcastic tone. "She said they are talking about what car he will buy her next year when she turns sixteen. I'm certainly not in a position to buy her a car. He's determined to spoil her. I guess most divorced parents want to be the most favored. She is pretty impressionable at this age."

"Sarah is driving? " Mother asked, gasping. "Our little

Sarah is turning sixteen? That can't be possible."

"She is and is also growing way too fast," Aunt Julia said with a sigh in her voice. "I meant to tell you, Anne, that I went to my neighbor's for a birthday party last week and Ted was there."

"Oh, lucky you," I said being curt.

"He came alone and didn't stay long," she said as she was threading her needle. "I think he had a little too much to drink before he got there. He was mighty friendly to me, I must say, and of course, he asked about you!"

"Yeah, I've been around when he's been friendly in that way," I said with disgust. "I was hoping he was getting his drinking under control." I wanted to drop the subject and Mother knew it.

"Please help yourselves to some of the goodies," Mother said, pointing to the sidebar that displayed too much food.

"I hear the merchants are planning a quilt show," Sue brought up. "Are you involved with that too, Isabella?"

"Yes, but I have to tell you, the quilt show committee has it all organized and Anne here is quite the ghost historian," she divulged.

They all looked clueless as to what she was referring to.

"Why does the show need a ghost historian?" Sue asked innocently.

Everyone had to laugh.

"Oh, it's for our raffle quilt," I explained. "We want to make something unique that represents the street, so we're creating it from motifs of some of the ghosts that reside in the buildings. Phil and his employee, Sharon, from Main Street Collectables are doing most of the work and Isabella has graciously offered to help find quilts if we need them as well as offering her machine quilting services. And a very generous offer it is, considering she isn't located on Main Street."

Isabella ignored the compliment.

"Portraying the ghosts was Anne's idea, and I think it'll be a big hit," Isabella bragged.

Judging from the looks on their faces and the silence, I wasn't so sure they thought so.

Two hours later, after having three cookies and a small lemon bar, I was ready to go home with my sugar high. Once I started the process of leaving, others followed with a promise to return soon. When I reached the door to leave, Mother said quietly that Ella was doing much better. I thanked her for not bringing up the accident. Mother said Ella would be back cleaning once her ankle healed.

"Yes, I'm going to call her tomorrow," I told Mother. "She has made it clear she doesn't want visitors. I did send her some flowers, however."

"I know how she must feel, but she'll probably like the flowers. Good idea." Mother said sadly. "You shouldn't blame yourself, Anne. Accidents happen."

"The least I can do, Mother," I nodded, going out the door.

CHAPTER 30

The first thing I did after coming back from my walk in our neighborhood was to call Ella. I dreaded the response but I knew it would feel better to address the situation earlier rather than later.

"Ella, it's Anne." I greeted her as normally as I could. "I'm calling to see how you are doing,"

"Not bad. Nothing a little time can't fix," she said rather calmly. "I still can't put all my weight on my right ankle and foot, but that'll get better in time, I'm told."

"Oh good," I said, relieved.

"I'm sorry to leave you for a bit without some help, but as I told Harry and your mother, I should be back fairly soon," she explained with some certainty.

"You're kidding, Ella. You are willing to return with all the craziness that goes on here?" I asked in disbelief.

She laughed a little at my question. "Anne Dickson, I

don't scare easily, so that is not the issue here," she stated seriously. "If you feel you need to replace me because of your needs, you should absolutely do that. I am just going to have to be a little more careful."

I couldn't believe her words!

"Of course we'll manage here, Ella," I assured her. "Just let us know when you are ready to return. Sam and I want to take care of any of your medical bills, and if you need anything else, just let us know."

"Oh no, my dear, I am well insured, so that is not necessary," she responded.

I was so impressed and shocked at the conversation we had just shared. I called Kevin on his cell and told him to drop off another ready-made floral piece and deliver it to her as soon as possible. Perhaps this would help my guilt, at least.

When I arrived at the shop later than usual, the workmen were hammering away. I was concerned about their production with the threat of rain coming later. Jason's last report to me was that the goal was to get the addition under roof as soon as possible and then they would tear down the back inside wall of the shop. That thought terrified me.

"Anne, Phil from the street is on the phone," Sally called from the front counter. Now what, I wondered. I didn't have time now for street issues.

"Yes, Phil, what can I do for you?" I answered.

"Well, Sharon and I will be over at Isabella's after the shop closes and we wondered if you could stop by to give us a little advice," he explained. "It won't take long."

"Sure, I just need to pick up Mother in time to get to the literary club tonight," I answered.

"Yes, Isabella said she is going to that as well," he

commented. "Meet you there, then."

Just as expected, the rain began to pour, taking all the workers away quite quickly before their regular quitting time. I called Sam and had to leave a message reminding him about my literary club tonight, and that I had some good news to share with him about Ella.

As soon as I walked into Isabella's Quilt Shop, she locked the door for the day. In the back classroom were Phil and Sharon, laying out all the black ghostly quilt blocks.

"Wow, are they all done?" I asked, surprised. "How cool they look!"

Phil was moving them all around and replacing some now and then. It was striking with all the black silhouettes.

"I wanted to get advice from Isabella to see which ones would be the most compatible together," Phil said as he rearranged. "I also wanted to make sure we would not slight anyone by our choices, Anne. You would be the best to tell us that. I think we need to narrow this to nine blocks," he said, staring at the quilt. "We might think of some way to incorporate the ones we don't use by doing something in the border or on the back of the quilt."

"They all turned out to be quite intriguing designs, don't you think, Anne?" Isabella asked. "I have to admit that I am partial to the mother-in-law silhouette. I'm sure folks will want to know about each one. I know I would. Phil, you may want to put that in the center block. Plus, she's probably the most famous ghost on the street, if I recall."

"Yes, I agree with you," I responded as I looked at them all. The mother-in-law sets the tone for the rest.

"Your appliqué is wonderful," Isabella complimented Sharon.

Sharon blushed.

"So, when do you think the top will be finished for them to quilt?" I asked Phil and Sharon.

"The rest won't take long, depending what we do with the borders, I guess," Sharon answered, putting her finger on her chin. I think this will be quite the quilt, if I have to say so myself."

"We want to debut it around Halloween because Kathy has advertised it as such," said Phil as he gathered up the blocks.

"That's great, you guys!" I complimented them. "The sooner we start, the better!"

We began to leave.

"Thanks for the encouragement from you all," Phil said, opening the door for me.

"Isabella, I'll see you at Jean's house shortly, okay?" I confirmed as I waved good-bye.

CHAPTER 31

꙳

As Mother and I were driving to Jean's house, I began describing the ghost quilt to her. Her response was as if she hadn't heard me—not that I thought she'd love the idea of the ghost quilt. I went to the next subject.

"I guess by now you've talked to Ella, right?" she asked before we got out of the car.

"Yes, I can't believe she wants to come back," I said, shaking my head in disbelief. "I'll be fine without her for now, but I'm not sure about you and Harry."

"I know she needs the money. Perhaps this will send a message to that mean spirit that likely had something to do with this," Mother snickered.

When we walked in the door, there was a room full of chatter and clinking teacups. Visiting Jean's house was like experiencing a taste of England, which I still had on my bucket list. Somehow, I knew I'd get there someday. Jane, England, and tea were subjects I wanted to know more about. Mother and I sat in Jean's charming love seat that only held two people. It was such a delicate antique. I think everyone else was afraid to sit on it.

Jean finally got our attention. "How are you all getting on?" she asked. Everyone responded in their own ways. "I have long wanted our club to converse about the sisterhood between Jane and Cassandra. I did not have a sister, but if you do, you should value it so."

Yes indeed, I thought to myself, as I had often wished for one.

"Cassandra was the most treasured soul in Jane's life," she went on to say. "Here is a quote from Cassandra after Jane's death: 'She was the sun of my life, the gilder of every pleasure, the soother of every sorrow. I had not a thought concealed from her, and it is as if I had lost a part of myself.' Silence fell across the room. Jean continued, "Early on, their parents decided to send Jane and Cassandra away to school for a spell so the parents could take in more male borders and increase their income. Jane was seven and Cassandra was ten when they tallied off to Oxford with their cousin, Jane Cooper. Their older brother was already studying there. They did not return home until Jane was eleven. I cannot devise the practice or reasoning with such young girls, if you get my meaning. I fancy it was quite so, however."

Odd, I thought.

"How coldhearted," Sue commented to me as I sat near her.

"When the daughters were apart, they wrote frequently to each other," Jean went on to say. "Unfortunately, after Jane died, Cassandra destroyed most of the letters between the two of them."

Sad sighs were heard.

"Cassandra was the artist that we read about, right?" asked Aunt Julia.

"Yes, in fact, one of the few pictures the world has of Jane is one that Cassandra did in watercolor one afternoon on an outing," Jean shared. "Jane had her back to Cassandra as she sat on a cliff. I am pleased to have a copy for you to see. She signed it in 1804. Jane, however, is faceless, but I like it, do you not?"

We all responded in the affirmative.

"Some people don't like their picture taken—like me," Sue jumped in to say. "I'll bet out of respect to Jane, Cassandra didn't show Jane's face. "I'm sure it's why few, if any, pictures are found of Jane. Some say she wasn't attractive; however, some say otherwise."

"Good point," I said, thinking about it for a bit.

"I want to insert a trivia question here, if I might," Jean said. "What were the precious gifts that Lieutenant Charles Austen gave to both Cassandra and Jane?"

There was silence.

"I think it was crosses. They were each on a chain, am I right?" asked Sue, raising her hand as if she were in school. "I saw a sketch or photo of them in one of the books on Jane."

"Yes indeed, Miss Sue," Jean said as she clapped her hands. "Jolly good! They were each a different shape, but both were quite grand and expensive."

"Wasn't Cassandra engaged? Or did she marry?" I asked.

"Cassandra was engaged to a man by the name of Thomas Fowle, but before they married, he died of yellow fever when he went to the West Indies. He was buried at sea, the poor chap. They said she quickly adopted widow weeds and abandoned all future thoughts of matrimony."

"Widow weeds? What's that?" asked Mother, trying not to laugh like the others.

"Settle down, ladies," Jean scolded. "They were garments that were worn during a period of mourning or time of sorrow. Some widows mourned a year and some never stopped, especially if they were quite elderly."

"This is most interesting," Mother noted. "It says a lot about how devoted Jane's sister was to her. I don't think it was that unusual for your siblings to be your best friends back then. I know the value of having sisters and how they become your friends as well. I have my little sister here with me this evening."

Everyone looked at Aunt Julia as she blushed. "Thanks, Sylvia," she said. "I love being the *younger* sister and treasure you as well!"

We laughed at the dig she threw in.

"There is so much more to learn about Jane and her siblings, but this sisterhood was so extra special. I thought you would delight in the discussion and would value it such as you read more about them," Jean said in closing. "I collect the more you gather about the chaps who surrounded Jane, the better one knows her. You all have been most engaging and I thank you! Please have a bit more tea and biscuits before you leave off!"

"Splendid program," shouted Aunt Julia. The rest vocalized their gratitude as we said our good-byes to great friends and family. Mother and I remarked about how much Jean appreciated and loved Jane Austen. When Jean shared information about her, it seemed to come straight from England, where her own heart remained. It was a night of warm and fuzzy feelings, along with some education. Jane and Jean sure had a way of bringing folks together!

CHAPTER 32

The next evening, I met up with Sam for dinner. I knew I had to make up my mind about this trip.

"So, can we book the trip to Door County or not?" Sam said as we were eating at Charley's. "We only have that window of time in October to be able to go."

"How long will we be gone?" I asked shyly, taking another bite of my chicken quesadilla.

He grinned at me, knowing I had succumbed to the thought. "We can make it a short or a long weekend. We could fly into Green Bay, but it's a wonderful drive this time of year," he said, trying to be accommodating. "It's really part of the experience of the area."

"I'll let you know for sure as soon as I talk with Sally," I replied. I was beginning to feel uneasy.

"You start getting busier at Thanksgiving and my mother will likely visit again, so it would be nice for us to get away before then," he noted, continuing to eat his salad.

"You're right, you're right," I said, frustrated. It was like someone was trying to make me take medicine because it was best for me. We dropped the subject, but I knew Sam was going to win this battle. I had to admit, it sounded wonderful. It would be a lovely drive, but if I went, I preferred to fly.

When I got home, Nancy had a wonderful thank you message on my phone. I had sent her a small pair of vintage flowerpots as a congratulations gift. One was a pink elephant and the other was blue. She loved older things as much as I.

Sam quietly went on up to our bedroom early to read, so I went to call Sally at home. I had to do it while this dilemma of the trip was on my mind.

"Anything wrong?" answered Sally at the other end of the line.

"No, silly," I said with a snicker. "Didn't mean to call this late, but Sam and I had a conversation at dinner about the two of us going to Door County near the last of this month. We wouldn't be gone long, but I wanted to discuss it with you first."

"So, what's the problem? And who's the boss here, Miss Anne?" she coyly asked.

I smiled, knowing it sounded rather silly. "Well, there are plenty of reasons not to go, but I'm under pressure to go, I'm afraid."

"Well, it sounds like pretty nice pressure, if you ask me," she teased. "It's no big deal, Anne. That's what you have me for." She was always so confident and positive. "Abbey was just saying she'd like more hours, and if we really have to, we can use Sue for a Saturday morning. I wish I had someone who wanted to swish me away for a vacation."

I laughed, wishing she did too!

So, speaking of wishes, what's up with Tim?" I boldly asked.

"The good news is he has called a couple of times to talk, however, it's usually to pump me for information about Paige. That's okay, I suppose. They say sometimes good friends become lovers at some point. How is that for wishful thinking?"

"That's the spirit." I wanted to cheer her. "I guess I'll tell Sam okay, then. We both are going to owe you big time."

She teased that she would take advantage of that.

I went directly upstairs to tell Sam but he was already asleep. I was not surprised. He had long stressful days and worked tirelessly without complaining. It was so easy to forget about Sam's health issues with all his normal activities every day. He could use a vacation, and the more I thought about it, I applauded his effort to do so. After I got ready for bed, I slipped in beside him and kissed him on the cheek.

"You just had your way with me, Sam," I whispered in his ear. "Door County, here we come!"

He smiled in his slumber.

I had reluctantly welcomed fall, as much as I tried to ignore it. But for the next few days, it was time to bring the rest of my spring and summer plants into the potting shed where they could rest for the winter. It made me sad. Leaf pickups were scheduled as I watched all the colors of the season fall away.

Today was hectic and ended with a merchants' meeting at Kathy's shop. Phil made sure I attended and everyone was hyped up about seeing the unveiling of the ghostly raffle quilt. The timing was perfect with the Halloween season approaching, I had to admit. Cheers and applause erupted when Phil and Sharon unveiled the quilt.

"I'm so excited they decided to put my ghost in the quilt," said Barbara from Buttons and Bows. "Thanks so much, Anne, for all you've done. This will sell tickets like crazy."

I was glad to hear she thought so, but I wasn't sure how other people would receive it. I wanted to sneak out from the meeting early, but reports kept coming from the quilt show committee and George encouraged everyone to stay for the entire agenda. Everyone was in a good mood and when this group had a focus, like the show, they showed up at the meetings.

On my drive home, Sue called to remind me of the cemetery tour. She, Sarah, and Aunt Julia were going, but Sue had no luck convincing Mother to go.

"I'm afraid I am going to miss that, Sue," I announced. "It really intrigues me, but Sam and I are going to take a quick trip to Door County, Wisconsin, to see the foliage and attend to some business that Sam has in Green Bay."

"Good for you, Anne," she said with some surprise in her voice. "I've always wanted to go there. Well, I'm sorry to say you will miss Mia's Halloween outfit."

"Oh no! What will she be?" I asked, excited.

"She loves Minnie and Mickey Mouse, so I found a cute Minnie outfit online for her. She is so excited. We'll take her by your mother's house, of course."

"Be sure to take pictures of Mia and also the cemetery tour, if you don't mind! I really wanted to hear what they would say about Albert Taylor's grave. Could you record that with your phone, if they let you?"

"Oh sure," she agreed. "Hey, you both have a good time. I'll want to hear all about it. You are one lucky lady!"

CHAPTER 33

 ❧

I did my best to prepare for a quick fall trip that promised color, charm, good food, wine, and precious time with my husband. I took comfortable clothes, hiking shoes, and one nice dinner outfit for a special evening, which Sam assured me would be wonderful.

When we arrived at the hotel in Green Bay, Sam left to meet with a client of Martingale while I soaked in the tub and took a short nap. I thought napping would occur on the drive, but it was much too pretty to shut my eyes. Before I started dressing for dinner, I called the shop, only to get our answering machine. It was not after hours, so I became concerned. Sam came back as I was hanging up. He brought plenty of tourist material and told me we would be staying in a charming village called Fish Creek. He said it was near the Peninsula State Park, a place where we could hike.

"The lady at the desk said shopping is the best in Fish Creek, so I thought you'd like to hear that," Sam teased as he connected the back of my pearl necklace. He was very pleased with the turn of events regarding his meeting, so I could tell he was now ready to start his vacation.

"I'm sure everything will be great, Sam," I said, giving him a wink. "I hope you didn't plan every minute so we can have some freedom to do what we feel like doing."

He just grinned, sending me signals of the control side of his personality.

We dined that first night at a nearby Italian restaurant that Sam had frequented before while on business. It was intimate, which I liked. Neither one of us liked places or events with big crowds, unless it was in my shop, of course. We had great wine made locally in their vineyard and a divine homemade pasta dish that made for a very romantic evening. It was my kind of meal.

As we drove in our fancy rented sports car to our destination the next morning, Sam shared with me that his mother would likely fly in for Thanksgiving. That meant we would again be planning a dinner for the rest of the family as we did last year.

"We do have the perfect house for entertaining, Sam." I did seem to remember having too many cooks in the kitchen last year. "We started a fine tradition and it takes the work away from our widowed mothers."

He nodded. "We have the perfect house for a lot of things, Anne," he said, as if I were supposed to get a hint.

"I know what you're hinting at, Mr. Dickson," I said with a grin. "I will have to see how well I do with those Barrister twins. I cannot wait to see perfect Nancy balance two babies!"

He laughed.

The curvy, scenic drive was indeed a visit to New England as we drove through charming villages viewing adorable bed-and-breakfast places, shops, and marinas looking out to the bay. As we got closer to Fish Creek, we drove through a picture-perfect village called Egg Harbor. The flowers were breathtaking. I told Sam to pull over on the side of the road a couple of times so I could get some photos. I definitely wanted to come back and visit some of the shops I saw along the way. The foliage was just perfect, providing a great view from any direction. One stop we made was near an antique mall located in a barn. With limited time, I managed to come out with three vintage flowerpots, a charming tablecloth, and a gorgeous ceramic watering can that would be perfect for displaying in my shop. Sam told me we could have things shipped home if I lost too much control. That was the wrong thing to say.

When we came around a sharp curve, we suddenly entered Fish Creek. The flower-lined shops and outdoor restaurants were so inviting. I was nearly starting to hyperventilate. Where had I been all my life to miss all this beauty? Our modern condo had the latest and greatest of new comforts, which was something Sam had gotten particular about with all his travel. I, on the other hand, liked the charm of old bed-and-breakfasts filled with antiques surrounded by English gardens. This condo, however, was nicely nestled at the front of the park, just as Sam had described. I liked it. We quickly unpacked so we could get in a walk before dinner. Sam put on a khaki hat that I had not seen before. He looked like a grown Boy Scout that needed a cute Girl Scout to accompany him. All I had to change were my shoes, and then we were off to explore.

The colors were of every shade, no matter what direction, as they glistened and crackled under the sun. Sam described every turn and historic point as if he were a professional tour guide. It was great to see him so relaxed and happy. We passed a secluded graveyard where very old tombstones carried the names of the founders in the area. That was an unexpected find, but I learned that Fish Creek was quite historic. It was a lot to absorb for one day, so we were truly exhausted when we returned.

A late dinner at the famous White Gull Inn was like walking into a historical magazine of the rich and famous in New England. Sam requested a table by the fireplace where we dined by candlelight eating fresh lobster, beet salad, and heavenly baked bread in cute clay pots. The waitress and waiters were dressed in period costumes. A harpist was playing soft music in the background. She tried to talk us into attending a fish boil dinner the next night, which Sam quickly dismissed. Sam said they were very popular with the tourists who came to the area for the first time, but he didn't enjoy the cuisine.

"Like me, Sam?" I asked innocently. "I don't want to miss anything. Why don't you like the fish boils?"

He snickered, knowing I would ask.

"Well, let's put it this way," he began. "It's a big huddle of tourists watching the help make a big fire before they throw in potatoes and fish. It's not exactly my idea of a good meal on vacation. Do you think you'd really like it? As you said many times, you don't want to miss anything!"

"You made a good choice," I kidded. "I can see how some would love it, though. This is where the best seafood should be enjoyed, not boiled!"

The perfectly charming waitress asked if we would like their specialty of bread pudding for dessert or one of their many other options that looked heavenly. We looked at each other like we were in pain from our indulgences. I had eaten enough homemade bread to turn into pudding. Sam ordered us an after dinner drink of amaretto on the rocks. The mellow sweetness was all the dessert we needed. We looked at the big bear rug placed in front of the huge burning fireplace and wanted to cuddle up right there before going home. Thank goodness we were just blocks away from our resting place.

After sleeping in the next morning, I took off to shop while Sam did a bit of office work on the computer. I wanted to bring back gifts for Mother and my Brown's Botanical family. Since the villages were just a few miles apart, I had fun stopping on an impulse at almost every one.

The village of Sister Bay had a famous Christmas shop that everyone talked to me about. When I walked into the restored historic church, I was in seventh heaven looking at three floors of colorful Christmas ornaments, trees, Santa's, and snowmen. There were more trains and unusual toys than any child could possibly wish for. As I went from room to room, I had no trouble finding décor for our big tree at 333 Lincoln in every shade or color imaginable. It was the perfect place to choose gigantic Christmas stockings for each of my employees as well as for Sam and me. While I shopped around, I had everyone's name stitched on them. I thought of Mia and of Nancy's twins. Christmas was for children of all sizes, but I would go nuts here for sure if I had children. I jotted down lots of ideas for my shop. Whoever did their displays was professional and artistic beyond belief. I drove home wondering why we didn't have a big Christmas shop on the street any longer. I would call it Trees on Main. I'd better not share that with Sam when I return!

On our last day, Sam wanted to show me a clever Swedish restaurant in the village of Sister Bay. When I saw the grass covered roof he had told me about, I was surprised to see live goats walking around on the top just grazing away. We asked a teenager standing near the door to take our picture with the goats. It was quite the tourist attraction that also had a wonderful gift shop with clever clothing and accessories. I found handwoven sweaters for Sue, Mother, and Aunt Julia that I planned to give for Christmas. The Swedish loved red and white, I quickly noticed. Red and white Christmas mugs were coming home with me, that was certain. The food was very delicious. They specialized in good soups and more homemade bread. Would everyone back home recognize fatty Anne Dickson when she returned? Right now, I didn't care. Sam graciously carried several bags of goodies back to the car from my visit. He was happy when he saw me happy. What was there not to be happy about?

To my surprise, I was sad to leave Door County and said my good-byes to places I didn't get to visit. I want to come back and soon. Sam was right—it was a slice of heaven that he knew I would enjoy, and he was so right.

We got back to 333 Lincoln at a late, dark hour. We were both quiet as we walked back into our other daily world. I couldn't believe that I was actually able to put the shop, the shop addition, and my potting shed aside to absorb another part of the world. There wasn't an intervention with Grandmother or any kind of negative conversation that entered our getaway.

"Next trip, London," Sam announced as we got into bed.

I snickered, knowing this man could talk me into anything. I snuggled up to him, whispering my thanks for a very special trip.

CHAPTER 34

꽃

When I returned to the shop, I couldn't believe the progress on the addition. The back wall was miraculously removed. However, a large unfinished area of cluttered construction and hanging black plastic was open for viewing. Sally quickly came to the rescue by explaining everything before I panicked. She said all was going well and there was no disturbance of the flow of business and production at the shop. Her excitement helped me adapt to what was really happening, and that it should be exciting for me as well.

Jean and Sally waited for my reaction and I didn't disappoint them. They wanted to know everything about the trip, which brought me to the large bag of goodies I had brought home for them and the shop. I pulled out their monogrammed Christmas stockings and was met with gasps of surprise and then laughter. Jean clapped her hands like a little kid.

"We'll line them up on a notch here at the shop and hope St. Nick will have a jolly time filling those toe warmers! I never had such a delight as this!" Jean said gleefully.

"Where are yours and Sam's going to hang?" Sally questioned.

"We desperately need them to adorn our fireplace at home," I claimed. "We had nothing last year."

Kip and Kevin arrived back from their delivery and walked in on the scene. They began teasing me about the large Christmas bonuses that would likely come their way with stockings the size of the ones I had purchased.

"So, are you pleased with what you see here?" asked Kevin as he looked at the changes made by the carpenters. "Kip and I helped out one day to make sure we had what we needed as things came tumbling down." They laughed like they were keeping something from me.

"Well, I'm thrilled, and thanks so much for helping them," I said. "Has Jason been around inspecting the progress?"

"Oh, yes," Jean inserted. "He was like a little red hen with you gone."

Everyone nodded.

"Well, we had a wonderful time, but it's back to phone calls and e-mails, I guess," I remarked as I turned to my desk. When the others got busy again, I decided I'd call Mother and let her know we were back. She was pleased to hear that we had a good trip and she said she had done some entertaining by having two couples over to play cards with her and Harry. Her update on Ella was good and the report was that Ella would be back to work soon. In a nutshell, it appeared all was well while the Dicksons were away. I told Mother I'd get my thoughts together about Thanksgiving and that Sam was pretty sure Helen would be coming. Mother seemed delighted.

Getting back to my e-mails, I quickly noticed one from Pat, Sam's sister. She had copied me on an e-mail she had sent to Sam telling him that she would be accompanying their mother to our home for Thanksgiving. She said Helen asked her to come along in case she needed help, so Pat hoped it would be okay to do so. She said she would be happy to share the guest room with her mother and for us not to go to any trouble. This was another curve for me, for sure, but Sam would love it since he didn't get to see Pat that often. We had no other prepared bedroom with furniture for another guest, which was pretty silly, with having all those empty rooms. Getting one furnished within a week was going to be impossible.

The next e-mail was from Nancy. Judging from the length of the correspondence, she had some free time on her hands. It was several paragraphs telling me every detail of her visits to the doctor and how she was rearranging the nursery. She was watching her diet very carefully so she wouldn't gain one extra ounce. Yup, that was Nancy. I couldn't imagine carrying one baby inside me, much less two. It did make me happy to share in her happiness. With her new life, she would likely be the one now to be too busy for me, for a change.

Phil's e-mail was next and he reminded me of a quilt show committee meeting tomorrow at his shop. That wasn't going to happen with my schedule, so I e-mailed him back asking if we could meet for coffee that next morning so he could report what had happened. That would certainly be more productive than sitting through each person's drama at a meeting.

"Julia is on the phone," announced Sally.

"Welcome back!" she greeted. "How was that New-England-in-the-Midwest trip?"

"It was better than expected and such fun," I reported. "You and Sarah must go sometime. It is such beautiful country, especially this time of year."

"We had a pretty good time ourselves while you were gone," she bragged. "The cemetery tour was so interesting. We sure wish you could have joined us. Sue and I entertained Sarah and her girlfriend, Megan. They thought it was a hoot, of course. It was pretty darn cold that night, but they had a nice bonfire at the end of the tour and served hot cider."

"That's great," I said, wanting to move on to the Taylor details. "I thought of you all. Who took care of Mia? And, I want to know all about the Taylor grave."

"Your mother was more than happy to watch her," she answered. "The tour was not her cup of tea, and besides, Harry was there. He got a kick out of Mia. She knows no stranger these days, and of course, your mother had just made cookies." She laughed and then remembered the Taylors. "They had one guide with a black cloak and a black top hat. It wasn't the talking dead as it was described in the paper. Anyway, we got to his grave, and they told us about the mysterious live lilies that remained there for years and years until one day when they mysteriously died. The guide said there were many rumors and stories about this Mr. Taylor, but they had no information to explain them being there in the first place. They just said he was very prominent in the community and that it is likely his ghost that resides in his home where he lived at 333 Lincoln."

"Oh, great. That's helpful. Did they all believe that? No mention of his mistress, I guess."

"No, not really. Plus, they all spoke of ghosts at nearly every gravesite," she said. "So much of what they told us was folklore, which they admitted. They did not take us to Marion's grave, by the way. Frankly, the most interesting gravesite to most of us was the fenced-in gravesite of the men who were killed during the construction of the old bridge here in Colebridge. A large cable broke, sending many men into the river. They had the actual pipe and cable right there for all to see. It has the men's names listed there. Have you ever seen it? Talk about ghosts being around! How would you like to die like they did?"

"I have driven by there going to Mr. Taylor's grave, but I never stopped to read about it," I said, thinking about the site. "It sounds like you really enjoyed it all."

"We did," she admitted. "It was fun sharing it with Sarah. I'm sure she told all her friends about it!"

Hanging up, I knew I'd been at the right place in Door County with my sweet husband instead of with the ghosts of Colebridge.

CHAPTER 35

I was really dragging the next day, trying to catch up from being gone. Sam was overwhelmed with meeting after meeting and didn't get in until late. I was figuring out where things were as the workmen put up plastic walls to hide their activity. Abbey expectantly stopped by to welcome me back and to tell me she had offered to help with the Christmas decorating committee on Main Street. As a resident, she was getting to know a lot of the folks and someone had talked her into helping.

"I've always loved Christmas here on Main Street, so it'll be fun, I think."

Just the thought of the beauty of Christmas on Main Street excited me. "That's wonderful. It's also my favorite time here on the street. We need lots of help with a lot of things. You know our shop supplies the greenery for the street, don't you?"

"I do. They explained it all to me and what the schedule is," she said, twisting her scarf.

"Do you mind coming in to work tomorrow morning for me, Abbey?" I asked, looking up from my desk. "I have a breakfast meeting and some things to do at the house for Thanksgiving. Do you have plans? You know you are welcome to join our family on Thanksgiving Day."

"I sort of do, I guess, but thanks for asking," she replied.

I could tell she wasn't sure she wanted to say what her plans were.

"Are you going to have a lot of people this year?"

"I'm sort of not sure, just like you," I replied, laughing. "When you have your mother-in-law and sister-in-law coming, any other guests are immaterial."

"Holy cow, Anne, I don't envy you," she said innocently. "When I hear about in-laws, it makes me happy I am a single broad."

I snickered.

"Who's a single broad?" asked Kevin, coming in from the construction area. He gave a wink, like he had overheard our conversation. He had a way of flirting with Abbey every chance he got.

"I'll be here first thing in the morning, Anne," Abbey stated as she still looked at Kevin. "I need the hours for Christmas money, so bring them on!" Out the door she flew.

"I'm glad she's getting involved on the street," I told whoever might be listening.

"Miss Anne, if I may interrupt, my Al was wondering if he should be on the lookout for another big tree for you and Mr. Sam this year," Jean asked timidly.

"Oh, my lands yes, Jean," I happily answered. "We

recently connected with a member of the Taylor family at our house, and he told us the Taylors always had a big tree there in the foyer, just like we did last year, so I want to keep up the tradition. Isn't that something?" Before she could answer, I said, "I purchased some wonderful ornaments in Door County that will be perfect for a big tree."

"Jolly good, then. I shall tell him so," she said, pleased with my answer. "We so enjoyed that party last year. Sam sure took pleasure with the mistletoe I brought. Will there be such a party this year, Anne? It's none of my beeswax, of course."

"I can't even think about it, Jean," I said, coming back to reality. "I have to get Thanksgiving out of the way. I have Sam's mother and sister coming from out of town, so I have my hands full. Abbey is going to fill in more with the holidays, so keep an eye on her for me, will you?"

"She's a sweetie, that Abbey," Jean said, smiling. "She dresses like they do in my London, which makes me homesick sometimes. She is a free spirit, as you sometimes say."

"Anne, I think I am going to be putting a good-sized tree in that corner there for the season. What do you think?" Sally said, joining us.

"Sure. We need to shake things up a bit since nothing will be quite the way it was, anyway. Plan a nice spot for those stockings, too!"

The door was locked and we were all engaged in finishing up our tasks for the day. Finally, Jean said *ta-ta* and it was just Sally and me.

"Hey, Anne, are you staying after for a bit?" Sally asked as she was sweeping up the last stems and leaves for the day.

"I think I have to," I said as I was starting the payroll. "I'm a little behind here, but I want to have those checks for you all tomorrow." I paused and looked at Sally. "How is it going with Tim?" I knew I was taking a chance asking, in case it wasn't going well.

"It's not going anywhere," she said firmly. "I'm just not his girly-girl type. It's obvious. He thinks of me like one of the jocks. He loves to talk sports, which is great, but he never gets personal. A sexy girl can walk by and he's all googly-eyed."

I shook my head, truly understanding what she was saying.

"Perhaps Paige and Abbey can give you some advice," I teased, hoping I didn't say the wrong thing.

"No thanks," she said walking to the storeroom.

I liked the way that Sally had principles. She was comfortable in her own skin with confidence and good focus. She was dependable, mature, and attractive in a natural sort of way. She had good basic looks that could be tweaked into being gorgeous, but that wasn't her style. Someday, someone was going to see her inner beauty.

CHAPTER 36

The next morning, I was determined to walk in the neighborhood before work. I really needed to think some things through. When I saw Sam at the kitchen table, he pulled me into his arms and said he missed me.

"I know, it's been crazy since we've gotten back," I said, taking a bite of his toast. "I hope you don't work too hard catching up, Sam. You don't regret that trip, do you?"

"Are you kidding?" he said, giving me a kiss on the cheek." "It was great. How's that addition coming along?"

"You need to see for yourself," I said, grinning. "I'm amazed they got so much done while I was gone. Will I see you for dinner? We could meet up at Charley's and you could stop by to see it!"

"Great idea, but I just can't say right now," he said sadly. "Hey, really great news on Pat joining us on Thanksgiving, huh?" He smiled while getting up and straightening his tie.

"I was wondering if you were going to mention it. You realize we have nowhere to put her unless you want a bed delivered before then."

He looked at me strangely. "Absolutely do not do that," he said firmly. "They offered to share the guest room and that will do nicely, Anne. They are only staying a couple of days because of Pat's schedule."

"Yes, boss," I teased back. "Keep me posted on dinner, okay?" Out the door I went, throwing him a kiss.

I walked into Starbucks and ordered my usual grande Pike Place and picked out a slice of lemon loaf bread. I noticed Sharon was joining Phil, so I greeted them and sat down at their table.

"Good morning. How did it go last night?" I asked, taking my first sip of coffee.

"Very good, actually," Phil said. "Everyone's on it. Raffle tickets are doing better than we thought. We decided that the quilt is going to move from shop to shop before the show. It's a darn good thing, because I'm happy to get rid of it."

"What's that supposed to mean?" I asked, enjoying the lemon loaf.

Sharon and Phil both laughed.

"Ever since I hung the darn thing for people to see, we've had nothing but constant rocking from upstairs. It's enough to drive us nuts!"

"Are you kidding me?" I asked with a laugh. "Did you go up there?"

"Oh yeah, a bunch of times," chimed in Sharon. "It's crazy. I'm ready to go home at night."

"George is picking it up this morning, thank goodness," he said, shaking his head. Kathy is doing some great public relations. We still don't have a count for Isabella on how many quilts we need, but she said she made up a list of folks who would lend their quilts. Hey, are you in need of one, Anne?"

"No, I'm in great shape. I was thinking of bringing the Potting Shed Quilt, which is a really crazy, crazy quilt."

"Hmmm, sounds like it could have been on the brochure," joked Phil.

We visited a bit more, and then I was on my way with a long list of errands. As I drove along, I was surprised at how my expansion took a back seat as I worried about the coming holiday. I pulled up to get some dry cleaning and reached for my cell phone to call Ella, the first on my list of people to call. "Ella, I hear you're doing better."

"I am," she immediately answered. "You can't keep a good dog down, isn't that what they say?" she laughed. "How was that trip of yours? Your mother was so pleased you took time to get away."

"It was perfect," I gushed. "Ella, I have to tell you that I have Sam's mother and sister coming in for Thanksgiving and I am at a loss as to how to get the house ready. If you are still recovering, I need some resources to help me."

"And take my job?" she teased. "No siree! No need to worry, honey. I plan to clean Harry's house tomorrow and then you are next. Now, it may take me a little longer, but I'll get it done!"

I breathed a deep sigh.

"Oh, Ella, that would be great," I said, relieved. "We have to put them in the same guest room, as I haven't yet furnished the other bedrooms, but they seem fine with that."

"I'll see to everything, Anne, if you'll just see to it that *everyone* in that household lets me do my job."

I got the hint and laughed slightly. "I'll do my best Ella. I don't know what we'd do without you."

Grandmother knew I was still upset with her for pushing Ella off the steps, so things had been pretty quiet since. It was a good feeling, for a change. I was pleased that Ella wasn't going to be frightened away like my previous cleaning lady, Nora.

Next on my list was reminding Kip to make sure that the grounds looked lovely and that the leaves were removed. We still had not had a deep frost, so the mums, begonias, and some geraniums were still colorful. He would do fine getting these things done, knowing company was on its way.

Food. Oh yes, there had to be food. Sam liked being in charge of the kitchen, which was fine with me. Our menu last year was a big hit, so we would likely repeat it. Mother could still supervise the gravy, which was always a critical menu item.

Now the guests had to be invited. Amanda and William were the first guests on the list to call. Most others knew of the scheduled dinner. It would be good to see Amanda and William again.

"Long time, no see," Amanda said, hearing my voice.

"I know, please forgive me, but it's also why I'm calling," I announced. "We are hoping you and William will join us again this year on Thanksgiving."

"Well, I will indeed be happy to, but William has moved to Omaha," she revealed. "I know he called your mother to give her his address. His company offered him a pretty good deal and he felt like he needed a change in his life."

"I'm so happy for him, but you must really miss him," I

said with some disbelief.

"Oh sure, but I have been dating someone and that makes it all easier," she explained. "I was thinking I may bring him to your dinner, if you don't mind."

"That would be awesome, Amanda," I said, feeling happy for her. "What's his name?"

"Allen Williams," she divulged. "You'll like him, and so will Sam. He's a boring engineer, but ever so cute!"

I could see her smiling over the phone.

"I'll bring champagne like last year, okay? I'm so glad you called."

"Sounds like a great plan," I said, feeling like things were starting to come together. "Your mother would be so happy for you and your brother. This is all good!"

After I hung up, I thought of the intimate conversation her mother and I had at the nursing home before she died. She wanted to make sure we always included Amanda and William.

Now Mother may have already invited Harry, but I thought it only proper to do so myself, so I clicked in his number next. It went to voice mail, which meant he was likely at the bookstore, so I left a friendly message inviting him to dinner.

So, the only remaining questionable guests were Mia and Sue. Sue was thinking of going to Ohio to be with Uncle Ken and Aunt Joyce. I was hoping she would go, as I'm sure they missed seeing Mia, who was growing up so fast. There was no answer and her phone also went to voice mail. If they were going, they likely had already left town. Mother would know. That means there would be around nine of us, if I included Sally.

CHAPTER 37

On Thanksgiving eve, Sam went to the airport to pick up Helen and Pat while I fussed over details in case they wanted a bite to eat when they got back. I probably went over the top with flowers everywhere, making sure I didn't have any lilies that could affect Helen's allergies. I placed a large new fern in the entry hall and one on the sun porch. Too bad a magazine wasn't here to take photographs. Every time I added something, it seemed to make our house come more alive and beautiful.

When they arrived, Pat was as classy and perky as I remembered. She always seemed down to earth and generally happy for Sam and me. Helen was now sporting a cane with her this visit. I tried not to notice or say anything until she did. Sam took their coats and made them comfortable near the fire in the study.

"Oh Anne, your house is magnificent!" cried Pat, who

had not seen it before. "Mother tried to describe it all to me, but that didn't do it justice. How do you manage all of this? I recognize some of the pieces from your loft, Sam." She walked around, looking at things closer. "This painting of the river is wonderful, as if it were the view you had from the loft."

"You're right," he said smiling. "Anne gave me that for Christmas before we were married.

I beamed as he told our story.

"We were looking in the window of a gallery on Main Street and both admired paintings we each liked. Lo and behold, we bought them for each other as a surprise that Christmas! In fact, we picked them up at the gallery at the same time."

"I love mine as well. It's hanging in your guest room. The furniture in there was in my bedroom at home and it went perfectly with it."

Pat seemed amused.

"You'll notice a special quilt on the quilt rack too, Pat. The next guest room will all be red and white, so it will be perfect in there. I really love it and will always cherish it."

"How wonderful," Pat said, looking at both of us. "I love red and white myself and have made myself a wall quilt with just red and white. I have a lot of blue in the house, so it goes well."

"Let me show you the rest of the house, Pat," Sam said, taking her in the kitchen and leaving me alone with Helen.

There was silence.

"How was the plane ride, Helen?"

"It was more uncomfortable with this cane and not being able to stretch my legs," she complained. "Pat was helpful, as much as she could be."

"How long have you been using the cane?" I asked timidly.

"Off and on since I had my knee done, I'm afraid." Then she gave me a serious look. "Anne, I am worried so about Sam. Is he really doing as well as he wants me to believe? The long hours he describes have to be stressful. Has he had any shortness of breath lately?"

"Helen, I know your concerns and I share them with you," I said, shaking my head. "I worry all the time. I have to say that I was so pleased at how relaxed he was on our recent little trip. Since we have been back, it's been one meeting after another. I'm surprised he sleeps as well as he does, but he hasn't mentioned any discomfort lately."

She smiled. "You're a good wife, Anne. I depend on you to keep him in line. He's turning out to be like his father, despite his determination not to be. He was a workaholic and didn't take health care precautions seriously."

This was not good to hear. Sam did not speak highly of his father and had mentioned that his father had cheated on Helen through the years.

Sam and Pat joined us with cups of coffee and some snacks I had prepared. Sam caught up on hometown news with his mother. After a time, we were ready to turn in early from a long day. I told myself that things were going so far so good, but the big day was to follow.

Sam was in such a good mood as we prepared for bed. He twirled me around and held me for a few seconds in his arms. "I am such a lucky guy, Anne," he bragged. "I have a loving family, a beautiful home, and a job I love. I am blessed." He gave me a kiss. "I have a little surprise for everyone at the table tomorrow." He said it in a teasing way, leaving an opening for me to inquire more.

I shook my head like he was crazy and climbed into bed.

The next morning, Sam was up early to attend to the turkey. Mother arrived early wearing a fresh apron and was ready to get started. Helen and Pat were late sleepers, thank goodness, as the kitchen seemed already crowded. Everything was going as planned.

Hours later, Aunt Julia and Sarah arrived, followed by Sally. Amanda and Allen arrived next, looking like the perfect young couple in love, bringing champagne. Mother took over the introductions as she reminded everyone about how pleased she is that Amanda is part of our family. Sam and Allen immediately bonded when they began talking about their work. Harry finally arrived, which eased Mother's concerns. He brought a delicious box of chocolates from Nick's Bakery, which he knew everyone would love. He said I couldn't be any sweeter, and I told him I felt the same about him. He gave Mother a little hug that made her blush. I didn't want to think any further about the two of them right now. Her day would now be complete with him here, I could tell.

CHAPTER 38

The aroma of the roasted bird was getting the best of all of us, and as we made our way to find our seats, I thought of Mia and Sue who were now in Ohio. I'm sure they would be thinking of all of us, just like we were missing them. Mia was always the little showstopper, which is what I was sure she was doing today at her grandma and grandpa's house.

We held hands with one another as Sam said the blessing. "We gather together on this joyful day to thank you for our many blessings. Thank you especially for bringing Mother and my sister this distance to join us, and also bless those who are traveling elsewhere. Bless this food that we are about to enjoy. We thank you. In Your name, amen."

We all repeated "Amen" as some of us kept tears from flowing down our cheeks. This Kodak moment would be hard to top.

The food was overwhelmingly plentiful and delicious.

The talk of the table was the delicious cranberry salad Aunt Julia had brought. I was miserably full, but awaiting Mother's pumpkin pie. I observed how Sarah and Pat had engaged in a quilting conversation. Sarah told Pat about her quilting with us and that she had her own ideas about designs she'd like to make for her room someday. I could tell that Pat was impressed. Harry blended in like he had been here many times before. I could tell he was tickled to be included. Amanda and Allen never took their eyes off of each other as they held hands under the table. I don't think I was ever smitten quite that way when I was younger. What was I thinking of in those days? Hmmm...

Just as we were finishing our meal, Sam stood and clinked a spoon against his glass. He said he had a little surprise he wanted to share with everyone. My heart was jumping out of my chest. Please, don't let anyone think it was an announcement of a new addition to the family.

"As I told my lovely wife last night, I have been very fortunate in many ways," he said, looking directly at me. "I have also worked hard, just like Anne, to achieve my career goals. Today, I can announce to you that I am now the new president of Martingale, Inc."

A quick and silent pause hit the room.

"What?" I was the first to say anything aloud. "You are? When did that happen?"

Everyone cheered and extended congratulations to Sam. I'm not sure anyone heard my questions.

He continued. "When I returned from a much-needed vacation, I went to our board of directors' meeting where Mr. Martingale surprisingly announced his retirement, effective immediately," he said with certainty as he grinned. "That's when they announced my new position. I was told this would happen one day, but frankly, I was so busy working, I didn't think about it. I sure thought Mr. Martingale would be around for some time."

"Oh Sam, that's wonderful," said Aunt Julia. "It is well deserved."

As I listened, I watched Helen's smile of concern as we looked at each other. What would all of this really mean? I cheerfully announced a toast to Sam's new position and that we would have our dessert and coffee in the living room. Sam took me aside to give me a hug. He knew I was thrown for a loop.

"This is for us, honey," he whispered.

After I told him I loved him, I started clearing some dishes while still thinking about Sam's announcement. Part of me wished he had shared it privately with me first. I wanted my expansion and Sam wanted to be president. There was no question; we were two people who wanted it all. Why wasn't I more thrilled at the thought?

After everyone left the happy get-together, Helen and Pat went up to retire for the evening. I looked at a spotless kitchen, thanks to Aunt Julia and Mother. Sam and I went into the den to put our feet up and assess the day. All was well. What was not perfect for this Kodak moment? Hmmm...

CHAPTER 39

The next day, I told Sam I really needed to go to the shop for a while, so he offered to show Pat his office and we agreed that I would meet them at Donna's Tea Room for lunch.

I skipped my much-needed walk to get to the shop early. I felt I was carrying around the whole turkey and half of Mother's pumpkin pie. It was nice and quiet when I got there, with the exception of one painter who was working behind our plastic wall. When I checked our answering machine, there were some lovely comments about arrangements folks had received for the holidays and then an urgent message from Phil. I knew it was early, but I picked up the phone at my desk to call him.

"Phil, how was your Thanksgiving?"

"Okay, I guess," he somberly replied. "Hey, you were having a bunch. How did that go?"

"Very good, very good," I quickly answered. "Hey, what's going on?"

"I didn't bother to tell you last week that George came in to complain about the raffle quilt in his shop and he needed to know who would take it before his time was up. He wanted to get rid of it fast."

"But, why?"

He said during the time he's had it, he's had nothing but bad luck with things disappearing, like when he first moved into that place. Some food has gone missing, the key to the liquor closet is gone, and a night's deposit bag full of money has disappeared."

"Well, I think that sounds like he's got a bad employee doing an inside job."

"He also said the quilt is giving bad vibes to his customers and he wants it out of there. I told him that Laura from the tobacco shop was next."

"Oh well, that's good," I said, feeling better. "I'm sure those things will show up."

"I'm not finished," Phil said with a serious tone. "Laura and Larry had it this past week and they said the noise from their crying ghost had not stopped the whole time they had the quilt. They said it had been quite a while since they had heard the crying, so it appeared very odd. Customers wanted an explanation, which they could not give, of course. Laura said they didn't think about the quilt being the problem. They had to change having Thanksgiving dinner at their home upstairs because of it. They went to a restaurant instead. Can you just believe it?"

"So, it is the quilt?" I asked innocently.

Phil continued with excitement. "They called George about who was to get the quilt next and told them about their ghost getting upset. George told them there were some other problems, but that Buttons and Bows was the next on the list. George told them not to say anything to Barbara, to see if anything happens. Do you think this really is about having the quilt or not?"

"I think we may be overreacting, Phil."

"I called Larry early this morning and he told me the crying stopped as soon as the quilt left the building. Tell me I didn't create a monster here, Anne. This is all too weird."

"Okay, I hear you. Frankly, I have had my own share of ghost occurrences, so I'm not making light of this, Phil, but we must keep this under wraps, you hear?"

Phil agreed and hung up, frustrated. So far, no one had been hurt; and, after all, we figured out that the ghost quilt didn't like being moved about. That could be fixed, I think. Hmmm...

When Sally arrived, she couldn't thank me enough for such a great Thanksgiving and congratulated me for having such a successful husband. She filled Jean in and then Jean reported on their traditional dinner with their neighbors on Thanksgiving. She said she told Al about finding us a Christmas tree.

When I arrived at Donna's Tea Room for lunch, I noticed Mother was there as well and had been graciously invited by Sam. They were having a great chat trying to decide if they were going to have Donna's special of beef brisket sandwiches.

"I told them I'd still be happy to make some turkey melt sandwiches, but I thought you might have had enough turkey by now," Donna said, her voice cheerful. "I have put aside your coconut cream pie before it sells out. It's my treat!"

Helen especially took to Donna and gave her a big thank you, squeezing her hand. She then began to describe the delicious pie to Pat, who hadn't had the honor of tasting it.

As I started drinking my tea, Pat asked, "So tell me about this quilt show I hear you're involved in. I also heard about that raffle quilt of yours and I am dying to see it and buy some tickets. Can

I see it before I go?"

"Sure, we can go look at it after lunch if you like," I offered. "It's just across the street at Buttons and Bows. You might even pick up a button there, too!"

She laughed and expressed her desire to go.

I went on to explain the whole reasoning behind having a winter indoor quilt show. Because of the poor winter retail sales, we needed something to increase income. I said we wanted the raffle quilt to debut at Halloween and it worked, selling lot of chances as a result.

"So none of the quilts will be hung on the buildings outdoors like they do in Sisters, Oregon?" she asked, somewhat confused. "You may not know about that hugely successful show, but everybody in town makes money when the quilts are out. I have been there and it is magnificent!"

"Yes, I've heard of it from Isabella who owns the local quilt shop," I said. "You may have gone to her shop when you were here for the wedding. It does sound amazing, but our merchants were determined to have it indoors, plus with Missouri weather, we could have a big snowstorm that day!"

She laughed and nodded her head in agreement. "If you all change your mind, I can give you lots of information on how it's done. I really want my quilt guild to do something like that someday."

We then talked about the dinner and how much everyone enjoyed meeting Allen. Sam said he was so impressed that he told Allen to send him a résumé for future consideration.

After lunch, Sam announced that he and his mother would go home to get the luggage while Pat, Mother, and I went to see the quilt at the shop across the street.

CHAPTER 40

Barbara was glad to see us come in the shop. She commented that she had hopes of a big retail day, as did others on the most successful shopping day of the year. She was making me feel guilty for taking time for lunch.

Pat was in awe of the many buttons lined up in boxes on the walls. She mentioned being partial to black glass mourning buttons from the Victorian era. Barbara showed her the case where there was a good supply of them.

"In the second room, you can get a good view of the ghostly quilt hanging on the wall with a sign on it offering raffle tickets for sale," I directed. "It looks good there, Barbara."

Barbara didn't respond.

"My goodness, Anne, this is quite something!" Pat said, looking closely at the quilt. "Is your shop ghost on here?"

"No, it's not," I replied. "So far, Brown's Botanical is ghostless, thank goodness."

Mother looked at me with a look of warning on her face that told me not to pursue the subject.

"I wasn't sure you'd have room to display it here in your tiny shop," I said to Barbara when she and I were alone.

"Well, if you must know, it's been in a different spot every time I've come in," she said, dismayed. "I'm used to my ghost moving things once in a while, but this is nuts! My antique display box on the counter keeps showing up in odd places, too. I had the hardest time finding it yesterday. I don't understand all this escalated activity! I don't want to say too much, if you know what I mean."

I just shook my head in wonder, not wanting to share the other shops' problems with her. "Where does the quilt go from here?" I innocently asked while looking at a charming white pearl button necklace.

"It goes to Kathy at the The Cat's Meow," she reported. "Frankly, I can't wait to get it out of here. Selling these raffle tickets is a disruption too, as I work alone most of the time. We sold a lot of them today, however."

"Anne, I want to buy you that necklace," Pat said as she watched me hold it up to my neck. "It will be a nice little thank you for your lovely hospitality. I also want to get six of these button pincushions for my quilting friends at home. Aren't they adorable? Include the black glass bracelet, if it's for sale. I didn't see a price."

Barbara was thrilled at Pat's purchases and quoted her an expensive price on the bracelet that floored me. Pat didn't bat an eye.

"Well, thank you, Pat," I said. "When I see it, I will always think of you. You know how much I love pearls."

"I'll take this pin, Barbara," Mother said as she put it

on her dress. "It goes perfectly with this outfit I'm wearing, don't you think?"

We all smiled with approval.

"I must get back to the shop, ladies," I said, kissing them each on the cheek. "I hope you have time to stop by the shop and say good-bye on your way to the airport."

"I do, too," Pat said, grinning. "Thank you for everything. I think that Taylor house of yours needs to take on a new name, if you ask me. I think the Dicksons have taken over and deserve the title. You all have done a good job."

We all nodded in agreement.

"Thanks, Pat. Please stay in touch and enjoy all your purchases," I said, going toward the door.

"Anne, remember to consider the idea of the outdoor quilt show," she reminded me. "I think you are making too much ado about the weather factor. Call me if you need more of my two cents."

We all laughed as I went on my way with my new gift.

As I walked back to my shop, I tried to visualize what Pat had suggested. The street was truly lined with lots of balconies and banisters where quilts could easily be folded over and easily taken down. Maybe we needed to have a balcony beauty quilt show with quilts just on balconies. Then I looked at other charming places sporting clever nooks at eye level that could also be enjoyed. Fences and porches were also intriguing on some buildings. "Quilts on Main" would say it all and it would be pretty amazing if it could be pulled off. I would have to file this in my memory bank, if there was room.

Main Street was decorated for the Christmas season the weekend before Thanksgiving every year. The lamplights were wrapped with pine greenery and topped with two red velvet bows. All the doors were provided with live wreaths with red bows so we looked unified and true to our historic roots. White lights were sprinkled everywhere, including our windows and flower boxes at Brown's Botanical. It was a taste of Williamsburg. Artificial decorations were heavily discouraged, and most shop owners complied.

Sally was glad to see me because the workmen needed to discuss with me some work that they thought they could do during the night, so as to not disturb the daily business. I was pleased and felt they could do a better job as well. As we were almost finished, Sam called on my cell phone, so I took the call as I was writing things down that the workman had told me.

"Anne, this is Helen. I'm on Sam's phone. We are running a little too late to come by the shop, but I just wanted to thank you again for a lovely visit." It sounded as though she was choked up as she shared her remarks.

"Oh, Helen, we loved it," I said honestly. "Come back anytime and have a safe flight."

"Please remember what we talked about, Anne," she said sadly. I knew immediately it was regarding her concern over Sam's health.

"I won't forget, Helen, don't worry," I said, hoping to comfort her. When she hung up, I knew so well how mothers never stopped worrying about their children, regardless of their age.

Jean, Abbey, and Sally were all working because of the post holiday rush. From all indications, we were going to have a very good day. Sally bragged about selling out of the Santa mugs and matching flowerpots. She wasn't sure she could get more delivered before the Christmas holiday. I went to the computer to check e-mails for the day and I also wanted to e-mail Phil about what Barbara had shared with me at Buttons and Bows. I informed him that the quilt was going to Kathy's next. Goodness knows what might happen at The Cat's Meow!

Jean came from the front counter looking very excited. "My Al thinks he has located a fine specimen of a tree for the Dicksons!"

"Wow, that's great, Jean," I said, realizing the timing was perfect. "Sam is so, so busy right now. Do you think Al could find someone to help him instead of Sam? I don't want him lifting anything heavy either!"

"Yes, my Al knows all sorts of chaps who would like to make an extra penny before St. Nick."

"We certainly trust his judgment. I'll get Sam's approval tonight so they can get started." It could not be there soon enough to suit me.

"I saw Abbey putting some final bows out on the street this morning," said Sally. "They are lucky not to be doing this in the snow and ice like we have had to do some years."

"I'm so glad she is helping the street. You have really done a great job decorating this shop, Sally, and I love the Christmas tree in front of the window this year, don't you? Change is good!"

"Yes, the extra lights through our windows at night look really cool from the outside," Sally concurred. "Everyone loves Christmas. It's like feeling hopeful, just like you feel when spring comes."

It was rewarding seeing Sally so happy with her job.

All the Thanksgiving cards were put away and fall

floral arrangements taken apart to make room for the red and green festive season. It was the beginning of the "feel good" season when folks thought about others in their gift buying. They were planning "feel good" parties and church festivities to celebrate the real purpose of Christmas. It was my favorite "feel good" time of year, for sure. I had to cancel out any negative thoughts about Sam's heart attack last year on Christmas morning. This year he felt good, and so did Christmas!

CHAPTER 41

✵

It was no surprise when Sam called to say he would be home late. Taking off extra time through Thanksgiving had put him behind. I told him I planned to work late as well. He was very pleased when I told him Al had found a Christmas tree and could find extra help to deliver it. Thinking about the big tree gave me such happiness. Knowing the Taylors had a big tree also made it extra special.

Weary from the day, I was about to leave the shop. Then, I got a call from Sue announcing she was now home from a great Thanksgiving with her parents in Ohio.

"We have enough toys for a lifetime, Anne," she said with a giggle. "We pretty much had our Christmas! Thanks so much for what you and Sam do for her, too, I might add. It really makes me feel more secure knowing I have assistance with her education because it will be here before you know it! Her grandparents worry, as you can imagine, especially since

I don't have a husband."

"Good, I'm glad you all had a great visit," I said, recalling our holiday. "We certainly missed you sitting with us at the dinner table. Your Mia will always be taken care of."

"You'd better think twice about that commitment, Anne," she warned. "There could be all kinds of little Dicksons that you'll have to educate!"

I laughed without giving her a response. "So, how are your folks doing?" I wanted to change the subject.

"My dad is slowing down, or maybe this is just the first time I've ever noticed, but Mother is like the Energizer Bunny. She never slows down! I worry about Dad's heart, as you know from what we've been through on that side of the family."

"For sure," I made an attempt at consoling her. "Mother sure has more energy now that she has Harry in her life. It really has been a good thing. I hear very little about the aches and pains she had before he came into her life. We invited him to Thanksgiving dinner this year and he fit right in, of course."

"I guess he took our place at the table, huh?" she teased.

"Well, as a matter of fact, we had a new guest brought by Amanda. She has been dating this guy named Allen, so she brought him with her. William, by the way, has moved to Omaha for a job opportunity there."

"Wow! That's a lot of changes with me being gone for such a short time," she noted. "So, the dinner went well?"

"Yes, just about perfect, as a matter of fact. Sam surprised us by announcing he is now the new president of Martingale. How about that?"

"Talk about someone's dream coming true! He has wanted that since I've known him. Please tell him congrats for me."

"I will, but I worry about how the extra stress will affect

him. This will add another layer and I've seen it already. The good news is that he said he should have to travel very little now. He really has been looking forward to that for a long time."

"Just don't let his stress become your stress, or you'll both be in trouble. I want to come by and see how the addition is going. I know how fast these things can occur. I somehow feel out of the loop. Maybe we can have lunch and talk a little about Christmas plans."

"That would be great," I said as we hung up. Sue was like the sister that I never had. It seemed she was feeling totally comfortable with being adopted. She hadn't learned that until recent years when she went home for a visit, but now she has an adopted child of her own and totally gets it. I realized I hadn't told her about Nancy's announcement of twins coming along. I guess a lot was happening. Hmmm...

The next few days were crammed with holiday demands at the shop. There were improvements to the addition every day. I could actually see my office now with its cute side garden window that Jason insisted I have. We chose a perfect stone-style floor that made the whole place look more like nature's outdoors and it was so much better to clean than the previously carpeted floor. The new refrigeration case had been delivered, and as soon as it was hooked up, Sally put it to use. I loved the new counters for our design area, and even though it was premature, we used them anyway. Every extra space was so appreciated. Sally was especially happy with our consulting room. After all, that was the main reason for the expansion. That was where the bridal consulting would take place. That scenario was not anything I ever wanted to be a part of, but with Sally's offer to take charge of weddings, I conceded. I was determined to keep that room uncluttered, other than the tools she would need for booking events. The way things were moving along, we could have our ribbon cutting with the Chamber of Commerce at the first of the year, as planned.

Snow flurries were appearing for the first time this season. I dreaded the first real frost because that was the killer for the season. As soon as I arrived at the shop, I went over to Nick's to get hot chocolate for everyone, especially since I knew Kevin would be there. It was his favorite. George was there getting a cake to go and asked if I had a minute to sit and visit. I agreed to chat with him for only a minute or so.

"Did you hear what happened at Kathy's when she had the raffle quilt?" he asked, his voice serious. I wasn't sure I wanted to really hear any of it.

"Forget any wonderful cooking smells she encountered there from the past," he said with concern on his face. "She said she has had a terrible odor to the point that folks wouldn't come in, and if they did, they left immediately. She said she couldn't have any of that, so she closed. Out of concern about the quilt ticket sales, she said she wanted to pass it on. She didn't think she could open again until they uncovered the source of the smell. She felt like the quilt might absorb some of the odor."

"Oh, George, I just can't believe all this! Did you tell her the smell would likely go away once the quilt was out of her building?"

He shook his head in the negative. "She took it on to Donna's Tea Room; but in all honesty, we have to tell Donna what's been happening," he divulged. "We can't let her suffer without some kind of warning. She may not want to have it. I'm afraid word is getting out on the street. Kathy also told me something else. Hopefully, this had nothing to do with the quilt, but she lost one of her cats that she keeps in the shop."

"Oh, no! Which one?" I gasped.

"It was Spiffy, the golden one," he said, shaking his head. "I doubt if the smell had anything to do with it, but I feel so bad for her and the timing of it all doesn't look good."

"George, you must go see Donna and tell her everything that's been going on," I suggested strongly. "She has a food business. We can't let anything happen there, with her excellent reputation."

George nodded and said he would stop there on the way back to his shop. There was some kind of message here with all the complaints. We had somehow upset the spirits on the street. Would it be my fault for putting them on display? Perhaps they were upset because we were profiting from them. Perhaps Grandmother could explain it. Hmmm...

CHAPTER 42

Mother and I tried hard to keep our regular hair appointments with Cherie. When I picked up Mother, she immediately went into a topic of discussion that she had obviously determined to introduce the next time she saw me. It seems that Mother was set on having the baby shower for Nancy. Also, she wanted to host it because, in her estimation, I was too busy to have it at 333 Lincoln.

"Mother, I'm her best friend. Don't you think she'll expect me to do that? After all, we have plenty of time to plan her shower."

"I think you're wrong," she responded. "She is pregnant with twins, and they typically come quite early. If her due date is February, we need to have it in early January. Frankly, the time to have it would be when her family is here for Christmas."

"Christmas? There is no way I can think of another thing

around Christmas! I have to make sure my ribbon cutting is done right after New Year's Eve. That is my priority."

"Okay, then. We'll do it at Donna's, just like we did with your bridal shower. We'll let Donna do it all. We will have to do the invitations, so I'll take that on if you can give me some names."

I looked at her in amazement. Mother was always positive and typically found a way to make things work. As much as the thought gave me an anxious feeling, her idea made sense. We were having lunch afterwards at Donna's, so we could get the ball rolling.

Donna's Tea Room was buzzing, but Donna found a table for two by the window that looked out onto the front sidewalk of Main Street. We told her we needed to book an event when she had time to join us and look at her calendar. After Mother and I ordered our usual menu items of turkey melts and salads, Mother went into plans about Christmas Eve. She seemed to be more excited than ever to plan the holidays, and I assumed it was because of a certain gentleman in her life.

"I hope William will come into town for Christmas," she shared. "I'll bet we'll see Allen continue to come with Amanda. They seemed to be quite smitten with one another."

A new waitress placed our lunch in front of us and Donna said she would be with us as soon as she could.

"Just so you know, Mother, the Dicksons will have another large Christmas tree in the foyer this year," I announced with joy in my voice. "Al and his friends are going to handle everything so Sam won't have to help. I can't handle a large party like last year, but this year I want to have the staff over to the house since the shop may still not be presentable. I want you to come also because you're part of that family, too!"

She grinned in agreement. "I bought some great decorations in Door County, including stockings for Sam and me, so I'm hoping Santa will be very generous this year."

We both laughed.

"Sounds like a good plan. If you need me to help with things, just let me know."

We finished our lunch and we were fortunate to catch a moment with Donna before we left. She was thrilled to have the business and said baby showers were her favorite events to host.

"I hope your Mother has more luck than I've had about getting some grandchildren," Donna shared. "I guess it's why I get such a kick out of having the baby showers here. My goodness, what they have today for those kiddos is amazing."

We laughed in agreement.

"I'm afraid I'm right there with you, Donna," Mother confessed. "I don't see any of those grandchildren coming anytime soon!"

I touched Mother's arm to give her the message to not go in that direction. I wanted to change the subject, as usual. "Did you decide to take the raffle quilt for display, Donna? And, did George visit with you?"

"He sure did!" she nodded, smiling. "We are going to put it up after lunch today, so we'll have it up for dinner this evening."

"I guess they shared with you that things have been happening at the shops who displayed it," I said cautiously.

"Yes, yes, Anne. He told me everything and it's a shame," she said, shaking her head in disbelief. "I've had my share of mysterious happenings around here, so do you think that's going to scare me when we need money so badly for our street? Now, if it hurts my people or customers, out it goes!"

Mother looked puzzled.

"We understand," I said as I nodded in approval. "Be careful and just give George or Phil a call if you want it to be picked up. We may have to think of a different way to sell the tickets if this continues."

"I must tell you though, Anne, I'm a little concerned about the indoor quilt show idea," she confessed. "I really don't want people in here just to look at a quilt if they aren't going to eat. My business is a bit different than a retail store, but I can see why they just want a warm body in their shop. I may just put a quilt in a sleigh by the side door to get them to look at the menu, and call it a day. What do you think?"

"You bring up an excellent idea, Donna," I said, visualizing her suggestion. "I like it a lot!"

I walked to my car, still considering what Pat had talked to me about when she suggested quilts be displayed outdoors, despite the season. For just one day, perhaps more suggestions like Donna's could be explored. How cool would that be? Very, very cool, and very, very cold!

CHAPTER 43

The scheduling for the Dickson Christmas tree installation couldn't have worked out any better. Al and his two friends arrived after lunch on Sunday. Sam and I were both home, which worked out perfectly. I didn't see the fuss and activity last year until it was all over. Today, when I walked into the foyer and saw it sprawled there, I realized it might be even bigger than last year's tree.

Sam helped clear a space for it and gave verbal directions to the men lifting the massive tree. It was lifted into place and they busily worked to secure it. I watched from the stoop of the stairs, trying not to yell out any warnings as they nearly hit the chandeliers and paintings on the walls. Maybe it was good that I was gone last year. However, with the tree erected and stabilized, Christmas had now arrived!

Two hours later, we were absolutely in awe of the beauty and intense aroma the tree provided. I offered cookies and sandwiches to the helpers, and they were very well received. After a quick clean up, they were on their way, leaving Sam and me alone to stare at a tree that seemed to say, "Well, I'm here, now what?"

It seemed that the installation alone was enough for one day, so Sam and I took our drinks into the study where a fire was going near our favorite love seat.

"Is my sweet Annie happy?" Sam asked as he kissed my cheek.

"Yes, yes, I am," I quickly responded. "Do you realize this is the first time since our vacation we have been home together for the whole evening? No meetings or dinners tonight! It's just the three of us—you, me, and the tree."

"I am very aware of that and hope to take advantage of the situation!" he said seductively.

"It's still early for any celebration, and besides, that tree out there needs to twinkle with white lights and needs all the ornaments I purchased in Door County! We can't quite quit now!"

"What?" Sam asked, shocked. "What a nagging wife you turned out to be, Mrs. Dickson! Is there no rest for the president of Martingale and the owner of the biggest flower shop in Colebridge?"

I shook my head to the contrary.

"It won't take long, and it will be decorated the way *we* want it this year," I pleaded as I remembered others putting their ornaments on the tree at the trimming party. "Please?" I jumped off the couch and went into the foyer. "Everything's here and Al left the ladder up for us."

He came toward me with his hands on his hips. "I suppose Albert Taylor had the same 'honey do' list years ago," he jested.

"He's probably looking down at me right now saying, 'Best of luck, sucker.'"

We laughed and began unpacking the strands of lights.

We were nearly finished when Sam pulled out the large angel tree topper from the box.

"I don't remember putting this on top of the tree last year, Anne. Did you do it?" he asked innocently. "Maybe Kevin did it."

I cringed, not knowing quite what to say. I knew it was a gift from Grandmother Davis. I was surprised it was still in the box.

"Neither do I, honey," I said softly. "I saw it for the first time during our trim-the-tree party last year. No one brought it in the door, if you know what I mean."

He looked puzzled.

"It was a contribution from a member of the family, I suppose, and that's all I'm going to say." I turned and walked to the kitchen.

To Sam's credit once again, he did not respond.

I peeked around to look into the foyer and saw him climb up the ladder to put the angel, holding lilies in her hands, on top of the tree. He paused to get a good look at it, and then looked down to me. When he descended the ladder, he shook his head in wonder of it all and didn't say a word.

After putting things back in the storage room, we finally made it up the stairs to our room. It had been a long day! I wanted the white lights to stay lit, but Sam insisted that they had a long season ahead.

"Thanks, honey, for being such a great sport and husband," I said, looking at him as he took off his shoes. "I love it that we are keeping the tradition alive, even though it's a lot of work.

Thanks so much, sweetie."

He grinned up at me. "You're a piece of work, Annie Dickson," he teased, drawing me near him. "I could do with one less tradition around here, like that grandmother of yours, but I guess we have no choice."

"Well, Mr. Dickson, you're not getting rid of this traditional wife of yours, that's for sure," I teased, moving closer to him. "That is what you asked for when you married me, and now you have it!" Lying in his arms was the best reward of the day, reminding us both that we were indeed in this together.

CHAPTER 44

It was so wonderful walking down the stairs the next morning and seeing all the ornaments we had placed on the tree. Sam was already gone for the day, having placed a note on the table that he had an early morning meeting. As I bundled up to walk out the door, my cell phone rang.

"You're the only one I know who would be up at this early hour of the morning," Nancy's voice teased through the phone. "I couldn't sleep again last night. I can't believe I'm already so uncomfortable."

"I'm so sorry. What can I do to help?"

"Well, now that you've asked, could you bring me a Starbucks coffee on your way to work?"

"You've got it, girl. Just give me an hour or more, though. I was just going out the door for my walk."

There were icy spots up and down our driveway from the night's freezing temperatures, so my walk was cautious and quick. I was wise to bring in the remainder of the plants last week. I checked the temperature in the potting shed when I returned and all was well. It appeared that some of the pansies planted outside the potting shed were going to survive this blast of cold. Their brilliant golds, yellows, and purples were so stark against the frosty white.

By the time I got to Nancy's, I was running later than I had hoped. I knocked on the heavy door of her elegant yellow home on Jefferson Street and handed her the cup. I stepped inside just long enough to tell her that Mother and I were planning a shower for her at Donna's Tea Room before Christmas, in hopes of including some of her out-of-town family.

"Oh, Anne, that is so generous of you with all you have going on right now."

"Mother and I are leaving most of it up to Donna, so don't give us too much credit. Please turn over a list of folks to invite to Mother as soon as you can."

We hugged good-bye and I was on my way. As I drove down Main Street toward the shop, I thought of Donna and the raffle quilt that was now in her possession. The shops lining the street were adding more white lights and red bows, creating an awesome sight. Maybe one of those shops would have a gift for my Sam. He had it all right now. What more could he possibly want in his life? Of course, a little Dickson heir would do the trick, but not just yet, or if at all!

When I arrived in front of the shop, I saw Jason talking to one of his workmen.

"Everything looking all right?" he asked, confidently.

"You bet, Jason," I said as we both walked into my warm, cozy shop.

"You can move into your office at any time now, Anne. We're

pretty much done with anything major. We just need to do some final touches here and there."

"Well, if we get caught up today, I may just do that. You have done such a wonderful job. I hope you will all come for the ribbon cutting."

"Wouldn't miss it, Anne," he said with a big grin. "I need to get going. I have an appointment with an old friend of yours, Ted Collins."

I stopped in my tracks.

"Their firm is doing an addition to the west office, so I've been dealing with Ted on that," he explained.

"It sounds like they're doing well!" I said, searching for the right words.

Jason mumbled something to my response and then left.

It was strange hearing anything lately about Ted. I wondered how well Jason knew him and if Ted was still drinking excessively.

"A good morning to you, Miss Anne," greeted Jean as she came in the door. "I'm a bit tardy because the car froze up and Al had to give it a battery jump. It got mighty cold last night!"

"Not to worry. I got a late start, myself. Sally will be late because she's making a stop at the license bureau, but if we can get Kevin's early deliveries ready, we'll be in pretty good shape."

"Good morning, ladies," Sue called out as she and Mia entered the shop. "I've got the day off and thought we'd stop by to see the addition on our way to the grocery store."

"Good morning!" I said cheerfully as I gazed at the happy pair all bundled up. "Take a look around, especially at the boss's own office! Well, Miss Mia, what color flower would you like today?"

She knew I let her choose a flower during each visit. Every time I saw her, she grew even more. She was going to be a very beautiful woman one day!

"Pinky, pinky," she said, running away from Sue.

"Everything is pink these days, no matter what!" Sue laughed.

"A special pinky it shall be, Miss Mia. Just follow me," Jean said, taking her hand.

"Anne, this place is so spacious now, I can't believe it!" Sue said while walking around. "If I come to help out now, I won't know where anything is! I love it!"

"It is all hard to believe myself, sometimes. I'm so glad Sally pushed me into doing this. Now, we just have to pay for it!"

Sue looked at me, shaking her head at the comment. "I am dropping off a few more little funeral quilts at Nancy's house on my way home," Sue announced. "Your mother told me about the news of the twins. Isn't that just wonderful? It's a ready-made family for a perfect couple. Are we going to try and make her a couple of baby quilts?"

"Not on my watch, I'm afraid," I confirmed, going back to my desk. "Mother and I have arranged to have a baby shower for her at Donna's Tea Room. I say we contact Isabella to find us a boy and girl quilt for that. We still have lots to go on Isabella's quilt; however, Mother said she has been quilting on it whenever she has a free minute."

"Sounds like a good plan," Sue happily responded. "I still have to make them a little something. I know how much she'd appreciate it. Those babies will be like a prince and a princess in that big castle of theirs." She then noticed that Mia was not by her side. "Mia, come here. We need to say good-bye now!"

With that, Mia started fussing as she came from the back room, indicating that she wanted to stay with Jean. At this stage, she didn't like anyone to pick her up. She was turning into an independent daughter in a family of strong women. I was not surprised.

"Will we see you at the literary club this week, Sue?" Jean asked before they went out the door.

"Probably so!" answered Sue, taking Mia's hand as she headed out the door. "Good-bye, everyone!"

Sally finally arrived and we stepped up our production for Kevin's deliveries. Just as I was beginning to feel like we were catching up, Isabella walked in.

"How do quilt shop owners get a day off?" I asked, teasing her.

"Lots of errands unfortunately, but I really stopped by to see if you had any late quilt show news," she inquired while looking at some of our plants. "Aunt Susan just had both knees operated on, so I want to take her one of these plants. She loves yellow roses, so maybe put a few in a bouquet if you have something like that ready to go. Wow, Anne, this place is looking fabulous!" She looked all around. We then walked to the display case.

"Well, I can help you with the flowers, but I'm not too informed about any recent quilt show news. Here are some red roses with baby's breath. How about if I add a couple of yellow roses to that?"

"Perfect. Love those two colors together," she said with approval. "I have those colors in my kitchen. Can you put that on my house account, Anne?"

"Sure," I said, handing the vase to Sally. "Would you do that while I visit with Isabella about the quilt show?"

Isabella and I stepped away to a quiet area of the shop.

"I hate all that talk about the raffle quilt," she confessed. "It really makes me worry about the person who will win this quilt. God help them!"

I listened, sensing she was making a good point.

"It's been at Donna's for several days now," I said. "I wonder how she's doing with it."

"You haven't heard?"

The look I gave indicated how much I knew.

"The quilt is now with Phil. The mother-in-law ghost wasn't happy competing with the quilt, I'm afraid. In these last days, Donna has had her roof leak, toilet back up, and her dishwasher break down."

"Yikes, but that sounds like maintenance issues, if you ask me," I decided. "That shouldn't have anything to do with the quilt."

"It got worse," she went on to say. "She has had one complaint after another with certain foods being too salty. She tasted the food herself and was horrified as to how it could happen, until she thought of the raffle quilt. She said she couldn't afford the risk any longer."

"Isabella, this has got to stop."

"That's what Phil said when she brought it to him," she repeated. "He said he would keep it himself and risk whatever. He feels so bad about it and he shouldn't. He and Sharon put so much work into the quilt and it's making our organization a lot of money. This whole quilt show has me uneasy, Anne."

"I have the same feeling and have some thoughts about that," I revealed. "Can we maybe visit before or after literary club about it?"

Sally stepped up to us. She showed Isabella the beautiful arrangement and had her sign the charge slip.

"She will really love this!" Isabella exclaimed. She then turned to address me. "Yes, I'll likely be there. We really do need to think about all this with what's been going on!"

CHAPTER 45

The next day, I was sitting at the kitchen table when Ella arrived to clean. Sam had made coffee before he left, and for some reason, the cold weather was telling me to stay home for a bit to plan my day, as my thoughts were all over the place.

"Well, I'm surprised to see you still here!" Ella said, taking off her coat. "It's about to sputter snow out there, I think. It must be winter, by golly!"

I smiled, knowing nothing could stop this lady from doing whatever she had to do. I was really beginning to like her.

"Did you ever have so much to do, Ella, that you didn't do *anything*? I said, taking another swallow of coffee. "Help yourself to some coffee and sit a bit."

"Oh yes, when I was younger, of course," she said, pouring herself a cup of coffee. "Is everything okay, Anne?"

"Oh, absolutely," I said, perking up. "I have nothing to complain about, Ella, especially since you're back with us."

She sat down in the chair beside me. "Well, it's a blessing, for sure!" she said, rummaging through her cleaning supplies. "I'll start down here if you're going up to get ready for work. I see you have a quilt out on the porch, Anne. That sun is hitting it pretty hard. You may have some fading if you don't move it."

"What quilt?" I quickly jumped up to see for myself. "I didn't put that there."

Ella gave me a strange look as I went straight to the porch to rescue it. I remembered Nora telling me the quilt was in a different spot each time she was here. Why was Grandmother doing this?

I took it directly upstairs, and when I put it back on the shelf in the closet, I also noticed something different on my writing desk. All my notes were back out on the Taylor book I was writing. I remember specifically cleaning off the top of the desk while preparing for Ella's day to clean. Grandmother had been quiet for quite some time, so what kind of message was this? I had to admit that seeing everything there made me want to sit down and start writing. I was a writer. Was someone trying to remind me of that? I may own a flower shop, but my yearning passion was with a paper and pen. Perhaps that's why I was also intrigued with Jane Austen. However, there was no time today. It would all have to wait in my waiting room until I returned.

I finally got off to work, and flurries did indeed start to fall just as had Ella had predicted. The flakes seemed to disappear as they touched the ground. When I drove past O'Connell's Art Gallery, I remembered the first Christmas gifts that Sam and I exchanged. Perhaps they could help me out once again, but what could Sam possibly want or need? What was special to him? Of course! It was 333 Lincoln. I could take them

Roxanne's drawing and have them frame something for Sam's new office. I had only seen his office once since his promotion, but I did not recall any artwork on the wall. I now knew it would be a perfect gift to have for him on Christmas morning.

I went by Phil's, thinking of his uncomfortable situation with the raffle quilt, but chose not to stop by just now. I had to work, as Sally had a day of vacation and Abbey and Jean had a full schedule. As soon as Kevin had time to hook up my desk computer, I could occupy my office. Phil would have to wait.

"I'm having a blast with the guys from the Christmas committee," Abbey announced as we were both working on a casket spray.

"You all have done a great job! Main Street is at its best at Christmas and springtime. I may need your help regarding the quilt show coming up, so I hope you'll be available."

She didn't have a chance to respond because the UPS man came in with five good-sized boxes. The driver complimented me on the shop's addition and then asked if I had taken my turn displaying the raffle quilt. That told me the gossip had indeed spread. I just shook my head, pretending I didn't know his reason for asking. Why were most salesmen and UPS men like little old ladies when it came to gossiping?

I stopped to take a call from Isabella who asked if we could meet at Charley's before literary club in order to talk about the quilt show. I agreed and then called Mother to tell her my plans and to let her know that I would not be picking her up. She sounded disappointed, but Isabella and I had busy schedules to accommodate.

Brad was happy to see me since I had not been there for a while. When Isabella arrived, we were seated quickly.

Isabella lost no time beginning the conversation. "Your

mother was in today to tell me to keep a lookout for a couple of baby quilts for Nancy," she shared as she found a place for her purse. "I can certainly do that. What a joy the babies will bring to so many. I sure hope everything goes okay. Your mother said she's been quilting on my quilt. I should be there helping her."

"I should, too, except that I'm a little busy," I said, making my excuses. "She loves doing it and she has the time to do it. My mind has been on our ribbon-cutting ceremony, which will be very soon. I hope you can come."

"Oh, I will indeed," she said. "I am so proud of you, Anne. Now, getting back to the quilt show, I spoke with Phil before I left the shop. He said that so far nothing horrible has happened with the quilt there, so that's good news. The bad news is he's not gotten it out of the bag to hang it. In other words, it's not making any money at the moment with the quilt still in the bag."

"Oh dear, I wouldn't get it out of the bag either, if I were him. I explained to Pat, Sam's sister, about our indoor show and she thinks we are making a big mistake by not hanging the quilts on the outside of the shops."

She looked at me with wonder on her face.

I continued, "I thought it was out of the question at first too, but this raffle quilt inside of the shops has been a disaster. No one is going to be too thrilled about showing any quilt in their shop with all of the rumors going around. I know it's just been bad luck with the ghost quilt, but it sure doesn't help with what we are planning."

"I know, but Anne, it's wintertime," she said, taking a sip of her drink. "It would be so much better in the spring, but I know everyone is determined to have it as a winter promotion.

They've already done some promotion of it too, I'm sure."

"Here's what I've been thinking, Isabella," I had started to explain when I saw Ted coming in the door out of the corner of my eye. I must ignore him. I turned my stool to his back and pretended not to see him. "I think we should hang at least one quilt on each building. The cold weather won't hurt anything, unless it's raining or snowing. I think the idea will blow people's minds to know it's outdoors, and they will want to see it. We could call it the Main Street Cover-Up or something like that. It's not too late to get the word out. Pat has been to Sisters, Oregon, just like you, only she has all the instructions about how they do everything. If we could assign two people to each city block and tell them where to hang a quilt, we could have the show up in one to two hours. At five, they go back to take them down. Abbey, who works for me, is so creative that she would know exactly where to place each quilt. She is open to helping us. I think if we keep it simple and assign one quilt per building, it's very doable."

Isabella was quiet.

"I know it's out-of-the-box thinking, but frankly, I don't think there are enough customers who care about what quilt is in each shop in order to get them to come in to check them out."

"Well, I have no say since I'm not even a member of your group," she began. "I think you could get a lot of criticism with the outdoor plan, Anne. If you do make this change, I'll have to make it clear from my perspective as a shop owner that it was a decision from the merchants' committee, because some of my quilt owners might not go for that idea. I told Phil I would help, so whatever you guys decide to do is fine with me."

"But Isabella, you are the quilt expert," I reminded her.

"We know nothing. We don't know what precautions to take or where to get quilts to display. We *need* you. You just can't leave it up to us. In a way, both of our reputations are at stake here. I couldn't stand by if someone was going to plant flowers in a terrible place or create a situation where there would be some neglect. Do you see what I mean?"

Isabella stared out the window, seemingly considering my pleas. She then asked, "Have you told Phil and Sharon about your idea?"

"No," I said, shaking my head. "This whole idea would go nowhere without your support. It's a risk, especially with the weather, but let's face it, if the weather is bad, they aren't going to come and shop on the street anyway. This crazy idea is something they won't want to miss. No one has done anything like this before. I think it would be safe to plan one rain date for bad weather. In Sisters, they have it rain or shine on that one day only. There is no backup date. They have so many people coming from all over the country that they have to stick to the advertised date."

Color was now coming back to her face, as if she may like the idea. "Oh Anne, we're going to be late for club! We need to go," she quickly announced after looking at her watch. "I'll have to sleep on this!"

"You're right, you go ahead. I'll settle up with Brad. Please think about this idea quickly and if you think it's doable, we'll go to George and Phil to present it."

"I will, Anne," she promised, putting on her coat. "You are one crazy mover and shaker. Do you ever sleep?"

I laughed.

Out the door she went. I was waiting at the table for Brad to bring me the tab when I remembered that Ted was somewhere in the vicinity. Sure enough, he was headed my way once he saw Isabella leave.

"Hey, Anne," he said, placing himself comfortably on the stool where Isabella sat just moments ago.

I nodded and barely smiled as I searched my purse for my credit card.

"I already took care of your tab, so don't worry about it," he said nicely. "Do you have a second to talk?"

Oh no, this was not good. "I'm late for literary club, Ted. That's why Isabella ran out ahead of me," I explained.

"I have so much to tell you," he began as I stood up to put on my coat. "I feel I owe you so many explanations about my behavior. I still care what you think. I don't care if you are married or not."

"Ted, please," I said as quietly as I could. "None of it is any of my business, and I really do have to go. Don't get me wrong, I wish you nothing but the best." I took a deep breath. "I will say that whatever you are struggling with, you will not find the answer here at Charley's bar!"

He stared and I was shocked at what I had just said.

"Have a good evening." I turned and went out the door. I got to my car and wanted to throw up. I hated being rude to him. I would always care what happened to him. What was I thinking? He was obviously struggling and I couldn't give him five minutes of my time. Was I becoming too high and mighty as Mrs. Dickson? Who made me Mrs. Perfect? What if Ted becomes devastated by my remark and hurts himself? When will I stop hurting him? What would Sam say if he knew about this conversation? I finally started my car to head home. Seeing the literary club was the last audience I needed to face tonight!

CHAPTER 46

When I arrived home, Sam was still out. I had two calls on my cell phone, which I could have predicted. One was from Mother and one was from Isabella. I'm sure not showing up for literary club was noticed by many. After I hung up my coat, I called Mother's home phone and left her a message that I was tired and not feeling well. I would explain to Isabella later.

I felt so frazzled and drained emotionally. I dragged myself upstairs, ignoring the big and beautiful Christmas tree. It might as well have not been there. I dropped my clothes to the floor and took a long, hot shower. It felt relaxing enough to help me sleep. However, I knew I needed to eat something. Lunch had been sparse at the shop and skipping dinner hadn't been smart. I went downstairs to find some crackers. Just as I sat down to nibble a few of them, I heard Sam come in the door.

"Hey, Annie, what are you doing home so early?" he quickly asked as he took off his coat. "Did they cancel literary club?"

I said nothing as he kissed me on my cheek with his cold lips.

"The flurries are starting to stick, so it's a good thing you're home." He gave me a look of concern. Perky Annie was not responding. "Are you okay?" He knew I wasn't.

I suddenly burst into tears. I was so confused. There was no way I could tell him how my encounter with Ted started all this. Was it Ted I was even crying about? I felt overwhelmed on every front. I sobbed with my head on the table and Sam was in shock.

"What is wrong?" he began trying to understand my behavior. "Tell me, sweetie, what has happened? Is it about you or someone else?"

I shook my head.

"I love you, sweetheart. Please talk to me."

I took a deep breath and got up slowly to get a tissue from the kitchen counter. Sam kept staring at me, hoping I would say something. I'm sure Sam never saw me like this before, unless it was when we lost Aunt Marie.

"I'm fine, just tired and overwhelmed," I said between sniffles. "I'm sorry. It's not any one thing, Sam. I have a lot on my mind and my hormones aren't keeping up."

He stared hard, trying to figure out my meaning.

"I had a drink with Isabella at Charley's. We wanted to talk about the quilt show before we went to literary club. When I got in the car, I decided to come home instead. I just wasn't up to talking to more people today. I just couldn't do it. I'm exhausted. I did call Mother when I got home so she wouldn't worry about me." Somehow, I knew I wasn't convincing Sam that this was my excuse for the outburst.

He finally spoke. "You do have an awful lot going on, honey, and I haven't been much help with all I've got going," he confessed. "I should have been paying more attention. You are always the one worrying about me and all my stress. You'll be the next one taking pills, if you're not careful."

"No, no, that's not it, Sam," I started to explain. "You are wonderful and you haven't been neglecting me at all. It's my doing. I told Ella when she saw me just staring into space the other morning I had so much to do that I didn't feel like doing anything. I'm sure a good night's sleep will help."

"How about I make you one of my omelets or a toasted cheese sandwich?" he said, coming close to me. "I'll bet you haven't eaten. I didn't have much dinner myself. Are these crackers your dinner?"

I nodded.

"Whatever you make sounds good, honey," I conceded. "It'll help me sleep better, I'm sure."

He immediately swung into action. He knew this was one way to be helpful and would hopefully fix things. Oh, how I wish a little food could do all that.

I went into the bathroom to wash my face and knew I was in good hands with Mr. Dickson here at home again. I told myself I had to regroup, be a big girl, get a grip, and get my act together. Where was that feisty Anne Brown when I needed her?

CHAPTER 47

A fter sleeping through the night in Sam's arms, I woke up refreshed. From the telltale aroma, I guessed Sam had made his way down the stairs to make coffee. It was Saturday, so Jean and Abbey were working until the noon closing. I had much to accomplish, however, so I planned to stop by the shop after my brisk winter walk.

"Good morning, beautiful!" Sam said as I entered the kitchen. "From what I can tell, you had a good night's sleep! I was thinking that the two of us should go out and have a nice dinner this evening. What do you think? We need to talk about our Christmas. The board at Martingale is doing away with the Christmas party this year. Did I tell you that? We're giving money to a couple of charities, which makes a lot more sense. Of course, they've been teasing me that since Mr. Scrooge Dickson has taken over, all the fun is taken away. My memories of that annual event were such that I could do without it happening this year. I would rather give the employees a bonus."

"I think it's all a good idea. Speaking of employees, I am going to invite my staff over for a light supper here one night if that's okay with you. I wanted to do a little more this year, considering all the help they have been with the addition. They would string me up if I gave their bonuses to charity!"

He laughed at my point.

"I want to share that magnificent tree we have out there. I'd like you to be here. Do you think it's possible?"

"I think any night but this Monday," he replied, putting away his paper. "We have a sales crew coming into town and we'll be taking them to dinner."

"I am so glad you are not traveling as much with this new position!"

He came over and gave me a squeeze. "Me too! Remember, there's a little snow on the ground out there," he warned as he watched me bundle up for the cold.

"I know. I'll be careful," I agreed, waving my gloves at him. "I'll look forward to tonight then!" I kissed him good-bye.

As I walked along Main Street, I was careful to avoid bricks that I knew could be very slick with the least bit of ice. Walking in the street was safer in some places, particularly if there wasn't much traffic. I couldn't help but look at each building again and picture where each quilt could be hung for the quilt show. The display would truly be for anyone driving down the street. The handicapped and elderly could see the quilts as they drove by. They would likely not come in the shops, but it would be a tremendous treat for them. Giving back to Colebridge was always a good idea.

When I passed O'Connell's Art Gallery it was closed, but

I would be sure to stop by later today to commission them to do something grand with my drawing of 333 Lincoln for Sam. I decided that a smaller print of it would be nice to have framed for my little office as well.

My toes were getting numb from the cold, so I headed back to my car and drove through Starbucks to get hot coffee and some muffins for the girls. As soon as I got to the shop, I started dodging questions about being a no-show at literary club. They soon changed the subject when the muffins appeared.

"Sorry, guys, I was really pooped last night!" I explained as I was getting ready to go into my new office. "Was it a good meeting?"

"Well, I took a shine to tell them a bit about the whereabouts of Miss Jane," Jean explained. "On a jolly big map, I showed them all the places where she lived. I brought in the historical timeline of King George III and so on. I suppose it brought on a yawn or two, but it is essential to our world of Jane. Last night, it was a mighty small group. Nancy was absent, of course, and also Sally and Paige. When you didn't show, I was a bit taken aback. You feel better, do you not?"

"Oh, sure. A good night's rest was needed," I assured her.

"I got the baby shower invitation from you and your mum, Miss Anne," Jean said. "I simply love to visit Miss Donna on any occasion, so it should be quite special!"

"Miss Donna is doing all the work, so I hope you can make it," I said from my office.

"Oh, Mrs. Dickson!" a voice called out from the front desk.

I peeked around the corner and it was Isabella standing

there with her hands on her hips.

"And you were doing what after we had our drink last night?" she teased.

"I know, I know! I fizzled out. Sorry," I said as she joined me in my new office.

"Wow, Anne, this is all very cool!" she said, observing my new surroundings.

"Well, it's all still a mess, but as of today, I hope to be all moved into this little piece of heaven."

"I have to say that this addition looks like it's been here for some time. I really like how you chose an outdoor feel for the décor."

I had to agree with her.

"Well, I don't want to keep you, but I have to tell you that I want to strangle you for keeping me up all night with your little outdoor show scheme!" she joked.

"Me?" I asked innocently.

"You sure did a good sales talk about the change to the quilt show," she confessed as she smiled. "I think it may just work! If you convinced me, chances are you can probably convince the rest of Colebridge to come and see this wonder in the dead of winter!"

"Yay!" I cheered, raising my arms in a show of victory. "Now we have to sell it to the rest of the group."

"Let me know when you want to go and talk to them," Isabella said, walking toward the door. Referring to me but looking at Jean and Abbey, she joked, "When this gal gets something in her head, you may as well concede, right girls?"

They laughed in agreement.

It was good to get my office organized. My computer was up and running, but I was determined to let e-mails go

ANN HAZELWOOD

for the day. My bare walls begged for personal touches like pictures of 333 Lincoln and my handsome husband. I might just have fresh flowers every day, I told myself. Two green plants were already in the little bay window.

Sam and I put on our best clothes and decided to go to Colebridge's newest restaurant, Rascinos. It was in a new, striking, contemporary building on the outskirts of Colebridge. The menu offered only natural entrées from Missouri-grown food. The building itself was made from recycled materials. It was a trendy concept that was proving very popular. We were enchanted with its atmosphere and energized by the anticipation of its delicious food. Sam was delighted to find a new place to entertain for business dinners and luncheons. We weren't disappointed as we enjoyed each course. We made every effort to not to talk about our work. Sam was sensitive when talking about our Christmas plans after what happened last year, so I kept my comments brief. The entire evening's experience was a nice change of pace and we knew we would be coming back.

We mellowed out in our home as we stood and admired our beautiful Dickson tree. I loved that it provided the only light in the house, and there were enough white lights to do just that. We settled in the study by the fire to snuggle and talk. God had indeed blessed me with everything I could possibly want this Christmas. At this moment, time could stand still forever.

CHAPTER 48

O n my way to O'Connell's with my drawing, I got a
phone call on my cell phone from Aunt Julia.

"Hey, Sylvia said we are going to try to quilt on Isabella's
quilt this Sunday afternoon," she said as soon as I answered.
"Are you going to be a no-show again?"

"Give me a break. I'm just a little bit busy these days. You
need to come and see for yourself. I moved into my new
office yesterday!"

"I will, soon! Are you pleased with everything?"

"I'm very, very pleased!"

"I have a little piece of gossip for you, unless your husband
already shared it with you."

Now what, I wondered.

"Did he tell you that Brenda has been promoted to vice
president, filling in the place vacated by Sam when he was
promoted to president?" she asked sarcastically.

"You have got to be kidding!"

"No, I'm not," she went on. "Harry Sims called to ask me out again a few days ago, and we talked quite a while on the phone. He learned this from Jim, who is feeling slighted, given he was doing the same work Brenda was doing." There was a pause. "No, I didn't agree to go out with him again. Hello!"

"Sam didn't tell me," I revealed. "He knows I loathe her for having an affair with your ex-husband. By the way, Sam has done away with the big Christmas party they used to have. He said they are doing something related to charity. Did Harry tell you that?"

"Yes, that I knew. Well, good luck with his plan! I don't think it'll stop all the affairs and who knows what else that goes on in almost every workplace!"

I hated to hear her say that, but it was probably true. Sam would try to set a good example, at least.

"How's Sarah?" I asked, hoping for a more pleasant subject. "I haven't seen her for a while."

"She's in seventh heaven these days because I'm letting her date on Friday nights. Jim is not as happy about that, however. Sarah and I are both coming to the baby shower, just so you know. What a great idea to have it at Donna's. I'll never forget your wedding shower and that incredible gift from your grandmother. Speaking of Mother, how is the old soul?"

"Aunt Julia, be careful," I cautioned. "She's stirring around, but not hurting anyone at the moment."

"Oh, that's reassuring," Julia replied, sounding sarcastic once again.

"I'm at my destination, so I'd better hang up. Maybe I'll

see you on Sunday."

A quilting day was not something I needed to put on my calendar; however, we owed it to Isabella to not delay her quilt.

The O'Connells loved the drawing of 333 Lincoln and their sales clerk suggested doing some tinting to it to bring it alive. I liked the idea and chose framing for Sam's picture as well as a smaller black-and-white print for my office. I told them it was a surprise and apologized for not giving them much time. They seemed to be grateful to have the business.

When I got to the shop, I called Phil to see if he could meet with Isabella and me regarding the quilt show. He seemed relieved to hear that we had some ideas and said he would call George to see if he could join us.

"I'm open to anything at this point," Phil confessed. "I feel this whole idea has gone sour with all that has happened with this raffle quilt."

I called Isabella and said all was well. We agreed to meet at Phil's and I decided that I would bring something to drink and have pizza delivered. It certainly wouldn't hurt to loosen everyone up. I was tempted to include Abbey at the meeting, but perhaps it was premature.

"So, we'll be stitching again for Miss Isabella, by golly," Jean said as she unpacked greeting cards. "Your mum called and I will venture that everyone will be a show, right?"

I had to snicker at Jean's way of saying things.

"Will our Sally be back today, Miss Anne?" she asked.

"Yes, she'll be here around eleven o'clock, and Kevin will not be coming in at all today unless we have an urgent situation."

"That Miss Abbey sure fancies our Kevin," Jean shared,

like it was a secret.

"How is he responding?" I asked, curious.

"He's a friendly sort to her, but I dare say he is courting that pretty Miss Maggie still."

"I'm hoping to have all of you over to 333 Lincoln on Friday evening after work for a little Christmas cheer, if you're available, Jean. I'll be telling everyone today. It's just for us, however. The only other person will be Sam, who is cooking and has agreed to wait on us!"

"Oh my! How gracious on your part and most generous and sweet of that Sam, I do say," she responded. "We'll have a much better time with just our little family, for sure! That Sam is such a good chap! What a merry time we'll have!"

CHAPTER 49

I left a message with Sam's new secretary to make sure he got my message that I would not be coming home for dinner. I was the last to arrive at the committee meeting, but no complaints were voiced when they learned that pizza would be delivered.

"This had better be interesting, Anne," George said. "By the way, is the raffle quilt still in the bag, Phil?"

Sharon burst into laughter as if there was an inside joke. "We got it out and kept it on the table back here until Mrs. Cane came in," Sharon explained through laughter.

"So, then what happened?" asked George, not seeing the humor.

"Ah, well, Mrs. Cane knocked over a whole shelf of glassware," Phil remarked. Silence fell over the room with all of us not knowing how to respond. "Thank goodness most of it didn't break, but it did about a hundred dollars' worth of damage. I thought immediately of the quilt's bad luck and put it back in the bag. Sharon thinks I'm crazy, but I wasn't going to take any more chances!"

"I can't say that I blame you," I said before anyone else could speak. "I don't know if I should laugh or cry."

"Mrs. Cane always presents a problem, you all!" chimed in Sharon.

The pizza arrived, and when we all got settled around Phil's table, I presented my ideas about having an outdoor show, rather than displaying a quilt inside each shop. Isabella helped explain how it worked at the Sisters, Oregon, show. She said they never advertised a rain date, but she thought it would be good if we did. She claimed that every business in town made good money on the one-day event.

They all listened intently.

"What do we do with the raffle quilt and where would we be able to even show it during the show?" Phil asked, still worried about the quilt's brief but troublesome history.

"I'll take it," I said without thinking. "It stays in the bag until the show. It's just on display for that one day, and when we draw the winning ticket at five, it's the next guy's problem."

"We can't let you do that, Anne," George said, concerned.

"I'll hang it on the outside of the building where I have no windows," I suddenly decided. "I'll have raffle tickets to sell until we draw for the winner. If my shop blows up in the meantime, I would suggest you draw the name sooner than show time!" They all burst into laughter and Sharon managed to spill her drink on her blouse in the process.

I then told them about Abbey creating attractive displays. They did light up knowing that someone was willing to take on the job.

"Where the group mostly comes in here is that we will need two persons for hanging and takedown in each block. Surely we'll get members to do that for a little bit. Each quilt will be in an identified bag with instructions about where it will hang. We could even include a photo of the quilt on the bag. That was Abbey's idea. She said she could take the photo as she planned where the quilt should go. When the quilt is taken down at five sharp, it goes back in the same bag and into the quilt shop, safe and sound for the owner to pick up."

"We can't expect Abbey to do that for nothing. She's not even a member of our group," said George.

"I'll pay her," I offered. "She lives on Main Street and needs the money. She was a big help with the Christmas committee, which she did for nothing."

"We'll have to get approval from the group, of course, and make sure our insurance will cover this in case there is any damage," George reminded us. "Can you get us enough quilts, Isabella?"

"I have a list already," she assured us. "Hanging their quilts outdoors may become an issue, so I'll have to get permission from them. I think I'll have them sign some disclaimer."

"So, this shakes up our publicity," said Kathy, who usually thought negatively. "We can't call the event the same name, obviously."

"It's up to the committee, of course, but you could call it something clever like Main Street Cover-Up," I suggested. "That may have a negative connotation to it, however."

They all snickered at the thought of a Main Street Cover-Up scheme.

"We can't call it Quilts Outside Main because it sounds

like we left them outside accidentally."

We were all absorbed in thought.

"The quilts will be along Main Street, so why not just call it Quilts on Main?" suggested Isabella. "It's simple and catchy."

"I really like that!" I said, hoping the others would approve.

They all perked up as if a problem had been solved. Picturing quilts all along Main Street was a visual they could all identify with.

"Let's go with that and call a special meeting to get this thing going as soon as possible," said George.

"Since I'm a sponsor, I'll be happy to pay for any changes we have to do, Kathy," offered Isabella.

Kathy smiled, so I knew she was relieved by Isabella's offer.

"In the meantime, Phil, I suggest you leave the quilt in the bag until the day of the show," George said firmly.

Everyone nodded in agreement.

"I'll send the quilt your way on show day!" Phil rhymed, smiling. "Here's to the first annual Quilts on Main!"

We all raised our glasses, hoping for the best!

CHAPTER 50

S am and I both took off early to prepare for the Brown's Botanical family Christmas party at 333 Lincoln. I put the finishing touches on a holiday table that was adorned with holly and red chrysanthemums. Sam prepared appetizers of shrimp and lobster that were divine. He made two options of hot pasta dishes, one with red sauce and the other with white. A large Greek salad in a silver bowl looked fit for a king. The smell of homemade garlic bread was a killer as we waited for our guests to arrive. Dessert was easy with Christmas cookies and candy from Nick's Bakery.

Kip and Kevin arrived together both wearing sweaters and khakis. Sally came in a conservative black pantsuit and Abbey stole the show with her red glittery minidress and black fishnet stockings. Perhaps she was trying to impress our dear Kevin. Sue and Jean were festive, choosing to wear what they owned in the color red. Sam took their coats and drink orders as they admired the big tree and all our decorations. This group always had something to laugh about, especially when Kip or Kevin were around. Abbey was taking photos with her phone every time I looked at her. She was so in awe of the house, and I told them they could wander through the whole place, except for our bedroom and the waiting room where the doors were closed.

After dinner, we gravitated to the fire in the study. The evening weather forecast threatened an ice storm, but no one seemed to be worried. I could hear Sam working at cleaning the kitchen. I was going to owe this man big time for all his hard work, despite how much he loved doing it.

"This is something from all of us that we had designed for you, Anne," Sally said as she presented me with a little wrapped box.

I opened the box to find a darling sterling flower shop charm with Brown's Botanical Flower Shop engraved on the back. It was precious! I blushed as I thanked them for their thoughtfulness.

"I have something for you that you may enjoy in later years," said Kevin, handing me another box to unwrap. He explained that he had taken pictures every day during the construction of the shop. He had put the photos in a red album rather than hand me a CD, which I so appreciated.

"Oh, I will cherish this, Kevin," I said as I hugged him. "I was so busy most of those days that I know I missed a lot of it. I love it! Thank you." I gave him a big hug.

Everyone rushed to join in looking at the photos, including Sam who came in the room in time to hear Kevin's presentation.

"Well, I have to say I didn't dare do anything other than

your annual bonus!" I said as I pulled my thoughts together.

They clapped and laughed.

"Thanks so much for all you do. I love each and every one of you!"

Sam looked at me, seeing my eyes well up with tears.

"This has been a special year with all of your help. Now, we can grow and grow, just like our plants!"

Sam felt the pride as well and knew I was very lucky to have this family.

"Merry Christmas and a Happy New Year at Brown's Botanical," Kip cheered.

We toasted each other, laughing.

"I can't take much more of the love in this room, you guys!" Sam said as we continued to hug. "I hate to be a spoil sport, but it's icing up really bad out there, and I want to make sure you don't slide down that hill into the traffic. Kevin, you could probably take the girls home in that vehicle you have out there if they don't want to drive!"

In the end, everyone was determined to drive themselves home. It was a special Christmas with a special family and my special Sam helped me make it so!

CHAPTER 51

✴

It was always a good feeling to come back to my former home on Melrose Street. My fondest memory of living there was coming downstairs each morning and seeing Mother at the kitchen table reading the paper. Coffee was always ready, and, no matter what, her face always indicated that she was happy to spend time with me as we shared what we anticipated was going to happen in our upcoming day.

When I arrived for the quilting, I walked in with Sue, Mia, and their cute dog, Muffin. Mia and Muffin always expected a treat from Mother as soon as they came in the door. Mia was now saying "cookie" as a not-so-subtle reminder.

We were hanging up our coats when Isabella arrived with her long-time employee, Norma. Most of us knew her from the quilt shop as a sweet elderly lady who made wonderful hand-quilted quilts. She usually had one or two on display in the shop.

Mother greeted her warmly and told her what a help it would be to have her stitches in the quilt.

"Isabella speaks so highly of you all. She thought I would enjoy your quilting bee and could keep the process moving along," she commented shyly.

As usual, we had carried all of the scrumptious desserts downstairs. Norma admired the quilt and Isabella showed her where she could sit. Mother had just rolled the quilt, so we were ready to go. We knew Norma was being kind when she admired our quilting stitches in the quilt.

It was always interesting to catch up on the latest news. Sue reported that Uncle Ken was having some tests done. Mother's side of the family struggled with heart issues, so I knew this would greatly concern her. The rest of us were silent, knowing what it could really mean. Sarah told us about her recent visit with Uncle Jim who had visitation with Sarah every other weekend. Jean bragged about the new shop addition and the wonderful Christmas party at 333 Lincoln. Isabella contributed to the conversation by telling them about Quilts on Main. They had many questions, which was to be expected.

"We need some of your quilts, ladies," begged Isabella. "We are about thirty quilts short right now. They don't have to be our very best. It's the color and design that will make the show."

"Oh, I can give you at least four," offered Mother. Other offers followed. I wonder what Aunt Marie and Grandmother Davis would think of us right now?

We stayed our usual two hours or so and then we began to leave and wander up the stairs. Mother reminded me about how she looked forward to having the Christmas Eve dinner this year and having Harry Stone joining us. She beamed at the thought.

"You may think I'm crazy, Anne, but I thought about asking Ella to join us," she said, tilting her head. "Harry always had her join him on Christmas Eve because she had nowhere to go."

"Sure, it's your party, Mother. Is William going to be in town?"

"Yes, he was nice enough to call me," she said with a smile. "He said he wouldn't miss it."

"Let me know if I can do anything besides send flowers," I said, kissing her good-bye.

It was good to get home to Sam who was answering e-mails on the computer in the study. He asked me about everyone before I went up to change clothes. When I returned, he said he was setting up arrangements for a conference call the next morning.

"Sam, you never told me that it was Jim's friend, Brenda, that took your place as vice president."

He paused for a moment. "Perhaps I haven't; however, it wasn't intentional. Who told you?"

"Aunt Julia."

He looked puzzled.

"Is Brenda still a married woman?"

"Yes, she is. I know for a fact that she is not seeing Jim, so what are you getting at?" He was sounding a bit defensive. "I'm glad to hear that. How did she get that promotion?"

He was looking irritated. "For starters, I think she's been at Martingale longer than I have. She's smart, ambitious, and frankly, she has brought us a lot of business."

I knew he was not happy with where this was going. "So

you supported promoting her despite her bad behavior as a married woman?" I asked accusingly.

"We can't inspect everyone's personal life, Anne, nor do I want to. If their job performance is not affected, it's really none of my business."

I didn't respond, but instead turned to go upstairs. I wanted him to have the last word on this. She'd just better leave my husband alone.

Later in the evening, while Sam was still working in the den, I wrote a few more notes at my writing desk. I wanted to be sure and write about the traditions that I was picking up on in the Taylor house. The Christmas tree was certainly one of them, and now we had a gardener as well. I wanted to know more about their other holidays, so I added the questions to my list. Perhaps I could write all of these questions in an e-mail to Edward, in case he remembered anything. Anything was better than trying to guess.

Somewhere in the book, I was going to have to insert something about the love triangle that existed between Albert, his wife Marion, and his employee, who happened to be my grandmother, Martha Davis. Did Marion really believe Albert when he denied the affair with Martha? I would probably never know that answer, I supposed. If women loved their husbands back then, they were likely to never rock the boat and thereby jeopardize their security. Were there other women in his life, as suggested by others? I had to remind myself this book was to be about 333 Lincoln, not just Albert Taylor.

The next morning, it was too cold and snowy to walk, so I answered my e-mails from home. Nancy was sending e-mails to me frequently, complaining of this or that. Her happiest comments were of how active the babies seemed to be. She was so looking forward to the baby shower, and I hoped nothing would go wrong.

As I drove to work, I was reminded of the extra Christmas carolers and characters the merchants' group had hired for this season. With my shop being closed in the evenings, I was missing out on some of the magic and activities that others enjoyed. I hated missing the merchants' party at the Q Seafood and Grill, but there was too much to do. I also didn't want to keep defending the outdoor quilt show idea.

When I went to Nick's for gift boxes of candy, he was actually bragging about what a tremendous Christmas season it had been so far. This was rare for him, but I had to agree, because our sales were up as well. I told him that Sally had added some seasonal products that made great add-on sales when customers would come in to pick up flowers. I also told him January 2 would be our ribbon cutting and that I would need some goodies to offer for those attending. He was delighted, of course, and said whatever I ordered would be his "shop-warming" present. I nearly gushed as I thanked him, which he abruptly dismissed. He was more comfortable being grumpy.

CHAPTER 52

Richard was quite the conscientious husband as he carefully escorted Nancy to the baby shower. Nancy was dressed in a lovely winter white maternity dress and was showing greatly in her pregnancy. I tried not to stare, but she was very large.

Donna's Tea Room was closed to the public in order to be able to accommodate the many family members and friends that Nancy had accumulated, plus her in-law's acquaintances in Colebridge. The shower had an appearance of a high tea with fancy sandwiches, puff pastries, and beautiful candied fruit. An enormous sheet cake from Nick's Bakery read *Welcome Barrister Babies*.

It was another excuse for Donna to use one of her sets of Haviland china, which she did on special occasions. The large, round gift table was piled high with gifts. It was adorned with swags of holly for the holiday season and the antique chandeliers had holly with pink and blue curled ribbons. Abbey

253

had prepared adorable centerpieces of assorted pink and blue flowers and holly.

Half of the Colebridge ladies in attendance were customers of mine and asked about my new shop addition. What would a shower for Anne Dickson be like, I wondered. I wasn't going there.

Nancy greeted everyone with a small speech about how long she and Richard had been desiring a family. "I wish I could convince one of my friends about how marvelous pregnancy can be," she hinted, looking at me.

I looked away as if I didn't know who she could be talking about.

Mother and I stayed until the last gift was opened and until the last person had left. Nancy didn't want the fairy tale to end. I was exhausted, plus I had promised the O'Connells that I would stop by and get my framed pictures. Thank goodness Richard showed up to haul off the gifts and take Nancy home. These babies were set for life with clothes and every conceivable nursery gadget known to man. Two of everything was over the top!

For the first time, I had chosen to close on Christmas Eve. I had to do last minute shopping for gift cards, which was the preferred way of giving for the Dicksons. When I arrived home, Sam was preparing a delicious crab appetizer for Mother's dinner that evening. I went upstairs to the waiting room to do last minute wrapping and then placed everything under the gigantic tree, which made a sparse presentation, to say the least.

I dressed formally for the dinner, which I seldom did. Somehow, it felt right to wear a silver metallic, long-sleeved top with a low neckline. My black long skirt had a deep slit on the side that Sam was already teasing me about. This called for my antique diamond earrings instead of my usual pearls. I bravely put on the diamond ring Mother had given me for my birthday, hoping Aunt Julia wouldn't notice since it was a ring that had belonged to their mother. It was just too perfect for this outfit and occasion. I was certainly getting Sam's attention as I completed my ensemble. Sam was truly handsome in his black dress suit and red tie that I had picked out for him in Door County.

We were pleased to see twelve festively dressed guests filling the table. There was Aunt Julia, Sarah, Sue, Mia, William, Amanda, Allen, Ella, Harry, Mother, Sam, and myself. I looked around the table where so much love and chatter was shared. Seeing Ella all dressed up was interesting for me. She looked elegant tonight. Mother said Ella had tears in her eyes when she was asked to join us. Mia's red velvet dress with white leggings was a striking complement to her very black hair. She had been to our dining room table enough to know a few manners that Sue was trying to teach her.

This year, the addition of Harry Stone broke a tradition that had once been handed over to Sam. Harry asked us to join hands during the prayer, obviously planned ahead of time.

"Thank you, heavenly Father for bringing us together to celebrate the birth of Jesus," he began. "We thank you for that precious gift, as well as friends and family that are gathered here this evening. Grant your blessing to this wonderful family hosting us today and to those who are not with us this evening. As we begin another year, we ask this in Your name, amen."

I was shocked to feel tears welling up in my eyes and I was afraid to look up. I first glanced up at Mother who was having the same reaction. I had no idea that Harry was at all spiritual. I guess we had a new man of the house on Melrose Street.

"That was pretty well done, Harry," Sam complimented.

We smiled with approval.

"If everyone will allow me, I'd like to make the first toast of the evening to my wonderful mother-in-law who is a great cook and hostess." Cheers and clinking of the glasses surrounded the table. Mother was blushing and Harry was beaming with pride as he looked at her.

Out of the blue, Allen asked if he could have our attention. "I would like to add to this special occasion by telling you that I have asked Amanda Anderson to marry me, and she has accepted!" The big surprise brought another round of applause and cheer. The two of them were all smiles, including William. This reminded me of when Mother announced my engagement at this very table. Oh, how Aunt Mary would have loved to be a part of this announcement.

The chatter grew louder and louder as everyone started their meal. Our pork tenderloin dinner was delicious and elegantly served with all the trimmings. Dessert was served in the living room, as always, where we opened the many gifts. One of the gifts Mother gave Amanda, Sue, Aunt Julia, and me was a beautifully framed black-and-white photo of her parents and young siblings. What a shame they didn't even know about their half sister, Mary, at that time. This was going in the upstairs hallway, where I had other family photos. Mia stole the show with her many cute toys. We all enjoyed her so!

Sam had made phone calls to his family earlier in the day, so the rest of the evening was all ours. Tomorrow, we would be celebrating our second Christmas morning together as man and wife. Sam's heart attack last year was going to escape my memory. All was well at the Dickson household.

CHAPTER 53

W ake up, sweetie, wake up," Sam whispered loudly, nudging my arm. "It's a white Christmas!"

I looked up at his happy face. At what age were men not like little boys, I wondered? I smiled at him. "Merry Christmas, Mr. Dickson," I managed to whisper.

"Merry Christmas to you, Mrs. Dickson," he said, leaving me to go look out the window. "I bet there's a foot of snow or more out there! I'd better call our service and make sure they get over here!"

"I just want to know if Santa made it here last night," I joked, getting up.

"Well, we'll have to see," he teased. "I'll start breakfast, honey, if you want to stay in bed for a while."

Now was a good time to tell me, since I was already up.

I made myself presentable for a Christmas morning, and then made my way down the stairs, admiring our tree all the way. The smells of coffee and sounds of Christmas music brought a smile to my face, knowing Sam was so into the holiday. I was so lucky to have someone that appreciated Christmas as much as I.

"I thought we'd have Christmas on the sun porch this morning," Sam suggested. "The view of the snow is beautiful and the sun has warmed up that room."

He was so right. It was a good idea. I got busy setting the table, taking my one of many poinsettias for our centerpiece. I could see my snowed-in potting shed. I will pay it a visit later and find out if my small heater is still working. We sat down to enjoy Dutch pancakes, bacon, and fruit. It was fit for a king.

"I think Harry has his dibs on that mother of yours, Anne," Sam ventured, smiling as he spoke. "I'm surprised he hasn't moved in."

"My mother would never do any such thing, even though he is there a lot!"

He laughed at me.

"Let's go see what's under that tree of ours," Sam said, taking his coffee with him.

When we got to the foyer, three striking red suitcases were stacked in front of the tree with a big white bow tied to each of them. Santa must have come while I was eating breakfast. They were so cool. In another package was a matching computer bag. The note with the bow said, "This is a wish for more travel with that wife of mine." I was delighted. I couldn't wait to examine each piece. Sam often made fun of my piecemeal luggage that I likely had from high school. I hugged and kissed him like he was Santa himself!

"Here's a little something from me," I said, handing him

my gift. "It isn't as splashy as your gift, so I hope you like it."

When he saw the picture of 333 Lincoln, he appeared to be very pleased.

"This is for my office, right?" he asked, holding it up. "It's so thoughtful and I know just the right place for it."

"Yes, it was so hard to think of anything you needed or wanted, Sam," I said as if I were apologizing.

He kissed me on the cheek and said it was perfect. "I see those gigantic stockings in the study are bulging. Should we take a look?" Sam asked, pulling my hand.

We continued to amuse ourselves by sitting on our large pillows and taking turns pulling treats from the stockings. My favorite surprise was a red and white striped pair of pajamas and Sam's favorite was a T-shirt with "president" in bold black letters on the front. He thought it was a hoot! Just as we were finished, we heard the arrival of the snowplow out front. Sam jumped up, of course, to be of assistance.

Christmas Day was a good day to be closed at Brown's Botanical. It wasn't a day off, however, for funerals or special occasions, so I went to the computer to see what had come in by e-mail or phone. I couldn't help but wonder what in the world we would do if this weather occurred for our winter quilt show. My goose would be cooked, for sure.

As I went to refill my coffee in the kitchen, a loud siren went off and got louder and louder, as if it were coming our way. I grabbed a coat to go to the front porch in hopes of an explanation. Sam, already on the porch, yelled that the ambulance had stopped at Mrs. Brody's house. It was a good thing the snowplow had cleared the road for them. What could have happed there?

"Should we go over there to see if we can help?" I yelled

across our drive.

"You go inside. I'll go over and see."

I went back into the house, sat near the fire to warm up, and said a little prayer for her. Christmas morning was not a good time for any kind of problem. Last year, an ambulance came up the hill to take my Sam to the hospital. What was it with this hill in Colebridge?

Fifteen minutes later, Sam came in, shaking snow off his shoes and clothes.

"What is it, Sam?" I asked as I took his coat.

"It's Mrs. Brody," he said with a sad face. "Her nephew found her dead this morning. From what they are saying, it must have been a heart attack."

"Oh no, Sam. She was such a sweet lady. Remember when she made us a berry pie for a wedding gift? I wonder how old she was."

Sam looked sad as he went silently into the study to get warm. I joined him, wanting to cry.

"I'm not sure, but she looked very, very old from what I saw this morning," Sam said, taking a swallow from his coffee.

She was a piece of the Taylor house puzzle for me and now she was gone. I should have asked her more questions. Why do we always value a person after it's too late?

CHAPTER 54

$\mathcal{K}$

The next day when Sally and I communicated by phone regarding the expectations of the day, we both concurred that the bad weather would kill street traffic; however, we also agreed that the staff needed to be there. I felt sorry for those shops that were counting on after-Christmas sales. Many shop owners would not be coming in; therefore, many sidewalks would not be cleared. I shared with her about the death of Mrs. Brody and that I needed to send flowers to whatever place would be appropriate.

Sam had left at his usual time. Weather was not much of a factor in his life like it was in his retailer-wife's life. Before I could leave the house, Mother called to ask about our Christmas Day and if I would be able to get down our hill to go to work today. She said that she and Harry had been dinner guests of Harry's sister, and that they had a lovely time.

"So, what did Harry give you for Christmas?"

"Several nice things, but I was very surprised when he gave me a gift card to the Green Spa."

I could imagine her blushing just telling me. "Well, I hope you use it," I said encouragingly. "You never did when I tried to give you something like that."

She laughed.

I chatted about our gifts and that Mrs. Brody had passed away. I looked at my watch and decided to pick up lunch on the way for everyone so we wouldn't have to get out in the weather once everyone made it into the shop.

"How sweet of you, Miss Anne," Jean said, eyeing the bag of goodies. "I'm afraid the jolly holiday has rolled some pounds on this old gal."

I had to agree that we all had overindulged.

When Abbey took her sandwich and sat down to eat a bite, I approached her about what I would like to have her do for the quilt show and that I would pay for her services personally.

"I'd be happy to, Anne, but it sure sounds like a risky event, if you ask me," she said, shaking her head. "You'll have to be careful how they are hung if there is wind or any kind of weather disturbance."

"Oh, we know," I started to explain. "Isabella is on top of that. We need your expertise concerning where to hang the quilt on each building and maybe some other advice, if necessary. We know it's risky, but we are going to try it if the group gives us permission. We have a meeting tomorrow, so I'm pleased I can tell them you will be willing to help."

"I love the title Quilts on Main, Miss Anne" voiced Jean, overhearing our conversation. "Do you have a quilt for us, by chance, or shall I bring something from my stash? I told Miss Isabella she could have some as well."

"I thought I would display the Potting Shed Quilt," I suggested. "It isn't finished, but it is still interesting and it hasn't been seen by the public."

"A mighty brave move, Anne, considering its history and activity," Sally said seriously.

I ignored her comment. "I will be the one to have the raffle quilt that day, so I think we should hang that on the north wall where we don't have a window," I suggested. "We'll see what Abbey thinks."

"Here is my list of people to be invited and the media notices on the ribbon cutting," I said to Sally after I printed it out. "I want you all to take a look in case there is someone I forgot."

"Is that Mr. Collins on there, by chance?" Sally said, trying to tease me.

"Don't go there, Sally," I warned, cutting her off. "By the way, do you have New Year's plans with anyone special?"

"As a matter of fact, I do," she answered fairly quickly. "One of my friends is having a party and Paige, Susan, and I are invited.

"So, is there any news on Tim? Will he be there?" I asked bravely.

"Well, he is also going, which I already knew. He said if I needed a ride, I could go with him," she said, grinning. "I guess that's the closest I'll ever get to something like a date with him."

"He didn't say 'we'?" I teased. "Isn't that called a date?"

She shook her head like I was crazy.

"It's called a *ride*," she quipped. "What are you guys

doing?"

"Probably work and a quick dinner, since the reception is the next day," I said without too much thought.

"That sounds like a married woman's answer," teased Abbey.

We laughed.

"Don't forget to factor in our date for inventory," I reminded them.

"Phil's on the phone," announced Sally.

Phil began, "I hope you'll be at the meeting tomorrow. We are going to need you there to help sell this thing. I'm already getting some flack over the outdoor idea."

"I'm sure you are, and it's probably to be expected," I said, dreading the thought of going.

He agreed.

"Hey, Phil, is the raffle quilt still in the bag?" I asked, picturing the last time I saw it.

"Yup, and it's staying there all closed up until you take it off my hands," he stated. "Sharon keeps threatening me by saying, 'I'm going to let the quilt out of the bag!'"

I laughed.

"Your secret is safe with me, Phil. I'll try to make the meeting."

CHAPTER 55

It was sad to hear there wouldn't be any kind of service for Mrs. Brody. Her nephew was the only family I knew of, and from all indications, there might not have been extra money other than the value of her property, which would likely go to him. Sam was already thinking ahead about possibly buying it from him if it went up for sale. I recalled my earlier visit with Mrs. Brody when she told me the Taylors were always trying to buy her property. She had resisted, and reasonably so, because it had always been her home, and I couldn't blame her. I instructed Kevin to leave a message on her door that we had flowers for them, whoever they might be.

I barely made it on time to the merchants' meeting, and the attendance was impressive. There was standing room only as I leaned against the wall next to Kathy. It never failed—there was always a good turnout when there was something to be against. After Christmas was when the whining would always begin on the street. The cold, dreary days ahead promised little traffic and business. My timing for making a change was not a good one.

George, our president, was great at controlling crowds as well as negative opinions. Because of the crowd, he moved the quilt show to the top of the agenda. I was glad to see that Isabella showed up to help present our suggestion. George began explaining that because of difficulty with the raffle quilt, the committee thought a new direction needed to be considered regarding the quilt show. As folks began to stir, he called on me to present the outdoor show idea. Before I could get very far in my explanation, I was interrupted.

"How in the world do you expect people to come into our shops if the quilts are outside?" asked Dan, representing the leather shop. He had a particularly negative tone in that one question.

Before I could respond, Isabella jumped up to introduce herself and explained that she had gone to the quilt show in Sisters, Oregon, where it was hugely successful. "What you had planned previously left the street bare and with no enticement to come into the shops. The visual you get from quilts hanging all along the street is colorful and enticing for most folks, and especially for quilters. I can tell you that attracting quilters from the region is very smart. They have money to spend on shopping and eating! By the way, I know some shops are going to have a quilt or two inside as well, so that makes it even better."

Before Dan could counter her remarks, George explained how Isabella had gotten permission from quilt owners to have their quilts hung outdoors and that our nonprofit status insurance would cover any liabilities. He then added that a rain date could be set for the following day.

"I say we wait until spring when this would be more appropriate," said Karen Maxwell, a Main Street resident. "You've got a great idea there, but just bad timing. You are setting yourself up for failure and possibly a disaster."

A number of people enthusiastically agreed with her.

"We'll have plenty of business in the spring!" Kathy was quick to respond. "We planned this for a middle-of-winter event, which we need desperately."

"I agree with that," voiced an employee from The Spice Shop. "We have got to do something!"

A few folks clapped.

"I really would like you all to support this," George said calmly. "We are so lucky to have the volunteer help of Isabella with the quilts and Abbey from the flower shop who will orchestrate the placement of all the quilts. We really don't have much to lose. Kathy, would you tell them about the publicity you are doing?"

"Sure, George," she began. "I have to admit that this idea threw me for a loop, too, but the more we've been working on this, the better I think it is. We came up with calling it Quilts on Main."

There were a few oohs and ahhs before she went on.

"I changed a few things, and whatever changes we had to make were covered financially by one of our members. Frankly, the press is going to jump all over this because the show will be for everyone, not just for people who choose to come into our shops. Think of the handicapped and elderly who maybe cannot walk the street. The goodwill here is immeasurable."

She had the audience in the palm of her hand, so I thought

it might be a good time to add my own two cents. "You all make very good points, pros and cons," I stated. "I know it's risky. Everything we do is. I do feel personally responsible here and I'll take full blame if this bombs. Keep in mind, I cannot control Mother Nature."

Some chuckled.

"I am taking the raffle quilt to place on my building so no one is taking a bigger risk then me!"

Most members in the room knew exactly what I was talking about and still shook their heads like I was crazy.

"You're a trooper, Anne," George said. "Now, if we approve this, know that all of you will have to take time to help in the block that you are located. It won't interfere with you being in the shop. We will hang the quilts between six and eight in the morning and take them down after we close our shops at five. The committee has a method for putting the quilts up and taking them down. Remember, another place has tried this before. I might also add that the quilt show committee could have very well just gone ahead on their own with where to put the quilts, but instead, they wanted you to be on board, and to help as well."

"Oh, so you are doing us a favor, is that it?" Nick Notto voiced in a nasty tone. "Seems to me this is signed, sealed, and delivered like everything else we have to put up with on this street."

"Hey there," scolded Barbara from Buttons and Bows, "there's no need to insult anyone in this room when they are doing all the work to bring us more business."

Some merchants clapped.

George now lost control of the chatter and emotions that were expressed. He reached for his gavel and banged hard on the wooden counter in front of him. This discussion had gone on way too long and I was getting concerned about its outcome.

"I move to support the quilt show's committee's recommendation to make it an outdoor quilt show," said Phil, who had remained silent up until now.

"Does anyone want to second that?" asked George in a firm voice.

"I'll second it," said Kathy with a big grin.

"All those in favor, raise your hand and keep it up until Sharon has a chance to count it," he instructed.

This was not looking very good.

"All those opposed, please raise your hand," instructed George. The room became totally silent.

"We have twenty-one in favor and fourteen opposed," Sharon announced.

"The motion passes," said George, trying to smile. Some clapped and some murmured things as George banged on the counter once again in an effort to restore order.

"Thanks everyone. I know you all will support this idea now that we have made the decision," George said with authority.

I looked at my watch and then followed Isabella out the door. I was not going to stay for the rest of the meeting, as it was getting late. I didn't want anyone to corner me with any more additional comments or concerns.

"What a fine situation you got us into, Anne Dickson," Isabella teased. "I am now your new partner in crime, I suppose. I guess we'd better put on a darn good show!" We laughed as we said good-bye, knowing that the pressure was on!

CHAPTER 56

The snow was melting as the New Year approached. All I had on my mind was the ribbon cutting on January 2. Sam was busy with year-end reports from department heads, so when he suggested we have a quiet dinner at home on New Year's Eve, I wasn't disappointed.

"I was talking to one of our executive chefs at a luncheon we had a few days ago and we were discussing restaurants," he said. "He asked where we would be dining on New Year's Eve, and I said we had no plans. He gave me a strange look followed by a big grin."

I listened, interested in what he had to say.

"He then went on to say that he did private catering on the side and that he could prepare a nice gourmet dinner for just the two of us in our own home. He said he provides full courses that include the china, crystal, and silverware."

I was trying to absorb what he was suggesting.

"He knows I have a more than adequate kitchen and he assured me he would clean up afterwards." He paused. "Okay. I'm trying to read those pretty blue eyes of yours."

I snickered and realized I wanted to kiss him at that very moment. "It is such a romantic thought, Sam," I said, smiling big. "Can we afford him?"

He laughed. "We can, my dear," he said, coming near me. "I'm sure the president will get a good rate and it sounds rather appealing, don't you think?"

"It sounds marvelous," I responded, giving him a hug. "We'll have to dress for that kind of dinner, that much is certain!"

"I thought about surprising you with it, but good luck with that. I guarantee it will be better than any restaurant fare."

The next morning as I took my walk, I couldn't help but think about what a romantic evening we were going to have. I watched the big chunks of ice float down the river as it was thawing. I glanced up to the sun to give thanks for the end of a beautiful and successful year. With God's guidance, he gave Sam and me the tools to accomplish our dreams. I asked that He be with us in the coming year.

I stopped at the shop to check e-mails when I ran into Abbey taking her walk on the street.

"I saw Nick last night and it sounds like I have a new part-time job with the quilt show," Abbey teased as we went in the shop and got away from the cold.

"Yes, I am counting on you, girl," I bragged.

She shook her head in disbelief as she smiled. "I was hoping to see you today because I have a bit of news to share with you," she said, taking off her gloves.

I waited patiently for the news.

"Kevin asked me out for tonight," she said, not looking at me. "Oh, maybe I should have kept it quiet, but I'm so excited. I know we are both so opposite, but I think he is so hot and a perfect gentleman, don't you?"

I laughed, watching her blush. I think it's great, Abbey," I finally said. "I'm not blind and a hundred years old. He's a great guy. Just don't bring it all in the shop, okay?"

"Oh, I hear you!" she quickly responded. "Don't worry." She nearly melted with jealousy when I told her Sam's plans for the evening. She threatened to crash our dinner until I told her that her job was on the line.

When I returned home in the late afternoon, I already smelled the activity going on the kitchen. I introduced myself to Chef Michael and made my way upstairs to call Mother.

"Happy New Year!" I said cheerfully when she answered.

"Oh, Anne, the same to you, sweetie," she said as I pictured her smile over the phone.

I explained our dinner plans for the evening and she said they, too, were staying in and that Harry had requested her pot roast dinner. That Harry was getting top billing with her and she loved every minute of it. She said she'd see me at the ribbon cutting and how proud the moment would be for her as well. She was so supportive.

After I showered, I chose to wear my best black slacks with a white cashmere sweater that was dotted with pearl sequins. Simple pearl earrings would be all that was needed. All of the pearl jewelry Sam had chosen for me was perfectly suited to my taste. When Sam and I looked at each other, Sam whistled and said we were ready for our night on the town—on top of Dickson hill.

CHAPTER 57

Michael told Sam he would serve our drinks and appetizers in the living room. When Michael entered the room wearing a formal tux and holding a silver tray in his hand, I knew we were on our way to a spectacular experience.

"This is called a royal gin fizz," he announced as he handed me a crystal champagne glass. "If you love this, I'll be happy to share the ingredients. It is a champagne base with some other goodies."

I had to believe it tasted as good as it looked.

"Have some appetizers of Brie and Merlot mushrooms on rye crackers, as well as crab salad in wonton cups. Be careful not to overindulge, as there is much more in store." He grinned.

Sam and I must have looked like vultures wanting to make a meal of the tasty delicacies.

"Oh, this drink is divine, Sam," I said as we started the evening. By all indications, Sam was hungry, so he told Michael we would be ready for dinner anytime. It was so relaxing by the fire and the delicious appetizers alone were truly enough for the evening.

As we were seated at the elegantly designed dinner setting that included white roses and candles as the centerpiece, he announced the menu for the evening. "We will begin with a roasted tomato soup garnished with roasted cherry tomatoes and heavy cream," he began. "It will be followed by a beet and goat cheese arugula salad. That, of course, will be enhanced with burned champagne. Your main course is roasted salmon served over leeks and fingerling potatoes, accompanied by blackened green beans. With that, you will enjoy a very dry Riesling wine."

Sam and I were quietly and overwhelmingly impressed as our mouths watered.

"For dessert, I kept it very light with almond tulles and mango sherbet. That brings us full circle with a bit more of champagne to bring in the New Year!" He grinned proudly as we waited for the circus to begin.

We enjoyed each and every bite as we listened to soft music in the background. Normal conversation went out the door as Sam explained the food and cooking process that he himself would have liked to prepare. I knew Anne Dickson would never measure up to this caliber, nor did she care to! It was a joy just to watch Sam love each and every bite. As we came near the dessert course, I was moaning from eating too much food. I became a bit mellower as the last bit of champagne was served. It was getting near midnight.

"May I ask you to please dance with me, Mr. Dickson?"

Michael dimmed the lights in the dining room to just the candlelight.

"Yes, Mrs. Dickson. I shall be honored," he said. He held me closely as he picked up on my unexpected romantic gesture.

"Thank you for such a wonderful, wonderful, wonderful evening," I whispered softly in his ear. "Why are you so very, very clever in everything you do, Mr. Dickson?"

"Because my wife has made me the happiest man alive," he whispered back. "I love my sweet Annie and want to live up to her expectations."

I hung on more tightly, feeling like I had arrived in heaven.

We danced slowly, as all the necessary words had been spoken. It was a Kodak moment that could not be greater or more enhanced by all the love we felt for each other. We truly complemented one another and were excited about our dreams that were about to happen in the following year.

Michael then rang the dinner bell on our table, announcing that the New Year had arrived.

"Happy New Year, sweet Annie," he said, taking hold of the champagne glass nearby.

"Happy New Year to you, my sweet," I said as I took the same glass out of his hand to taste.

Just then, all the lights in the house began to flicker off and on. We laughed as we both looked up.

I raised my glass and said, "And to you as well."

Sam shook his head in disbelief as always, as the flicker now stopped in response.

CHAPTER 58

"This is the day the Lord hath made; let us rejoice and be glad in it." I said, driving myself to the shop on the big day of the ribbon cutting. Having rested well on New Year's Day, I was focused, along with my staff, to make this a very special day.

The minute I arrived, early well-wishers were stopping by to take a peek at the shop and congratulate us. I glanced at my flower shop family who were dressed in their finest clothes for the occasion.

"Anne, did you see the gorgeous flowers on your desk?" Sally asked.

I gave her a blank look. "Flowers *from* someone, you mean?" I asked innocently.

"Yes, I didn't put them there, but someone did," she explained, following me into the room.

"Oh, red roses," I said with admiration. "From Sam, no

doubt."

Sally shrugged.

I opened the card and it read, "I'm so proud and happy for you! I wish I could be there to see your face and share the happy occasion with you. Always, Ted."

Sally watched my face fall.

I looked at the large bouquet and then back to her. "Ted," I finally said.

"Oh, Anne, I'm sorry. This is none of my business," she said, turning to leave.

I took the note off of the flowers and put it in my pocket so no one would see. Why did he have to keep inserting himself into my life? It was touching, yes, but so out of place.

"Anne, the chamber director and mayor have arrived," Abbey announced.

"Oh thanks," I said, getting back my train of thought. "Abbey, how did New Year's Eve go for the two of you?"

"Oh yeah, awesome," she replied, putting her thumbs up in approval.

I had to laugh.

The place looked beautiful as I looked around. Jean was working with Nick Notto as they arranged an elegant refreshment table on the main design counter. The white tablecloth displayed fancy silver serving pieces full of chocolates, cookies, fruit, and Jean's delicious tiny orange scones. On another smaller counter nearby, Jean had put on hot coffee and tea for the chilly day and champagne for after we cut the ribbon.

"Miss Anne, I was a bit taken aback when I saw the lemonade in the refrigerator all made up and the like," Jean revealed. "Did you want me to put it out? I'm afraid I was not prepared with the proper glasses, as all I have are these paper cups."

"Oh dear," I said, not thinking clearly as the place became more crowed. "No, leave it in the refrigerator unless someone requests something cool to drink."

The gift shop area was chosen to cut the ribbon because it had flowers blooming in every corner. Sam arrived as I was about to take my place in the line of dignitaries for the ribbon cutting. I motioned for him to join me.

"One, two, three, cut!" they all yelled as my hands maneuvered the scissors to cut the ribbon. Cheers and clapping erupted as Sam grabbed me for the first hug of congratulations. I looked over at Mother, whose eyes were tearing up as she approached me. All of a sudden, I felt someone tugging at my skirt. I looked down to find little Mia dwarfed by the tall crowd, trying to get my attention.

"Annie, Annie, me too," Mia cried out as she stood by her mother. I picked her up to get a big, wet kiss. I then handed her to Sam who got in line and waited for the opportunity to get them each a cookie.

"Anne, this is perfect. I love it," Sue bragged.

I gave my sweet cousin a hug.

"Are you pleased?" asked Jason.

"I am if you are," I teased. "Thanks for everything, Jason."

"So, now what, Miss Flower Child?" asked Aunt Julia as she gave me a glass of champagne.

"Hmmm, good question," I answered smiling. "I guess I first have to make sure I can afford all this additional space. What's next for you?"

"I'm tossing some things around," she said, surprising me. "Keeping an eye on my teenage daughter is a full-time job."

"Where is Sarah?" I asked, not realizing it was a weekday.

"She'd better be at school," she answered. "She'll have to see this at another time."

"Well done!" said Phil as he and Sharon came my way. "You are quite the superwoman to achieve this!"

"Thanks, you guys," I said, blushing. "I guess I now have to focus on the quilt show."

He nodded in agreement.

"I hope we can have a sunny day like today," said Sharon. "I love this flower quilt on the wall, Anne. Did you make that?"

"Oh, no. You can thank my mother over there," I said, pointing her way. "Please tell her. She'd love it."

The celebration was over quickly, considering all the trouble it took to plan. Sally was very pleased about selling the amount of merchandise that we did and Jean bragged about the scones all being devoured as she cleaned up. Kevin was moving things back into place as folks were leaving. I said good-bye to Sam as he headed back to the office.

I was about to admit to myself that I had a headache, so I went into my office and closed the door. This was a luxury I had never experienced. Before, I would have to go the restroom if I wanted some privacy. I left the chatter behind and sat down at my desk. I stared at the red roses, which had a heavy scent. Ted was still here, despite the fact that I am now happily married. I jumped when someone knocked on the door.

"Can I come in, Madam Shop Owner?" Nancy asked in a silly tone. "Sorry I missed the ribbon cutting. I had Richard drop me off for a bit. It's getting too uncomfortable to drive."

"Oh, Nancy, now my day is perfect!" I exclaimed, giving her a hug. "Please sit down. Are you okay?"

"Big and sassy, as Richard says. I couldn't miss this, girl! I am so happy for you. I love your office and that picture of your house. I should have known that the boss gets her favorite flowers on her desk every day!"

I laughed.

"That's another story, I'm afraid," I answered, frowning. "They're from Ted and that's all I'm going to say."

She looked shocked. "Well, some things don't ever change, I guess," she lamented, shaking her head.

"So, have you picked out any names?" I asked as I looked at her tummy. "It's almost time."

"Well, we're close. We decided we would say for sure after they were born. You have got to come over and see the expanded nursery. It turned out really well."

"I will," I agreed. "We have the street quilt show coming up shortly and I really have to help pull that off. I'm afraid I am in over my head again."

"That's you, girl," Nancy laughed. "If I can help just a little bit, let me know. I have to get going. I'm so glad we had this private moment together. I am so, so proud of you!" She hugged me as I felt her ever-so-big tummy greeting me. She was the best friend ever!

CHAPTER 59

The start of the New Year was extra exciting to think about now that the expansion of the shop was completed. I was hoping for a normal day with the pressures of the holidays and ribbon-cutting ceremony behind me. We had a good start on the year-end inventory, leaving just what we had in the gift shop to be counted.

Skipping my walk to get an early start was a good idea because the weather report was frightful once again. It promised freezing rain, eventually turning to ice. Ice was always much worse than snow because of our steep hill from Lincoln Street, and it was the best reason to keep customers off of Main Street. I went to Starbucks to pick up coffee for me and muffins for Jean and Sally as I traveled the deserted streets to my shop. I noticed Sally had arrived before me. I noted again how conscientious she was with her manager's position.

After handing Sally the welcome treat of muffins, she

predicted that the day would be slow and mentioned how she wanted to get the inventory out of the way so she could begin setting out Valentine's Day merchandise.

"I haven't had a chance to ask you how the party went with you and Tim," I commented, surprising her.

"Oh, not too bad," she said, smiling. "We spent most of the evening together, which surprised me. He rarely noticed Paige, who ended up going home with some Asian guy she just met."

"Really?" I said, somewhat amused. "What did Tim have to say about that?"

"Nothing to me, anyway," Sally said, munching away at her muffin. "He wanted to know if I wanted to go to the band blaster concert next weekend, which floored me."

"Great. Hang in there," I encouraged her. "Have you heard today's forecast, by the way?"

"Yup, trying not to think about it," she responded. "Should we call Jean and tell her not to come in? You know she and Al are not fond of getting out in this weather."

"Good idea," I said, nodding. "Would you call her?"

I looked out the window and saw Abbey heading toward our door.

"Morning!" she yelled as she shivered. "Got the coffee pot going?"

I laughed and nodded.

"Were you out walking in this sleet?" I asked, taking her coat.

"Well, I started, but the sidewalks are already a sheet of ice," she complained.

"So, since you're here, would you like to help Sally with the rest of the inventory?" I hesitantly asked. "We told Jean not to come in."

"Why not? Beats what I had planned today," she offered. "Muffins are here for us, right?"

"Go for it," I nodded. "You can have Jean's portion."

"Phil called early this morning and said we have a quilt show committee meeting tomorrow morning at the coffee shop," Abbey shared. "Did he call you? I still have a couple of blocks to do on the hanging plan. I sure hate to think that this could be the weather for our quilt show."

"Stop it," I demanded. "I won't hear of it. It's a ways off. A lot can change." I went to the window again to watch the icicles forming on my gutters. It was then that I noticed Ted driving by very slowly as if he were observing our addition or me, I wasn't sure. I backed away from the window in hopes that he didn't see me. His office wasn't near Main Street. It reminded me that his accounting firm was also going to be celebrating an addition, according to Jason.

It was noon when I got a phone call from Sam asking if we needed lunch and if everything was okay. I told him we were fine because we seemed to have tidbits of food hidden here and there.

"Let me pick you up after work so you can leave your car there," he suggested. "Is there any traffic on the street?"

"Thanks, Sam. I don't think I could drive up our hill," I told him. "And no, other than the UPS driver, I have not seen much activity."

The rest of the afternoon was productive with few interruptions. Most of the telephone calls seemed to be people checking on us personally instead of folks needing flowers. I teased Sally that our idea to do weddings must have flopped because no one was calling. She didn't think my little joke was funny.

Mother was spending her afternoon quilting on Jean's quilt, thinking she may even get it completed. Nancy called to say she was bored and uncomfortable. Kevin called to check on delivery times and was pleased he didn't have to go out. He reported that he had the hardware to install on the side of the shop where we planned to hang the Ghostly Quilts on Main Street during the quilt show. It wasn't bad enough that I had talked the merchants' group into having an outdoor show in the dead of winter, but I took on the most controversial task of taking the quilt for my building. What if something really bad happened to my newly renovated flower shop? I had to erase the scary thought.

"Staying in tonight?" asked Sally, holding her clipboard of numbers.

"Absolutely, if we make it home," I said with fear in my voice. "It would be a wonderful night to continue my writing. I still haven't finished all the information that Edward Taylor supplied me with when he visited. That reminds me to check my potting shed when I get home. That little heater had better be doing its job or all my green friends will be dead."

"I hate winter," cried Abbey from the design counter. "It's like time standing still as if it were frozen."

"I agree, Abbey," I said, pouring my third cup of coffee for the day. "Other than a few little white flakes for Christmas morning, you can have the whole season. Spring will continue to be my favorite with shades of green and buds that want to pop. It is the season of hope. Who would possibly plan a quilt show for the deadly season? She should have her head examined!"

"Yes, she should," chimed in Abbey and Sally in unison.

CHAPTER 60

T he weather continued to get worse, making it impossible to drive up the hill from Lincoln Street with all the ice. We left our car parked on the street and climbed up our hill hand in hand as we hung onto bushes and tree limbs. It was certainly a good workout for the day.

Sam planned on making his great spaghetti sauce for a pasta dinner while I changed my clothes and set up a spot for us to eat in front of the fire in the study. Phil called on my cell phone as I was about to join Sam in the kitchen.

"With the forecast for tomorrow being much the same as today's, it looks like the street will likely shut down tomorrow, so I'm calling everyone to cancel the meeting planned for the morning," Phil explained.

I gave him my support in doing so and described the icy climb up our hill.

He then went on to tell me how complaints were

mounting about the outdoor quilt show. He was certain that the majority of it was fueled by the bad weather.

"Just remind them that the sun will come out tomorrow!" I said, repeating a line from one of my favorite songs. "We have lots of days before then, and no matter when it is, there is always a risk. Is the quilt still in the bag, Phil?"

"Yes indeed. I don't need any more challenges these days," he reported.

"Just so you know, Abbey just has a couple more blocks to do on her hanging instructions. How is the volunteer list coming along?"

"Not very well," he said, sounding down. "It's still a little early to panic."

"I'll make sure Kevin and Kip help on our block. They may have friends that could also help if we really need it."

"Great. I'll put them on the list."

By the time we hung up, I think we both felt better.

After a warm, relaxing dinner, Sam and I felt ready to retire for the evening. Sam grabbed a book he was trying to finish on the Civil War and I took my last notes on the Taylor book to look over. We snickered about how we were behaving like an old married couple. Little time passed before we were sound asleep.

The next morning, we were awakened by a truck coming up our hill that was spreading salt. We had slept later than usual, but then sprang into action as if we were really going somewhere. A look outdoors told us differently.

I called Sally to confirm closing the shop for the day and said that I would have the calls forwarded to my house. Fortunately, the few current orders I knew about were for future delivery.

As I sat with Sam having coffee at the kitchen table, I was reminded of the Potting Shed Quilt that had fallen so frequently on the sun porch floor. I remembered taking it upstairs and putting it into the waiting room closet. I planned to get it down and take to the shop while it was on my mind.

I went upstairs to change clothes and then checked the closet where I had put the quilt on the shelf. It wasn't there, so I proceeded to check the other closets. My next thought was to check with Ella to see if she had seen it anywhere. I had a notion that Grandmother was playing games with me again. What was going on?

I came down the stairs in jeans and an extra heavy sweatshirt to find Sam multitasking in the kitchen, which he always seemed to master. He was pecking away at his laptop while preparing chili for lunch. This guy was all about food—good food! How much bigger will I be each year living with this guy?

Sam picked up the landline phone when it rang, and after a short conversation, said it was for me.

"Anne, how are you?" a familiar voiced asked. "Sam said you are all iced in, which means the two of you are actually home together!"

Her remark made me chuckle. By this time, I knew it was Pat, Sam's sister.

"What a pleasant surprise," I responded. "Is everything okay?" I was thinking of Sam's mother and wondering if all was well.

"Oh, sure," she said to calm me. "I thought I may do a stopover on my flight so I can be there for your quilt show! I feel like I got you into this, so if I can be of help, I'd be happy to. I'll be staying at a hotel near the airport so I can fly out the next morning."

"That's great, but you don't need to help," I quickly explained. "We're in pretty good shape, except for the naysayers, I guess."

"That's understandable," she added. "Trust me, when they hear the cash register ring, they'll all be as happy as clams!"

After we hung up, I went upstairs to visit the waiting room. I sat down to revisit the day Edward came. I had so many more questions. How did the Taylors handle the icy weather? How did so many of their plants and trees survive? On that note, I quickly ran down the stairs to the sun porch where I had snow boots and a heavy coat. I had the potting shed on my mind. What if everything was frozen and dead? Why hadn't I checked on the heater sooner?

"What's up, honey?" Sam asked, looking at me strangely.

"The potting shed! I forgot to check the heater!" I announced as I rushed to get dressed for the cold weather.

"I'll go, Anne," Sam said, getting out of his chair.

"No, I'm all dressed," I replied, opening the back door.

"You be careful, Anne. Take it slowly, you hear?"

"I will," I yelled in return. "If I don't come back shortly, it means I'm frozen somewhere!"

"That's not funny," Sam yelled back as I got nearer to the shed.

I lifted my boots carefully and hung onto various bushes to secure my footing as I got closer to the frozen shed. The windows were totally frosted. I didn't know if that was a good sign that there was warmth inside or not. I pulled and pulled on the frozen door, almost falling, when to my surprise, it opened to a warm little nest of green plants that eagerly greeted me. I quickly closed the door and grinned from ear to ear. Thank you, Lord! The ferns were shedding some of their brown leaves, which was to be expected. I knew they would be just fine, come spring. I checked on each plant, giving them a little water as needed. I swept up the accumulating leaves and wanted to hug each one of my little surviving plants. I had so many wonderful memories here in this little tiny place. I remembered sitting on my counter stool writing away one long afternoon. I remember arranging all the stacks of clay pots, and, of course, admiring the new garden tools that Grandmother had given me for my birthday. This was my little piece of heaven, left from the Taylors, which I wanted to keep as much like it was originally as possible. As I prepared to leave, I told them I would be back soon and it would be no time before I took them all outdoors in the springtime.

As I approached the house, I saw Sam looking out the window at me. I waved my arms with a big smile on my face and gave him the thumbs up sign that all was okay. He opened the door to let me in. His warm hug and the smell of chili and corn bread made me a very happy camper.

CHAPTER 61

✣

It took a couple of days of consistent sunshine to get Colebridge back to being a functioning community. Jean, Sally, and Abbey were all on the schedule for the day in order to catch up with pending orders. Kevin and Kip were also kept busy with deliveries, shifting their hours since we had just one delivery van. It had been a long time since Colebridge had experienced such a bitter and long, cold winter. Record snowfalls up north threatened spring flooding, but none of us wanted to hear about that possibility.

A lunch meeting at the Q Seafood and Grill brought our quilt show committee together for the last time before the show. Abbey gave me her report to read, which looked very doable if we provided the right tools for the volunteers who were hanging the quilts. Phil said he was still short a few men, but he hoped to have the slots filled by the time of the show. Kathy, our public relations person, bragged about how well things were going. She said she even landed an interview on a local television show. She said Quilts on Main was a catchy title that had many folks curious, especially since it was to be held outdoors. She said many would be watching to witness our success and perhaps failure. It was agreed that Phil and Kathy would be the spokespersons for the event, and they should be prepared for the right response no matter how the show goes.

Kathy also showed clever T-shirts with the ghostly raffle quilt displayed on the front. She had already sold some and thought it would be a great seller during the show. We teased her in every way possible about what could happen to the poor souls who wore the shirts. She was not the least bit amused.

When we concluded the meeting and our lunch, Phil handed me the raffle quilt that had been kept in the same bag all these weeks. I hesitated to take it since it was not quite the time of the show date. I took it as a favor to Phil. I knew he was so done with that quilt by now.

When I returned to the shop, Sally looked at me, concerned. "Is that the quilt I think it is?" Sally asked when she already knew the answer.

"Yup, now the question is, where do I put it to keep it safe until we take it outdoors?" I responded as I looked about the room.

"Why not keep it with your other quilt that's in your office," Sally said innocently. "We won't need them both for a while."

"I don't have a quilt in my office," I replied as I went to look in my office door. "Oh no, I can't believe this. When did that get here? I have been looking everywhere at home for it. Who put this here?" In the chair next to my desk neatly folded was the Potting Shed Quilt.

By now, all of the staff had heard my remarks and stood there staring at the quilt.

"That's the Potting Shed Quilt, isn't it?" Sally asked to break the silence. "You said you were going to display it here for the show, so I assumed you brought it from home."

"Right, but I am not the one that brought it here!" I said, almost yelling. "Do either of you know anything about how this got here?" I looked directly at Abbey and Jean.

"You've not had any callers while you were gone," said Jean politely. "Isn't it quite so, girls?"

"Right," answered Abbey. "Where is the quilt supposed to be? I'm confused."

"At home in my closet, where I put it!" I said in an angry tone. "I've looked everywhere for this!"

"I would venture that Grandmother Davis did you a nice favor and you should value that," Jean suggested.

"Okay, okay, but I don't like playing games with her!" I said in an even louder voice.

The girls slipped away from my sight since they knew my mood was unpleasant. Nothing more could be said. I picked up the quilt from the chair and opened a deep drawer in my desk that was still empty from the move. I put the raffle quilt right on top of it and slammed the drawer shut, wishing the ghostly quilts well in their dark and crowded locked drawer. I put the little key back in the front of my middle desk drawer. I wondered what would be next with their ghostly games. Jean then walked in the door with a hot cup of tea in her hand.

"I know you are trying to take meaning of it all, Miss

Anne, but you should just take a shine to a good deed," Jean said eloquently. "I brought you some of this special tea that my cousin in Bath sent me. She said it soothes the soul and is very calming to the spirit." She smiled, wanting to be helpful.

"Thanks, Jean. You're right," I said smiling back at her. "I do need to soothe my soul. I just wish my grandmother would do the same."

"Your mum rang earlier to give you a reminder for a pick up this evening," Jean said as she also sipped her tea. "Will you be popping in at club this evening? We missed you so at the last meeting."

"Oh, I forgot it was tonight," I said, not surprising her in the least. "Mother is probably anxious to get out after being in so long with this weather, so I'd better go."

"Jolly good!" Jean said as she left my office.

Before I left the shop, Nancy called, asking for a ride tonight as well. She was going crazy staying in and Richard would not let her drive anywhere. I agreed to do so and then called Mother back for confirmation. Sam was my next call. I had to leave a message. His little wife was as busy as he was. It was a good thing we'd had those iced-in days together.

CHAPTER 62

Everyone was in a jolly mood when I arrived at Jean's house with Nancy and Mother. Nancy's additional baby growth was the topic of conversation as everyone got their tea and biscuits before the meeting. When we sat down, Nancy said she had wanted to ask me if she could do something for me during the quilt show.

"I just want to be there in all the action," Nancy pleaded.

"You'll have to have someone sit and sell raffle tickets, won't you, Anne?" Mother suggested. "I'm sure all of your girls will be busy working at the shop."

"Yes! Perfect!" Nancy quickly responded. "I can sit and do that."

"Oh, Nancy, you don't have to work to be there!"

"No, I don't want to be in the way. I want to be useful," she demanded.

"I wouldn't fight with a pregnant woman if I were you!"

teased Mother.

"Okay, okay," I said as Jean was trying desperately to get our attention.

Jean began the meeting by asking us what lessons we had learned by reading Jane Austen. She reminded us about how differently we had interpreted our quilt blocks and her sayings. When she asked again, there were whispered giggles around the room.

"I guess Jane made me feel better because she proved that you don't need a man in your life to be happy!" Aunt Julia shared.

Several others agreed with her.

"I read about a frugal Jane that lived within her means and I really liked that," voiced Sue.

Nancy was the next to speak. "I think she reminded me how important the written word was at that time and should be today. People are getting away from writing thank you notes and love letters. I think it's a big mistake."

Everyone clapped.

"I agree, Nancy," I said quickly. "She has certainly inspired me to keep writing. The written word is the best legacy one can leave, I think."

More applause erupted.

"Well, as I read on and on about this Jane, I realized you sure don't have to have your picture everywhere to be famous," Abbey noted. "Isn't it something how they had to put a description together to get anything close to what she may have looked like? Cassandra's sketch shows just her backside, for heaven's sake!"

Everyone agreed with the analysis.

"I think I read more carefully after reading Jane's books,"

said Mother. "Her books are not easy reads and many can't handle the thought and attention it requires to absorb everything."

"Mighty good observation, Miss Sylvia," noted Jean.

The discussion continued as we brought another enjoyable meeting to an end. On the way home, Mother mentioned that Harry had been under the weather and hadn't been out much. I then felt better that I had not disappointed her tonight by not taking her to the meeting.

Sam was sitting by the fire staring when I arrived home. I offered a greeting to him as I went into the kitchen to get something to drink. As I chatted about the cold weather, I could tell he had his mind on something else. Out of the blue, he told me he had been home for some time now. In the early afternoon, he started having shortness of breath. I stared at him, concerned.

"When do you go back to the doctor again?" I asked as calmly as I could.

"I'm not due back for a few weeks or so," he said quietly. "Don't worry, I took something and feel a bit better now. I don't need an earlier appointment."

"Is that what you would tell your wife if she came home with symptoms like that?" I asked, leaning back as I spoke.

"I'd tell her she was just trying to get attention from a husband who was probably ignoring her," he teased. "I would take her in my arms and tell her how much I loved her." I blushed as he drew me close. He always had a way of coming out on top of a conversation.

The day before the quilt show was dark and dreary with light snowflakes sputtering about. The forecast was for clearing up the next day, but it was hard to believe. We all had our fingers crossed.

The shop was turning red again for Valentine's Day. Sally ordered heavier with gift items that included flowerpots with quilts on them. She arranged a display in the window in hopes of attracting quilters the next day. We had a small table and chair waiting for Nancy with the raffle tickets available for her to sell. Abbey made a cute sign that would be attached to the quilt outdoors, telling the public to purchase their raffle tickets inside the flower shop.

Abbey spent her afternoon instructing the hanging volunteers. When she came back in the late afternoon, the snowflakes were sticking on the sidewalks. I tried not to look outside or panic. Phil told us that a decision would be made at six in the morning if we were going to cancel the event. The whole town was watching the weather and every other call at the shop had a question about the quilt show.

Isabella walked in about four o'clock looking pretty stressed. She asked if her partner in crime could go take a break with her. We all laughed and declared that we were all ready for that break!

"We can't let up until the shop is completely ready, you know," I teased. "The show must go on!"

"My part is done!" she claimed. "George said he'd bring back all the loaned quilts to the shop around six or seven. I'll check them all out then so folks can pick them up in the next few days. I reminded Phil that we cannot put out one quilt if there's moisture out there!"

Oh dear, I thought.

"Yes, and I told them they have to wipe down every line before they hang a quilt on it," warned Abbey. "It will all be fine."

I agreed to go for a little while with Isabella to have a bite to eat at Charley's. We ordered artichoke dip and shrimp with cocktail sauce to nibble on. We kept looking out of the window giving different assessments on whether the flakes were dying down. From a distance, I saw Ted going into the bar area, but I kept talking in hopes that he would not see me.

Isabella suggested that the two of us leave town if the quilt show had to be cancelled. When I told her, Pat, Sam's sister, was coming in that night for the show, she really freaked out.

"Well, the more the merrier. She knows what's at stake here!" replied Isabella. "We'll just go home with her!" It was no laughing matter. The want-to-get-away option had entered my mind more than once! Hmmm...

CHAPTER 63

Waking up at five in the morning on the day of the show was difficult, dark, and frightening. I looked out of the window as soon as my feet hit the ground to see if there were any snowflakes, but to no avail. As I dressed, I looked at Sam who was soundly asleep. I couldn't believe this handsome man could possibly have any health issues.

I bundled up for the cold before I opened the front door. The air hit hard, but thankfully, there was no precipitation. So far, so good! I drove down Main Street toward my shop to find cars pulling in to park in each block. This told me that folks were showing up for the task at hand.

When I arrived at the shop, I turned on all the lights, which was a rare occurrence for a shop that kept only daytime hours. I started the coffee before taking off my coat, still shivering from the outdoors. I began thinking of my list of duties for the day and knew it was time to get the Ghostly Quilts on Main Street out of my desk drawer and out of the bag. We also needed to find just the right spot to display the Potting Shed Quilt.

I unlocked my drawer to see only one quilt. There was the bag containing the ghost quilt, but the Potting Shed Quilt was gone. I almost fainted right in my desk chair. There was no way anyone could have gotten in this drawer. Even Sally didn't know where I kept my key. I took a deep breath, trying not to panic. This was indeed a paranormal occurrence. There was no other explanation. Grandmother did not like this quilt and continued to send me messages to make that very point.

"Okay," I said aloud as if she were waiting for my response. "I get that you don't like Marion and the quilt she made, but why would you want to ruin my day and my plans to show it off?" I was sounding very angry. "So Grandmother, I was hoping you would stay out of this affair, because this show is important to me, and you are *not* going to spoil it!" Thankfully, no one was in the shop to hear me.

I jerked off my coat and made my way to the front desk where I laid down the quilt bag for Kip or Kevin to hang the quilt. Sally arrived minutes later. I tried to calm down and enjoy some coffee.

"I think the weather's going to be fine, Anne. Did you see the sun coming up?"

I had gotten so distracted, I hadn't even seen the best part of the day! "Really? Oh, that's great!" I responded, going to look out the front window.

"I brought some brownies that I made last night," Sally offered. "I figured this was going to be a long day."

Jean and Kevin then arrived as they bragged about the sunshine.

"Anne, do you have the raffle quilt?" Kevin asked. "I can put that up right now if you want."

"I think we'll leave it in here for a while until Nancy comes to sell tickets," I suggested, feeling a bit cautious. "I want to keep my eye on it for as long as possible."

"Okay," he said, pouring himself some coffee. "I'll go ahead and get the order from yesterday delivered then, if that's okay."

"Yes, good idea," I said. "I'm sure Barristers will be open by now.

"Are you sure Nancy will come by ten?" asked Sally, as if she found it hard to believe.

"Oh, knowing her, she's not going to want to miss a thing," I joked.

"Did you get out the Potting Shed Quilt?" Sally asked innocently. "It will look great over that chair over there, don't you think?" I had to think for a minute as to how to respond.

"I had second thoughts on whether to use it or not," I started to explain. "It is so messy. Those little papers still fall out and I don't want anyone to handle it."

She was not bothered by my decision, nor did she ask any questions, thank goodness.

"Your lovely flower quilt made by your mum is plenty enough," Jean said. "Do you suppose Miss Abbey will be in today or is she working the street, as they say?"

We laughed.

"She will likely be in and out, but I do have her scheduled."

I could hear the street coming alive, even at the early hour. I glanced across the street at the Spice Shop to see a quilt being hung on their balcony. The bright yellow and red star design looked like the sun rising in the dead of winter. It was striking, to say the least. It was a good choice for that building.

My cell phone rang and it was Pat saying she was at the hotel waiting for Sam to come join her for breakfast. Her excitement was uplifting and she predicted that the day was going to be wonderful. She said she and Sam would come down to the street right after breakfast. I was glad they chose to make plans on their own, as I had a one-track mind where the show was concerned. When Kip came in the door, he said quilts were lining the street!

"What a cool thing to see, Anne!" Kip bragged. "You should see all the colors! Everyone's freezing out there, but I imagine the quilts will warm things up!"

"Pretty clever, Mr. Kip," Jean said to him.

Just like clockwork, Nancy and Richard arrived right on time. In her excitement, Nancy was trying to describe all the quilts she saw as she drove down the street. As she said good-bye to Richard, he cautiously told her to stay put and not to walk the street to see all the quilts. As Sally showed her the table and the tickets, I gave the Ghostly Quilts on Main Street quilt to Kip to hang on the side of our building. I followed him out the door to make sure all went well as I secured the ladder. He placed the wooden clothespins very closely and I pinned Do Not Touch and Tickets for Sale signs to the quilt at eye level. Kip had so many questions about each of the ghosts, but I was freezing and declared that we needed to get back into the shop.

When we arrived inside, we already had three people browsing around looking at merchandise. I took Nancy some coffee and noticed how adorable she looked as a pregnant lady. She wore a coffee-colored sweater dress that made her look like she was carrying more than two babies. She immediately asked the browsers if they'd like to buy a raffle ticket, and they were more than happy to do so without even seeing the quilt. She was good—and who could refuse a pregnant lady?

CHAPTER 64

꙳

The shop continued to draw folks in from the street, which made us all busy, in fact, too busy to take in viewing the quilts displayed on the street. We were glad to see Abbey arrive and I put her right to work making some small containers of flowers that had nearly sold out. Sally had a clever special for the day that advertised twenty percent off on the customer's next order if they took home a ready-made floral arrangement. The approach seemed to be working. We also were interrupted by many who came in just to ask questions about the ghostly quilt displayed on our building. Our answers were kept short and they could see we were busy with customers.

Sam and Pat walked in around lunchtime with a long submarine sandwich for us to share. Needless to say, we were more than ready after getting up at such an early hour. Pat immediately complimented the placement of all the quilts.

Abbey was thrilled to hear it and I made sure she received the credit.

"People are definitely going into the shops, Anne," Pat stated. "Don't let them tell you otherwise!"

"They're probably freezing, for one thing," I teased.

Everyone laughed.

"I'm dying to talk to Phil. I hope everyone's having a good day."

"The quilt on the wall out there is pretty unique," said Sam. I wasn't sure just how he meant that. "I hope you don't win it, Anne. I think we have enough ghostly activity at our house."

I snickered, but Pat seemed to be in the dark.

"We'd better let you get to work," Pat suggested. "Sam is going to drop me off at the airport when we leave here."

"You were so helpful with this project, Pat," I said, giving her a hug. "I am honored that you made the trip just to see the show."

"Well, the bonus was spending some time with that brother of mine," she said, grinning at Sam. "I will e-mail you some photos and everyone said to tell you hello. I hope someday soon you'll be back to visit."

"Please give everyone my love," I said as they walked out the door. I followed them to the car and then went around the corner to check on the ghost quilt. It seemed to be behaving itself as everyone stood by admiring the cleverness of it all.

The day was going very quickly since we all stayed so busy. All of a sudden, I heard Nancy cry out loudly, "Oh no, oh no!" I dropped what I was doing and went to her side. She was looking down as water appeared on the floor. I didn't know a lot about pregnancies, but I knew her water had broken.

Everyone nearby became silent.

"Don't panic, Nancy. Just sit here a bit," I said calmly.

She was bending forward.

"Are you in pain? Should I call an ambulance?"

"No," Nancy exclaimed. "Call Richard!"

Sally noticed what had happened and ran to get some paper towels. I told Jean to lock the front door when the lady she was helping finally left. Nancy let us all know that the next pain was very uncomfortable. I went to my desk and called Richard's office. The receptionist said he was out, so I went back to Nancy and said we needed to call Richard on her cell.

"My purse, it's in my purse!" she directed, a sweat breaking out on her forehead.

None of us had ever had a baby, so we didn't know how serious her situation was or wasn't.

"When did you start having pains, Nancy?" I asked as Sally handed me Nancy's cell phone, which I handed to Nancy.

"I guess when we had a little lunch, but I didn't think too much of it," she explained. "I frequently have pains that come and go."

When Nancy dialed Richard, it went straight to voice mail. I thought she was going to throw it at us. She was so exasperated.

"I've got to get to the hospital. Oh no, oh no, it hurts!" she moaned.

"Okay, off we go," I announced. "Jean, you come with me. Get her coat from my office. Can you walk?"

She moaned, but she got up and went toward the door.

"Just get me to the hospital before the next pain comes!" she ordered.

"I'll stay here and get this cleaned up," said Sally. She had a look of helplessness on her face.

The car was parked right in front of the shop and Jean sat in the back seat with Nancy.

"I'm so sorry to ruin everything, Anne," she said tearfully as we drove off. I had to dodge people walking everywhere as I carefully made my way down the street.

"Hold on, girl, we're nearly there!"

We pulled up to the emergency room door and I went in to get someone with a wheelchair to collect my dear friend. I might have been more frightened than she, but at least I was not the one to have to deliver two babies. She looked a wreck and her lovely dress was ruined. When they took her away, I called Sam on my cell phone and told him to get to the hospital. I gave him little information other than I needed his support.

"This has been a scary moment in the course of one's day, huh, Miss Anne?" Jean said, shaking her head. "She's in good hands now, by golly. A coming out of one baby would be a pig's ear, but two would be terribly horrid!" We both laughed heartily, feeling greatly relieved to have Nancy in a safe environment.

We went to sit down and collect our thoughts in the waiting room. The thought of Nancy in there alone was very concerning to me. Where was Richard?

"Is she okay?" asked Sam, joining us in the waiting room. "Is Richard with her?"

"No! We've left messages!" I complained. "I'm sure glad to see you, though. I think I need to get in there to be with her, Sam." I got out of my chair and went to the nurse's station. I explained that there wasn't family here, but that I was a good friend and had brought her to the hospital.

"Please let me be with her for a while," I pleaded. "She has no one else here right now."

Just as she was going to tell me her decision, a doctor walked in my direction and asked for my name.

"Mrs. Barrister is going into labor early, which is not unusual for twins," he explained. "I told her some time back that we may have to have to do a cesarean. I would like to have her husband's signature on the procedure, so do you know if he's on his way?"

"No, but I will call the funeral home again in hopes that they can track him down," I reassured him. "May I go see her?"

"I'm afraid she is already out of it with the medication I gave her, but go in for minute if you like."

When I saw her, she was moving her head back and forth and moaning as if she were really in pain and going into lala land. I grabbed her hand. "Richard's on his way, Nancy. I'm here with you. Be strong for those two little Barristers that are about to be born! I won't leave you."

"Anne, Anne," she whispered.

"Her husband just arrived," the nurse announced, coming into the room. "You'll have to leave now, Mrs. Dickson."

I said a thank you prayer and kissed my brave friend on the forehead. I left Nancy's room to return to the waiting room to be with Sam. When I saw his worried face, I ran into his arms.

"Sam, she is so scared and is in such pain!"

"Richard's with her now," he consoled me. "You are a good friend to her, Anne. I love you!"

CHAPTER 65

Entering the main waiting room again, I saw Mrs. Barrister, Nancy's mother-in-law, sitting next to Jean. She was quick to jump up and tell me how thankful she was for me getting Nancy to the hospital.

"Her father is out of town," explained Mrs. Barrister. "Thank goodness Richard stopped by our house after his meeting. He had his cell phone turned off, so no one could reach him. The home called us to see if we knew where he was and told us that Nancy was taken to the hospital. He was quite alarmed, as you can imagine. She was not due as yet, so it caught all of us off guard."

"She's in great hands now," I said, assuring her.

"Anne, this is Millie Cramer," she announced. "Millie is going to be the babies' nanny.

"Pleased to meet you, Millie," I said, taking her hand. I quickly assessed a rather young-looking woman who didn't have the look of what you might picture as a nanny. Leave it to Nancy to have help right away.

Sam and I decided to walk down the hall to the little coffee nook to get a cup of coffee while we waited on news of the delivery. We sat there in silence until I asked Sam if he knew about Nancy's water breaking at the flower shop.

"Yes, it's quite a story, Anne. Thank goodness you all knew exactly what to do," he bragged.

"We had no time for an ambulance, plus the street was crowded with the quilt show," I explained. "Oh no, I forgot about the quilt show. What time is it?" I looked at my watch. "The show is over and the quilt might still be hanging on the building." I reached for my cell phone and called the shop. I got the answering machine.

Sam just watched me panic.

I called Sally's house and she had just gotten home. She tried to ask me questions, but I interrupted her, asking about the raffle quilt left on our building.

"Not to worry, Anne," she began. "Gayle saw you leave with Nancy and she helped Kevin and me take the quilt down in front of quite a crowd. Phil came by to draw the winner. It was Terry Doyle who lives somewhere in Illinois, so Phil said he would mail it to her. We all joked about how glad we were it was leaving town. George and Kathy were there, too. There were disappointed folks who really thought they were going to win! So, what about Nancy? Did she deliver the babies yet?"

"No, we're all waiting, including Sam who is here with me. Thank goodness Richard arrived, which is the important thing."

"Good," she replied. "You'll be tickled to know that despite our early closing, we had a fantastic day at the shop! I think everyone on the street did well from what George said. Phil said it was the best Saturday he's had in a long time!"

"Oh, I'm so glad," I said, breathing easier. "I'll talk to you later. I think we are about to get some news here!" I hung up without saying good-bye. Jean was coming toward us, beaming.

"The Barrister babies are here!" she announced, excitedly. "The little lassie weighed in at six and one-half pounds and the laddie at seven. Not bad for early birds!"

Sam and I laughed.

"I'd best be getting back to Al now, Anne," she said. "It's been quite the jolly Quilts on Main day, has it not?"

"That it has, Jean. Thanks for all of your help!"

"I cannot wait until we are talking about our own lassie or laddie, Anne," Sam said, taking my hand as we walked back to the delivery waiting room.

"I know, Sam," I said, understanding his emotions right now. "It will happen one day. It was a bit of an eye-opener though to watch Nancy in such pain. She felt so bad that she caused us to close the shop on such a big day."

"Weren't you envious of her bringing into the world those babies that represent Nancy and Richard's love for one another?" he asked. There was an earnest tone in his voice that was unmistakable.

This was going to be a tough one to answer. I had to somehow find the right words. "I had no time to think of any such thing, Sam. This was all about Nancy." I explained best I could. "I will know when the time is right and so will you. Let's enjoy these babies right now. I promise I will give it more thought. Can you settle for that?" I knew I sounded way too defensive, but I had experienced enough stress for one day.

"That's all I ask, sweet Annie," he said as we got closer to go see the new little darlings.

CHAPTER 66

I slept like a log from the very long, eventful day. The first thing on my agenda was having a conversation with Isabella and Phil. I really felt I had dropped the ball when I went off to the hospital. Later in the day, I would go visit those Barrister babies, leaving some time for Nancy and Richard to get acquainted with their new family.

I left Sam at the kitchen table and headed to Main Street. The winter sun was no longer with us, making me realize more than ever how we lucked out with a very special quilt show. Since it was Sunday, I wasn't expecting to see Phil at his shop in the morning, but there was his car, so I pulled over and knocked on the locked door. He laughed, shaking his head when he saw me.

"The word on the street, Anne, is that you had quite a show of your own going on yesterday!" he teased. "Come on in. You need coffee?"

"I do, actually," I said with gratitude. "I had planned to go by Starbucks. I have so much to do today and suppose you do as well."

"For sure! We have some orders to ship tomorrow, all from a good day! I'll go on home when Sharon comes in at noon."

"That is so good to hear, Phil. I'm glad everyone had some decent business. Do you still have the raffle quilt?"

"Yup, it's still in the bag. I cannot wait to get that shipped off tomorrow."

"I'm off to find Isabella," I stated, going toward the door with my coffee. "I guess all went well with her?"

"I think she said she was leaving town for a few days, but she did have a bit of a scare, I guess," he said, sitting down at his desk. "She called me in a panic about a quilt that didn't show up at the shop."

I stopped in my tracks. "What? What happened?"

"All is well, Anne, but when it was five o'clock, an owner of one of the quilts decided to be helpful and took her own quilt right off the rail of the gazebo. She took it home without saying anything to anyone. Isabella went through everything, thinking it could have been in another bag or maybe they left it on the gazebo by mistake. She was beside herself and the volunteers didn't have any answers. She didn't want to call the owner of the quilt until she was absolutely sure it was missing. I told her she had to do it or it could get worse."

I was floored at the news. "Well, when she told the lady of her loss, the lady laughed, saying she had taken it home, thinking she was being helpful."

"Oh my word, Phil, what was she thinking? Well, there's a lesson to learn for the future. We should all make a list of suggestions because Sally said folks wanted to repeat the show."

"Oh, for sure, that message was loud and clear, especially from the restaurants!"

"Well, I'd better be off and take care of some things at the shop before Jean and Abbey come in. I am so pleased about Abbey's help. She is turning out to be a pretty good street person."

Phil laughed, though it was a phrase we used for all of us that lived or worked on Main Street.

Later that afternoon, I walked into Nancy's flower-filled room to see a bright-eyed, happy mother. She complained of being sore, but bragged about her accomplishment. Her hair was beautifully combed and her pretty bathrobe was so Nancy. She probably chose it years ago for this very occasion.

"Are you ready to meet Amelia Anne Barrister and Andrew William Barrister?" she asked proudly.

"I love the names! They both start with an A, which is very cool. Are those names you planned all along?"

"Yes, and I'll have you know the Anne is a tribute to you, my friend," she said with a big smile.

"Really?" I gasped. "Oh, Nancy, I'm so honored!"

"William is a family name," she continued. "Richard picked Andrew and I have always loved the name Amelia. I'll imagine they'll end up being called Andy and Amy, which is kind of cute. The names fit their personalities already!"

"Well, let's go see!" I said as we walked toward the hallway where the nursery was located.

The tiny, tiny creatures were so pink and fair featured, just like Nancy. Andy had more hair than Amy, but they appeared to be identical, which Nancy claimed they were.

She said Richard was bragging about how much they both looked like her.

"You really have created more pressure for Sam Dickson to have a family, Nancy," I divulged. "I knew that would happen."

Nancy looked at me strangely. "When will it ever be the right time for you, Anne?" she asked, her tone serious.

"Maybe soon, maybe never!" I said, staring at the two cribs side by side.

She frowned.

CHAPTER 67

I wasn't sure what to call my falling spirit as I drove home that evening. I decided post-partum depression had a hold on me at the moment. Isn't that what new mothers sometimes had? I had just experienced all the drama one could possibly handle.

I first had the challenge of creating a ghostly quilt that was not happy here, but was finally on its way out of town and I was glad it was OVER! The unknown weather for the quilt show was truly a success, but that concern was now OVER! Nancy's anticipated delivery was over the top, but it was now OVER! I couldn't throw myself back into my expansion project because it was completed and OVER! I couldn't look to enhance Sam's climbing the ladder at Martingale, because he had reached the top and it, too, was OVER! The Anne Brown Dickson that always had many irons in the fire at all times seemed to be OVER, at least for now anyway. Hmmm...

Why wasn't I in a joyous mood for all the success God had given me? All these worries had great results. Did I appear ungrateful? I certainly didn't want to be. I was just out of gas, I told myself.

Ella was finishing up in the kitchen when I walked in the door. It was good to see a warm and friendly face on such a cold, somber day. Ella was beginning to feel like family.

After a little hug, she said, "You look exhausted, Anne, as you should be, by golly. How about I fix a hot cup of cocoa for you before I leave? I bet you don't treat yourself to that very often, do you?"

"No, you're right, Ella," I responded, sitting down at the kitchen table with my coat still wrapped around me. "That sounds good. I heard on the weather report that another storm is heading our way. I may just go on up to bed after I finish this since Sam is not coming home for dinner. I think I am more exhausted than Nancy is after birthing two babies."

She laughed. "Do they look alike, Anne?" she asked sweetly as she put my cup of hot chocolate in front of me.

"Oh my, yes," I quickly said. "Nancy said they are identical. She is on cloud nine. I am so happy for her."

"Your day will come, my dear," she said as if to comfort me. "My, I'd better get going. Say, I see you found the crazy quilt. Where was it?"

"I did?" I said, almost choking on my drink. "Where?"

She looked at me strangely. "Where it's been many a day since I've been here," she said, looking out onto the sun porch.

I got up to look closer as I saw my own ghostly quilt folded nicely on the drying rack instead of in a pile on the floor where Grandmother seemed to prefer it. Somehow, nothing more today could shock me.

"Oh yes," I said calmly. Exhaustion and dismay kept me from telling her it had been locked safely in my desk drawer before appearing here.

After she left, I went upstairs with my half cup of cocoa. I set my cup near the answering machine where a light was flashing. I clicked to hear the message of Mother's happy voice asking me all about the Barrister babies. She then reminded me we needed to be thinking of a bridal luncheon for Amanda. I wasn't in the mood to call her back. I just wanted to crash.

The chocolate was like the final drug to take me straight to my bed. I did take the time to pull the covers back, but I left the lights on behind me as I pulled the sheets over my head. I could hear the wind pick up speed as some of the branches hit the bay window. I wanted to escape the quilts, ghosts, and babies that were whirling all around me. Perhaps when I awoke, I would find the center of myself again. Hmmm...

CHAPTER 68

I didn't move until the next morning when I heard Sam stir at his regular early hour. I sat up in my sleepy haze and started making excuses for not hearing him come home. He laughed them off and told me how pleased he was that I was getting some needed rest.

"Looks like we got a few inches of snow last night," Sam said as he began brushing his teeth. "It was a very slow hike up the hill last night. The wind likely created some snow drifts, so you may want to check your potting shed this morning."

I tried to picture it in my clouded mind.

"I hate February. Always have," I responded to his dismal report. "I'm not going in today. Abbey can help Sally if she needs it. I guess I'd better make some calls. It's cold in here, Sam!"

He looked around the corner at me from the bedroom

and remained silent.

I quickly put on my thickest robe and heavy socks to go downstairs. I told myself that I might never change clothes for the day. I was not up to fighting old man winter and planned to stay in my cave for the rest of the day.

Sam had the coffee going and was lighting a fire in the study when he announced that he, too, had decided to stay home for the day and review his reports from his computer at home. It was an unusual step for both of us.

Sam's good nature had him whistling as he toasted some English muffins and he offered some to me as well. I shook my head and sat down at the kitchen table to enjoy my black coffee. I could see right out onto the sun porch where the Potting Shed Quilt rested for the night. I wanted to process how it was possible for it to be there, but my mind still seemed to be asleep and uncaring. Did other people have ghosts living with them and they just never said anything about it? Could anything possibly make this nuisance go away?

"Anne, Anne," Sam said as he waved his hands in front of me to gain my attention.

I calmly looked his way and stared.

"You look like you are miles away from here. What's on your mind?"

"Nothing and everything, if you really must know," I said with a rude tone.

"What's that supposed to mean? You aren't yourself this morning. Are you feeling okay?"

"I'm fine, okay?" I snapped. I got up to go look into the refrigerator to see if there was anything I wanted to eat. I quickly closed the door, realizing that food was the last thing

I wanted. I turned around to Sam's stare.

"So, what's up with your agenda today?" he asked in an even tone to change the subject to a safe and normal conversation.

"Nothing, absolutely nothing," I stated firmly as I picked up my cell phone to check e-mails.

"A day off? I don't believe it!"

"I can do that! I need a break from meetings, quilts, ghosts, flowers, and even babies, so how about that?"

Sam glared as he tried to figure out how this monster had appeared.

I had never raised my voice to him, but this time, I didn't care. "Glad you reminded me about the potting shed. I'd better get out there and see what's going on." I put on my boots and then put on my heavy jacket over my robe.

Sam remained in shock as he watched me.

"Now? In your pajamas?" he asked in amazement. "If you want to get dressed first, I'll be glad to go out and help you. That door is probably frozen shut. You may need some help, Anne."

"No thanks, I can handle it," I said as I put on my gloves. "I can handle anything!" I brushed past Sam, opened the door, and was immediately hit by a gust of cold air. If Sam responded, I didn't hear him.

I marched through the few inches of snow on the ground. Light flurries were still coming down with a good wind. Sure enough, a snowdrift of a good foot was planted firmly in front of the potting shed door. The windows were frosted as I tried to look in for some sign of warmth. I pulled and pulled at the door as I swept snow away with one hand. It was not about to budge. I took an iron plant rod that was nearby and used it to help pry the door open. With a swift yank, the door opened and I landed flat on my backside. I didn't know whether to laugh or curse. I had a feeling Sam's eyes could easily be watching this crazy attempt. The minute I got inside, I felt and heard the heater still pumping away in the small, humid space. I heaved a sigh of relief. After I closed the door, I turned to find a white gorgeous lily in a green pot sitting by itself on the potting bench. It was the last thing I expected to see, and yet it was no surprise to find Grandmother waiting in here for me. She had appeared here several times before. My emotions were hot and cold as I burst into tears. She knew. She always knew what was going on with me.

"What's the matter with me?" I yelled out loud to my invisible grandmother. My sobs were now increasing as I cushioned my head on the counter. "I'm on a treadmill and I cannot get off! Sam thinks we need a baby and I cannot even take care of myself and my commitments in life. I can't tell anyone, not anyone. They think I have it all and I do! What's wrong? I pray all the time to God and thank Him every day. He continues to be good to me, and I don't deserve it! *Tell* me what's wrong with me, Grandmother, don't *show* me."

I started to feel really strange talking to her like this, but I knew she was here, right in this potting shed! I took a deep breath, and as I sniffed, I felt extra warmth as if someone had put their arms around me.

A soft voice seemed to ask me, "What do you love to do?"

I repeated the question to myself aloud to make sure I heard it correctly. Why this question and why was it now in my head? Answer, answer, and don't ignore it.

Okay, when I think of my first loves, I realize I am no

longer doing what I love. I always loved working with flowers, so I got myself a flower shop. Now I own a building with an office and a door that can close me off from the flowers I love so much. I love to write, but it is impossible to do so with other priorities. There are many times I want to grab a pen to describe a thought, a poem, or a clever idea, but there is no time, no time. Wanting to write a book on the Taylor house is a nice thought that will likely never happen.

The longer I gathered my thoughts, it seemed to bring calmness over me and my head was becoming clearer. I had to get back to basics and throw out the clutter that filled my everyday life. Clutter. Good word for it, I thought. I looked at the white innocence of the single lily without any other plant to enhance it and it gave me peace.

I blew my nose and decided I could leave the lily behind as I began my walk back to the house. How could I explain it otherwise? I managed to smile as I looked back at the peaceful lily. I had gotten the message loud and clear.

CHAPTER 69

*

Sam was in the den working when I came in the kitchen. He was on the phone and had not heard me come in. I took off my winter garb and filled up a cup of hot coffee. The comforting aroma assured me all was well as I went upstairs.

I went straight to my waiting room as if someone was truly there waiting for me. I sat down, still in my robe, and looked at the notebook full of papers on the Taylor house. My laptop had remained closed for some time now. I knew my ambitious plan would take some time. Part of the story would unfold as I lived in the house and got to know its history, bit by bit. After all, this was an adventure that should be enjoyed. I had to be patient, yet stay focused on my mission.

As I thought again of Grandmother, I thought about how all the ghosts on Main Street had consumed me and so many of the folks who did business and lived on the street.

Just like Grandmother did sometimes, the ghosts had their way of rebelling when we used them for our fund-raising efforts. We were exposing the street ghosts for our own gain and not giving them the respect they deserved. They were happy or unhappy, doing and living as they pleased in their place in history. They couldn't seem to move on, just like Grandmother. Why was that? I picked up my pen and began to pen my thoughts.

WHY DO THEY REMAIN?
Why do the spirits remain on Main,
for a reason we must know?
Why do they stir at certain times,
just to make a show?
Why do the spirits want their say,
instead of going on their way?
Why not smile and greet them,
and encourage them to stay?
That spirit might be us one day,
if our spirit chooses to remain.
Let's hope they will welcome us,
and let us stay on Main.

I was so engrossed in my thoughts and words I didn't hear Sam come up the stairs. He came up behind me, putting his hands on my shoulders.

"I love you, sweet Annie," Sam whispered softly. "It's nice to see you writing again."

I put my pen down and turned toward him. Sam looked

like a little boy who had lost his best friend. Somehow, I couldn't find the words to tell him I loved him too! He knew that. I got up from my chair and looked at him.

"I'm sorry, Sam," I said with in earnest as I held back tears. "I got lost, way lost, but I'm okay now." I paused to think how I was going to describe my thoughts. "Did you ever spread out in every direction until you lost the center of who you are?"

Sam looked like I hit him with a gut-wrenching thought. He walked over to sit on the side of the bed. Then he looked down toward the floor in thought. "Oh yes, oh yes, honey," he sadly repeated. "You said it well. One can lose oneself very easily with the tugs and demands of everyday life. I realized that after I got my second chance with my heart disease. I really thought I was going to die. It puts things into perspective real fast, just like they say. I really have to discipline my stress or my heart and lungs send me signals accordingly. When you feel great, you think you can do it all." He paused to smile and shake his head. "I have a few quotes around the office to help remind me, but you, Annie, are the real center of what my life is about. You have helped give me a purpose, and sharing life with you is so much better than without you. You help me stay centered, whether you know it or not. I can't afford for you to get lost. I know who I fell in love with and I don't want her to go away or to be unhappy."

"I don't either, Sam," I said, joining him at the bedside. "I have to make some changes and I sense you'd like for me to make some as well. I have to make them for me, though, not for you. I have to get back to the center of what I love, not what I *think* I should be loving and doing."

He nodded as he looked me in the eye.

"I need to write. I was writing as a little girl. My best presents were pads of paper. I was never bored when I knew I could write. It's part of who I am. I have to write. Now I have created a spot here just for writing and it can't happen. I miss it. I also want to be more creative in this beautiful house. We still have rooms that need to be filled and decorated. I love this house like I love the gardens and flowers around it."

Sam was happy to hear what I was saying.

I took a deep breath to continue. "Sam, you cannot pressure me about getting pregnant. It makes me crazy!"

His sober look returned.

"I will promise you that when I regain my center, I will go off the pill, and we'll see what happens. I refuse to put that on my to-do list. I want my mind and body to be in sync with the idea. You must understand that."

He grinned.

"I'm sorry if you were feeling pressured," he confessed. "I wouldn't want it any other way. It would only mean further trouble for us if we didn't agree on that. We have all the time in the world. You don't know how happy it makes me to hear you say these things. You are smart to stop your treadmill before you really get burned out." He put his arm around me. "Remember when we first got married? We said we'd make sure to set aside one date night a week in our busy schedule. Then we put things off until I stopped traveling. I don't think we made that happen, did we?"

I shook my head. It made me sad to think about it.

"Do you realize we are both still in our robes and it's noontime? When is the last time that ever happened? Do you also realize we've managed to have this talk without any cell phones going off or computer interruptions?"

I smiled.

"It's a good day to play hooky, if you ask me! How about I go to my customized kitchen and make us some soup, which I happen to enjoy doing, while you stay up here and write for a while? After that, I'll bet we'll find other things to do that we love!" He reached his arms out for a big hug. It was a bear hug like my father would have given me when I needed it. He turned to go downstairs as I went back to my waiting room to continue writing.

Life was feeling better right now, but there was the same whisper that I heard in the potting shed that told me challenges were ahead. Somehow I knew that, but it didn't scare me. It was all the more reason that I had to find my center regarding what I really loved. It was always love that sustained me and my family. Grandmother knew much more from the other side, but I would have to live my own life, through the good and the bad, as the Colebridge community continues.